Jolene's Adonis

J. Jaden

"A woman knows the face of the man she loves as a sailor knows the open sea."
Honore de Balzac

Jolene's Adonis

DISCLAIMER

JOLENE'S ADONIS IS A WORK OF FICTION. NAMES, CHARACTERS, AND INCIDENTS ARE THE PRODUCT OF THE AUTHOR'S IMAGINATION OR ARE USED FICTITIOUSLY. ANY RESEMBLANCE TO ACTUAL PERSONS, LIVING OR DEAD, OR EVENTS IS ENTIRELY COINCIDENTAL.

ISBN- 978-1-962490-09-2

To my husband, my Adonis, with almond-colored eyes and wavy hair.

Content Warning

This novel contains mature and graphic content intended for adult readers only. Themes include:

- Explicit sexual content, including consensual BDSM and bondage

- Violence and depictions of murder

- Emotional and psychological manipulation

- Profanity and adult language

- Suicide

- Stalking

Reader discretion is strongly advised.

This story is a dark romance and may be triggering to some. Please prioritize your well-being and skip this book if these themes may be harmful to you.

J. Jaden

Playlist

"Superstar" – Sonic Youth

"Uninvited" – Alanis Morissette

"Haunted" – Poe

"Every You Every Me" – Placebo

"Criminal" – Fiona Apple

"Rock the Boat" - Aaliyah

"Closer" – Nine Inch Nails

"Business" – Eminem

"Soldier" – Eminem

"Shoop" – Salt-N-Pepa

"I Want Candy" – Bow Wow Wow

"I Try" – Macy Gray

"Butterfly" – Crazy Town

"Fighter" – Christina Aguilera

"Thank You" – Dido

"Survivor" – Destiny's Child

"Jolene" – Dolly Parton (New String Version)

1

Jolene: Unsatisfied

The mast looms like a watchful sentinel, cutting into the sky, and rising from a sea that knows too many secrets. But it's not the height or the waves that twist my stomach. It's Wesley. It's always Wesley.

Suspended forty feet in the air, I squirm in what he proudly calls a bosun's chair. "Chair" is generous. It's really a sling for my ass made from a square of fabric with ropes and straps, holding me just tightly enough to remind me who put me here.

When he gave it to me for Christmas, I thought it was a sex swing. I laughed. He didn't.

I was wrong. So wrong.

It wasn't for pleasure. It was for work. For control. For him.

He uses it to haul me up the mast to do the things he won't like painting, sanding, inspecting; jobs that don't suit his pride or his schedule. At first, I resisted. "Absolutely not!" I snapped. "I'm scared of heights, Wesley!"

But I went up anyway. Not because I'm weak. Because with Wesley, I always give in.

That's the part I hate admitting the most.

The first time, I cried. The second time, I cussed. Now? I drift. I let the rope bite into my hips, let the wind tug at my hair, and I stare straight ahead. The trick is to fix my eyes on the horizon. Don't look down. Don't look back. Don't think about the dizzying drop. Don't think about the vast blue beneath me, or how easily it swallows everything, like truth, time, and even love. Just imagine how many women came before, staring into that same shimmering blue, asking themselves how the hell they got here… and whether they'll survive it.

I finish the last careful stroke of paint and glance down. The deck sways far below, small and uncertain, like a paper boat caught in an endless sea. The sight tilts the world beneath me, and a slow dizziness unfurls in my chest, rising like a tide I can't control. To calm the rush of vertigo, I close my eyes and exhale, letting my full weight sink into the harness, praying it'll hold.

I gave up so many battles with Wesley just to keep him close. The more I pushed, the more he distanced himself. So, I stopped pushing. Stopped resisting. Stopped being the girl who always had to win.

Why? Why did I relinquish my control? My power? My voice? I gave in because Wesley is the only man who's ever made me feel truly seen, truly loved. He's my undoing; my wilting, maddening, seductive weakness. If not for him, I'd be trapped on that God-forsaken farm, married to the man my parents handpicked, who was an NRA bumper sticker in human form with a Bible in one hand and a leash in the other. That wasn't the life I wanted. I wanted more. I wanted freedom. And somehow, I thought Wesley was the answer.

Gripping the small walkie in my hand, I press the button. "Hey!" I raise my paintbrush like a weapon, aiming it toward the deck below. "Why the hell are we doing this out here? Couldn't we paint the damn mast at the dock where the boat isn't swaying and trying to shake me loose?"

Crackling through the speaker, his voice cuts back. "Because, Jolene, you know why." There's irritation in the way he says my name, like it tastes bitter in his mouth. "I can't take you with me when I work. This gets you out of the marina, out of the condo, and out of that precious metal shop where you shut yourself off from the world. Out here, I get time with you... alone. Plus, free labor."

I don't hesitate. I hurl the brush toward him. It misses, bouncing on the deck with a dull splat I can barely see, but I know it left a smear across the teak.

"What the hell was that?" he snaps through the handheld. "You just got paint on the deck. You know it won't match."

Jolene's Adonis

He disappears into the cabin and reemerges with a towel, scrubbing at the stain with one hand while lecturing me through the walkie with the other. The radio crackles before his voice snaps through, tight and clipped. "I oughta bring you down and make you clean it. But no! I'm leaving you up there. Maybe you'll learn not to throw shit when you're forty feet in the air."

My stomach clenches. "Wesley," I call into the walkie, breath catching. "Don't leave me up here. Please. Bring me down."

He doesn't answer.

He doesn't bring me down.

He's changed.

The Wesley I married used to listen. He used to ask. Now he just tells.

My fingers tighten around the rope. I'm here because I said no, and he said it wasn't a request.

Until a few months ago, he stayed out on the Gulf of Mexico alone for days at a time. When he was home, he took calls behind closed doors and then left without telling me where he was headed. "Work," he'd say. "Imports, exports." Like that explained the cash, the penthouse, or the stack of designer dresses in my closet with the tags still attached.

He gave me a storefront, something to keep me busy. A little metal art shop with a workspace in back. Said it was mine. Said I could make something for myself. And I do, just not enough to pay the bills. Still, that workshop is the only place that feels like it truly belongs to me.

Lately he's around all the time. Talking about getting away. Saying he wants to vanish down the coast for a few days. I should be grateful for the time, for the quiet, for the sunsets he pretends are just for us.

But something's changed.

He's restless. The money's slower. The tension clings to him like the salt in the air. He doesn't talk about it. He doesn't talk at all unless he's giving instructions. So, I obey. I climb the mast. I paint where he points. I pretend I'm not scared of falling, or worse, of what I might see if I look too closely at the man waiting for me on deck.

Leaning back in my chair, I let out a sigh of relief, knowing that Wesley, the neat freak, will be occupied with his meticulous cleaning for quite some time. As I drift away, desperate to escape my current predicament, my mind wanders back to when I first noticed a shift in Wesley six months earlier.

****

Jolene's Adonis

Steam from the shower seeped under the bathroom door as Wesley hummed to himself. In the seven and a half years we were married, I knew him so well that I could anticipate the exact moment he would finish his shower and exit the primary bathroom, wearing nothing but an erection and a smile.

In anticipation of a night filled with passionate lovemaking, I removed the comforter and top sheet from the bed, folded them, and placed them neatly on the zebra-printed chaise lounge. Grabbing my favorite perfume atomizer from the vanity, I sprayed the fitted sheet and pillowcases, and then squirted it onto my abdomen and just below my breasts. I then climbed onto the bed moments before Wesley opened the door. His smile broadened when his eyes rested on me, kneeling in the center of the four-poster. I wore a black bra with lace, feathers, and holes that exposed my nipples. A matching black lace thong highlighted my pubic area that I waxed earlier in the day.

He walked toward me as I circled the right breast with my thumb and forefinger. "Want this, sailor boy?" I beckoned him closer with my left hand.

"You know I do." His erection bounced with each step as he made his way toward me.

I licked my finger and stuck it underneath the lace thong, caressing the bald, sensitive skin. "You wanna make me purr?" I asked.

"Hell yes!" he growled. His pace quickened, and he reached the foot of the bed and grabbed my right hand, pushing it down to my clit that was now wet. He then pulled my forefinger to his mouth and placed it on his tongue, which folded onto my finger and caressed it, tasting me. My pussy clenched in response, making it even wetter. He then guided my finger to the soft, mushroomed crest of his cock as his mouth found my right breast. My nipple grew taut as he teased and licked it, circling, nipping. His hand guided my finger around the tip as his cock shuddered in response. My body tingled. I wanted to feel it inside me. I ran my finger up the shaft; my eyes closed in expectation. They flew open when Wesley released my nipple and pulled himself away from my grasp. He pushed me backward onto the soft bed as I moaned.

He pulled a silk tie from under the mattress and covered my eyes, tying it loosely behind my head. I could see nothing, but I felt a shift as he positioned himself at the top of the bed and brought his lips to mine. His nose rubbed against my chin as our mouths locked and tongues entwined. The taste of toothpaste and me were on his lips. He then pulled himself further down my body as his mouth reclaimed my breasts. He teased and licked while I sucked on his nipples, one at a time. His chest was tight and smooth.

"I could eat you up!" I told him as my tongue traced his muscles.

"You could?" he teased.

"Yes," I said, breathless.

He laughed and raised himself up before sliding his body further down. I jumped at the feel of his mouth on my now soaked pussy. "I could eat you all night!" he said. His fully erect cock touched my lips.

"Ahh!" I sighed as his tongue found my clit.

"I want you to come," he said.

I felt for the shaft of his cock and guided it into my mouth, sucking hard. His body flinched, and I became even more aroused. I cupped his balls and stroked his penis with the same rhythm that his tongue stroked my clitoris. With every movement of his tongue, my mouth moved up and down the shaft of his cock. Occasionally, I stopped and licked his cock like it was an ice cream cone, slowly, deliciously. We moved harmoniously up and down, sucking, licking, becoming more excited with every stroke. Between licks, he told me exactly what he wanted. "That's it, baby. Suck that cock!" He patted my clit with his right hand as if to spank it. I shivered and pushed my hips upward, begging for more.

I then felt him move. His hand joined my lips on his cock. He stroked his penis, pushing it in and out of my mouth until he stiffened. He pulled out and exploded onto my chest before once again burying his face into my pussy. His sweet beard tickled my newly waxed bare skin, making me hypersensitive.

His tongue went deep inside me while his chin massaged. I couldn't take it any longer! I grabbed his hair and pushed his face further into me. My body wracked with orgasmic waves as I found my own release.

Spent, I lifted the tie from my head and patted him, signaling him to stop. He pulled away and collapsed onto his back as we both released a satisfied sigh. For a few moments, we were still: our feet at opposite sides of the bed.

I pushed myself off the bed and made my way to the bathroom for a quick shower to wash the semen from my chest. When I returned, Wesley had replaced the blankets and was curled up, resting on his left side. Naked, I slipped under the covers and positioned my body against his with my breasts touching his bare back. With my right hand, I reached around him and stroked his now soft penis. It didn't grow. Trying to arouse him, I traced the lines of his back with my tongue and wrapped my leg over his body, rubbing myself on his firm buttocks. As I stroked his cock, my voice filled with a seductive whisper, and I playfully nibbled at his earlobe, coyly remarking, "My pussy craves more, sailor."

Wesley let out a low groan but remained motionless. A few moments later, he took heavy breaths, just like he did when he was in a deep sleep.

****

Jolene's Adonis

That night was the first time he was satisfied after a single sexual encounter. Before then, we made love half the night and stroked each other in our sleep. He couldn't get enough, and it excited me to have a man who wanted me that much and who was uninhibited in the bedroom, ready to play and fulfill my fantasies. But since that night, when he fell asleep on me, the disappointments in the bedroom continue. His libido has fizzled, and when he initiates sex, it's only about his wants and needs. I'm left unsatisfied. At some point, he quit caring about whether I got any pleasure from the encounters. That's when my Adonis took over…

Wesley pulls me out of my thoughts by lowering the rope that is securely holding me near the top of the mast. As I descend, my anger and frustration simmer just below the surface. I went up there for him! And this is how he treats me? As if I'm not worthy of kindness or consideration?

The moment my feet touch the deck, I pivot on my heels and make my way into the cabin, immediately flopping onto the bed in the stateroom and burying my head into the pillow. As I breathe in deeply, the weight of my circumstances becomes palpable in my thoughts. I roll toward the picture resting on the bedside table, and I'm instantly transported to my daddy's farm, surrounded by the familiar sights and sounds of the countryside. I can recall every detail of that day as if it happened just moments ago.

It was March 13, 1994, eight years earlier. Wesley and I posed together in front of a herd of cattle Wesley purchased from my dad. Smokey eyes and charcoal-colored strands peeked out from under his white cowboy hat. With his custom-tailored shirt, he exuded confidence and sophistication, while his knee-high cowboy boots hinted at a life of adventure. His snug jeans left little to the imagination, hugging his form in all the right places.

With my tank top, cut-off jean shorts, and tall rubber boots, I was ready to tackle the horse stalls. My long blonde braid trailed behind me. To anyone else looking at the picture, we appear to be the epitome of a harmonious couple, capturing the genuine spirit of rural Texan living. But to me, those smiling faces concealed a deep well of heartache and disappointment soon to come.

I still feel like that 25-year-old corn-fed girl, my sun-kissed skin a testament to life spent under the open sky. My calloused hands, revealing years of hard work on the farm. Before meeting Wesley, I existed in a state of limbo, yearning for the opportunity to break free from the emptiness that engulfed me since birth. Confined within a fifty-mile radius, I relied on him to broaden my horizons and steer me away from the path my family planned for me.

In my quest for liberation, I viewed him as a version of Adonis himself, a vivid fantasy come to life. From the moment he arrived on the farm and stepped out of his sports car a few weeks before we posed for the picture, he captivated me. I made a vow to follow wherever that man went. And I did. At twice my age, he was handsome, tall, and lean with prominent cheekbones. At first, he exuded charm and sophistication, promising a life full of thrilling adventures and new opportunities far beyond the confines of the ranch and the church.

As the years passed, Wesley's behavior and mannerisms have increasingly mirrored those of Daddy, causing me to draw unsettling parallels between the two. According to the church elders, girls select partners who bear resemblances to their fathers. My family expected me to marry a devout man… a farmer. I thought I escaped that destiny by running away and eloping with Wesley, a man with no religious affiliation, and a man who traveled for work. I was wrong.

While I yearn to get swept away in the sentimental recollection of happier days, the undeniable sensation of Wesley's erection against my back serves as an abrupt reminder of the present. He strokes my hair in the dimly lit cabin. "I know, puppet." He coos. "Everything is fine. I cleaned it up. I understand you get anxious about going too high and I know you're sorry. No need to apologize. I'm not mad. Now get in there and take a shower."

I roll over and face him, offering a smile, knowing that the smile doesn't reach my eyes. No matter how much I pretend to be the good woman, the one who's always here to serve her man, the subservient lady my family raised me to be, my eyes betray me. They're like the truth tellers of my soul. They won't allow me to lie. No. I'm not sorry.

I turn away from Wesley and slide to the edge of the bed. Standing up, I walk into the bathroom, or what Wesley calls the "head" and I turn on the shower and undress. The water cascades down my body, mingling with the salty taste of tears on my lips. As I work to control the storm raging inside me, the soothing scent of lavender fills the air, calming my senses.

When I exit the bathroom, Wesley stands at the side of the bed, waiting to strip off my clothes. It's the same routine every night. I slip into a nice dress, and he peels it off like wrapping paper. Honestly, it'd be easier to go to bed naked—skip the charade entirely—but this is the part that gets him going. The undressing. The control. Treating me like his little doll, his little puppet, as he likes to call me, excites him.

I lay flat on my back and wait for him to enter me. His fevered breath wafts onto my chest, adding to the stifling temperature of the small stateroom, now illuminated by a vanilla-scented candle. The air is a heady blend of musky wood, salty sea breeze, sweet vanilla, and sex. The sound of a seagull's lonely call echoes outside the porthole.

"Jolene, you're so tight!" he murmurs as he pushes his cock into my crevice. When he says my name this time, there is a distinct shift in his tone. It's no longer filled with regret and loathing, but rather with a deep desire and overwhelming lust.

Sweat pools on my bare skin as he pounds into me harder, deeper. Wesley grunts as the friction builds a fire at my core. With closed eyes and parted lips, I release a soft moan, fantasizing about a different man writhing between my legs. Dark, wavy hair drips with perspiration. Walnut-colored eyes burn into me…hungry, wanting. His jaw clenches, smoothing out full lips. His chest muscles ripple. He's exotic. He's on top of me. He's mine.

Wesley breaks my trance as his lips search my face. I seal my eyelids and turn my head, freeing myself from his moist kiss. I'm not ready to lose the vivid image of my dream man, my Adonis. He soon returns, and I pant as my thighs ignite, causing the flames to move higher. I'm ready. Opening my long limbs fully, my hips match the rhythm of his. I thrust myself upward, welcoming the sweet gratification that I hope will soon come. Just when I feel myself on the verge of letting go, Wesley stops.

"Turn over, little puppet." He withdraws his erect penis. I whimper but oblige. My Adonis vanishes.

I bury my frustration into the cream satin pillowcase and Wesley positions himself behind me, slapping my ass hard before shoving into me. My skin stings and my insides ache with sudden dryness from the intense pressure mingled with disappointment. *I was so close! He doesn't care, not anymore.*

I count his thrusts like the beat of a choreographed routine. Wesley moves with mechanical precision—one, two… thrust. Four, five… thrust. Seven, eight… thrust. Ten, eleven… thrust. Thirteen, fourteen… thrust and hold. By sixteen, his fingers dig into my hips, his body shudders, and the dance ends.

He groans, goes limp, and collapses onto my back. I let out a quiet, disheartened whimper, burying my face in the pillow. It's over. Relief floods me, but satisfaction never comes. He always finishes. I never do.

Wesley places a gentle kiss on the back of my neck, then rolls off me and onto the other side of the bed. I pull the sheet over our naked bodies and gaze at the man lying next to me. He's not the Adonis I conjured so I can feel pleasure while having sex with him. He's a mere shadow of his former self. A lifetime of hard labor, maintaining his yacht and working with cattle, keeps him active. At 58, he's still virile enough to toss me onto the bed and have his way. Yet, his saggy skin and balding forehead reveal his advanced age and the slow, but steady and irreversible descent into his twilight years. His thin lips part, and he breathes deeply as he drifts into a satiated sleep.

My gaze lingers on my partner, lover, and occasional captor. Being with him feels like a constant state of loneliness. So why do I choose to stay? I rationalize that it's because he rescued me. Without him, I'd have to return to the farm and potentially marry a widower in the church, if anyone would even consider marrying me. Where I come from, divorce is a moral transgression. A sin. If I leave Wesley, I'll spend the rest of my life as a woman trapped in misery and under someone else's thumb. Someone else's puppet. Is that what I am now? Sometimes. Yes. But not always. I do have some control over my life. Sometimes.

I sigh as I get out of bed and slip into the bathroom to take another shower. This time, I don't cry. Water runs over me from the sprayer, and again, I close my eyes.

He returns.

As I move my hands over my silky-smooth skin and the scent of lavender soap fills the air, my body tingles under what I fantasize is my Adonis's touch. My left hand cups a breast as my thumb caresses the taut nipple. My right hand slides down my abdomen and my fingers find the swollen bud between my legs and stroke. The liquid soap moistens me, washing away every trace of Wesley.

Only Adonis remains.

I can feel him as my forefinger continues to stroke. The sound of rushing water hides my moans as I find release.

Alone.

I return to bed, cleansed, invigorated, and satisfied. Before long, I drift into dreams of my Adonis.

2

Jolene: Death

The pink sky is barely visible through the porthole as my eyes flutter open and I hear a faint sob. "Wesley?" I call out, patting the empty spot next to me on the bed. He's nowhere to be seen.

"Wesley!" My voice cracks, echoing my concern as I stand on my tiptoes to peer through the open hatch. I can barely make out the backside of Wesley's nude silhouette on the deck. A heavy rope winds up the length of his body. A large object goes overboard and then something clangs as it hits the rail and then falls with a heavy splash into the Gulf of Mexico. What appears to be a dark shadow darts in front of Wesley and dives off the boat. "Wesley?" I call again, uncertain of what's happening and trying to rationalize what I saw. *Was it a person? Was it a bird's shadow? What did I see?* I blink and rub the sleep out of my eyes. With a loud clunk against the rails, Wesley tips forward and falls into the water.

It seems as if time races ahead, and reality straggles behind as I make my way up the steps to the top of the hatch and then onto the deck. My feet feel sluggish, chasing time, and too slow to reach the rail. I lean over and peer into the murky water, searching for any sign of Wesley. He disappears into its depths.

Damn him!

For a few seconds, I pause, unsure what to do. What did I see? Did someone do this to Wesley? I shake my head free of the unthinkable possibilities and inhale deeply before diving into the unknown. The early morning surface water is freezing, chilling my bare skin, and causing me to shudder. With only one goal on my mind, I ignore the cold. A few feet down, my husband sinks quickly, but I can't reach him. After coming up for air, I dive again, this time deeper into the water.

He's gone.

Kicking my feet frantically, I swim to the surface and try to focus my thoughts. My head spins. Did I awaken in someone else's reality, or not awaken at all? How can I distinguish between reality and a nightmare? The chill sets into my bones. This is no nightmare. I'm awake. Freezing. Naked. Alone? I kick my feet and, with my arms, pull myself in a circle, surveying the deep waters around me. The ocean is vast and empty. There are no other vessels in sight, and I can't identify any landmarks. The sails on the boat wrap around the masts, but it seems to have broken free of its anchor and drifts away.

Jolene's Adonis

Panicked, I power through the water toward the boat. The waves are unusually high for a calm morning.

What is Wesley always saying?

"Red sky…Red sky…fuck!" I yell at the burned sky above. "Red sky at night, sailor's delight. Red sky at morning, sailor's first warning."

I fill my lungs and rest on my back, floating on the waves long enough to regain my strength as my mind reels. I want to scream at him! I want to cry out to the world! But I can't give in to hysteria. I need every dose of energy my body holds to get out of this alive. I'm not ready to sink into the unknown with Wesley. I'm not ready to die. I said on the day I met Wesley Brown that I'd follow him anywhere, but not into the deep. Not now. Not this new Wesley that I don't even recognize on most days. I want to live!

Exhaling, I sink the lower half of my body into the water and turn to face the boat. Inhaling, I propel myself into the waves and pull the water toward my body with my arms. With each breaststroke, I gasp for air as my head crests the waves and then I dive into the surf, pushing myself forward. By the time I reach the stern and the lowered swim ladder that dips into the waves, my body is numb.

I'm thankful that the ladder is down, but why is it down? Wesley always pulls it up when we're not swimming, so he doesn't forget to raise it when the boat moves. If it drags in the water, it will snap off or damage the hull. *Did he know I would follow him, so he left the ladder down for me? Damn him!*

Pulling myself onto the deck, a seagull mews protectively as it hops from the stern to the bow and perches on the rail, watching me suspiciously.

"There you are. Where did you come from?" I ask through clattering teeth. The seagull just stares, never looking away as I step into the cockpit. For a heartbeat, I cling to its gaze as if it might anchor me, the only living witness to the madness I just saw.

I grab a towel and wrap it around my body before reaching for the radio and flipping it on, tuning to channel 16. With fingers trembling from the shock of the cold water and seeing Wesley jump, I press the button. My voice quivers. "Mayday, Mayday, Mayday! This is sailing vessel My Knotty Jolene at 27.82 degrees north and 96.99 degrees west. My husband is overboard! He jumped! I'm alone! A storm is coming! Please help!" Salt water still burns in my throat, but it's nothing compared to the hollow ache spreading through my chest, as if the ocean swallowed not just Wesley, but the last piece of certainty I had left. Releasing the button, I crumble onto the floor.

3

Jolene: Rescued

"Ma'am?" Something taps my face, and I open my eyes to a young man bent over me and a sky that's dark, except for flashes of lightning in the distance from an approaching storm. Bright search lights shine onto the boat, which rocks violently. "Ma'am?" the young man repeats. He's dressed in a Coast Guard uniform. Helping me to my feet, he asks, "Are you Amy?" in a raised voice so I can hear him over the crashing thunder that draws closer.

"No. Jolene. Jolene Brown. Wesley's wife. Amy's his daughter….my stepdaughter…my husband…." I search the deck. The gull is gone; the rail stands bare, and I swear the ocean has taken it too, just like Wesley.

"Where's my husband?" I swallow hard, remembering. The image of Wesley standing on the deck with the rope wrapped around him scorches my memory. *Am I dreaming?* I stare at the anchor tattoo on the man's forearm. It's identical to mine, just above my bikini line. I pull the towel tighter, recalling the fact that I'm naked underneath, and why.

"I'm Lieutenant Miller with the United States Coast Guard, Mrs. Brown," he says. His voice is compassionate but laced with authority. "What happened here? We received a distress call but couldn't understand the circumstances. Did you call us?"

"Yes!" I cry. "My husband, we…" I stagger backward.

Supporting me with an arm around my waist, the lieutenant speaks in a calm, yet raised tone as he leads me below deck and to the main salon. "Take a moment. It's okay. We're here. What happened? Take me through it one step at a time."

"I woke up. Wesley wasn't in bed."

"Okay." He encourages me with a nod.

"I saw him on the deck." My voice cracks. "There was a rope." I make a circling motion with my hand, winding it in midair. "He went… into… the water," I sob. My words barely distinguishable through the tears. I stand sobbing, shaking my head. "I tried!" I scream. "I to follow him! I jumped in. He sank too fast. I couldn't reach…" My head falls into my open palms. I feel like a failure. Could I have done more to save him? There were no signs of this coming, not that I recall, not that I noticed. Could I have stopped it if I wasn't so lost in my own misery? Guilt washes through me, causing my skin to prickle.

"Okay, ma'am. We have a remotely operated underwater vehicle on board, which will help us in our search. My team and I will do everything we can to find your husband, but it may take some time due to the storm. We should be clear to dive in the next hour. In the meantime, I'd like to ask you a few questions." He glances at my towel. "Would you like to get dressed first?"

I lift my head and nod. The motion triggers the acid in my stomach to rise to my throat. I swallow it down, suppressing a sudden urge to vomit.

He leads me to the stateroom and closes the door to give me privacy after I step inside. I lean heavily against the wooden frame and tremble, trying to ground myself and stop the room from spinning. A cold, empty feeling envelopes me. The room's heartbeat is gone. All that remains is a dull ache—a hunger for life.

I find my footing as something intrinsic guides me through the mechanical motions that coexist with the reality of surviving. I know it too well. When Katie, my best friend in junior high, suddenly collapsed in the school hallway from an asthma attack and died, I wasn't at her side. I wasn't holding her hand, telling her not to go. Katie was surrounded by strangers, and so young. Too young. During the weeks following her death, I feigned life. I didn't know how to go on living without Katie. Instead, I essentially became numb while everything around me seemed to carry on as if nothing happened. Katie was gone, and I didn't understand how anyone could smile or laugh.

How could they continue to live when Katie—who dazzled the world and made it incandescent—disappeared?

Eventually, I went from numbness to survivor's guilt. Katie would never experience her first kiss or her first time with a boy. We stayed up all night during sleepovers, giggling and whispering about what our first kiss would be like. We never came close. After Katie's death, I was determined to live for both of us. By the time it finally happened, I wasn't plagued with guilt that Katie would never taste a boy's lips. Instead, I craved more. My appetite was insatiable. In high school, I funneled some of my excess energy into art. It kept me from going too far over the edge in my constant quest to feel invigorated, to feel alive. I could get lost in the process of creating and block out the world without anyone trying to pull me back. Also, a girl that knew how to work with torches, hammers, and vises was hot…or at least, the guys at school thought so. I was the epitome of a brooding artist. I played with fire. I was dangerous.

When I met Wesley, he fulfilled me and tamed the wildness inside. For a while, he was enough. Now, even as we drift apart, whenever I get lost in my art, he gives me a reason to find my way back.

Now, he's gone too. And the numbness I felt after losing Katie creeps back in, familiar and unwelcome.

Pushing away from the wall, I stumble to Wesley's side of the bed and pull on the black baby doll dress he tossed to the floor as he undressed me in what seems like a lifetime ago. The silk chiffon cools my sun-burned skin, but the dress resembles a shirt on my tall frame. The hem falls just above the thick part of my thighs, leaving my legs exposed. It was okay for last night, but this morning? No!

I rifle through the small closet and pull out a pair of knee-length shorts, slipping them on with a sigh. In the mirror, I catch my reflection and swipe at the black smudges circling my emerald eyes. My hair hangs in a tangled mess down to my waist. It's wild and windblown like I've been shipwrecked for days.

I look like I've washed ashore. *God, how I wish I were back on land.*

I grab the picture from the bedside table and open the stateroom door. The lieutenant steps inside, glances around the room and toward the rumpled sheets on the bed before escorting me into the main salon.

After taking a seat at the galley table, I stroke the images in the picture, whispering incoherently to Wesley, while the lieutenant fills a teakettle with water and then places it on the small stove, turning the knob to ignite the burner. He moves through the galley like a seasoned sailor, never losing his balance. I look up from the picture occasionally and direct him to the location of the tea bags and mugs, which he fills and places into the built-in cup holders in front of me. I carefully set down the picture and grab a mug and lift it to my lips, welcoming the warmth it provides.

"Are you up to answering questions, Mrs. Brown?" he asks, sliding onto the bench on the opposite side of the table.

I take another sip, careful not to drink the hot liquid too fast, and nod.

The commotion going on around us is distracting as Coast Guardsmen prepare for the search mission. Waves crash against the sailboat, and it bangs against the buoys on their large cutter, which is lashed to the port side.

The lieutenant picks up the picture and looks it over for a few minutes before placing it back in front of me. He asks a series of questions such as, "When did you last see your husband?" and "What was his state of mind when you last saw him?"

With a detached calm, I recount the events to the lieutenant, repeating what I told him earlier, but carefully leaving out the more intimate details. The process is slow, even grueling. Sometimes, I don't even recognize the sound of my own voice. The words feel mechanical, like they're coming from someone else entirely.

The questions taper off, and for several long minutes, neither of us speaks. I stare at the photo again. Grief rises without warning, crashing over me, and I break—sobbing uncontrollably. The lieutenant says nothing. He simply waits.

I've read enough true crime books to know investigators sometimes build rapport before pressing harder, before pushing for a confession. I'm innocent. I have nothing to hide. *But innocent people go to prison all the time. Don't they?*

My body shifts restlessly in the chair, and I suddenly become hyperaware of how robotic I sound. Too precise. Too practiced. *Could they mistake that for guilt? Could I really end up in prison for something I didn't do?*

When I finally finish answering the same questions asked a dozen different ways, the lieutenant reaches across the table and slides a clear evidence bag toward me. Inside is a folded piece of paper, creased and smudged, with a short length of rope still tied around it.

He nods toward it. "We found this secured to the ship's wheel."

The name Amy is scrawled across the front, unmistakably in Wesley's handwriting.

"Can I read it?" I ask.

"No," he responds. "It's logged into evidence. But I can tell you what it says."

I nod, unsure if I want to hear.

Softly, he recites, "'My dearest Amy. I'm sorry I failed you.' There's nothing else." He sits back, arms crossed.

I stare at the lieutenant, puzzled. "That's it? 'Sorry I failed you?' What does this mean?" I glare at him.

"I was hoping you could tell me," he answers.

"Why would he just leave a note for his daughter? Nothing for me?" I sob, searching his eyes for an explanation. I pick up the picture. "Nothing for me?" I repeat. "Why?!" I scream at the man in the photo. *Why would he do this?*

The lieutenant remains silent, watching me intently.

"Someone has to tell her," I whisper, setting the picture on the table and looking at the lieutenant, my eyes pleading.

"Pardon me? Tell who?" he questions, uncrossing his arms, and leaning forward.

"Amy! I can't be the one to tell her. She hates me!" I cry. "She was expecting us this morning. I'm sure she'll be waiting for us at the dock. You have to tell her!" I beg, glancing at the clock. It's already past noon.

"Mrs. Brown, she would take the news better from a family member." He leans back and re-crosses his arms on his chest.

"Not from me. She hates me. I was twenty-six and Amy was twenty-three when we married," I explain. "I was her new stepmom…three years older and I was her new mom. You can just imagine how well she took that news." I wave my hand, like waving away the responsibility.

Lieutenant Miller nods. "I'm sure that was a difficult time for her."

"Yes, it was. She showed up drunk at the wedding and vomited all over our cake. You have to understand." I say, leaning forward. "Amy believes that I'm after her daddy's money, her money, and nothing else. She's made it her mission to get rid of me." I lean back, struck with the fact that the lieutenant now has a motive for murder. I want to shut down, stop talking, and quit digging myself into a hole of suspicion, but I need this man. Lying to him about my relationship with Amy will only make things worse. I must be honest.

"I see," he says. "Is there anyone else? Any other relatives?"

"No." I shake my head. "Wesley's family is gone. Amy's mom has been out of the picture for years.

I'm all she has left…" The realization hits me hard. *I really need this man.*

"Perhaps she'll be more accepting of you now," he says, his demeanor softening. "Considering the circumstances."

"You don' know Amy. Once her mind's set, that's it," I drawl, letting my southern roots that I worked to hide slip momentarily into my accent. "She holds a grudge like a hound on a scent."

"I see," he repeats. "I'll do whatever I can to make this easier on both of you."

"Thank you," I say, exhaling. "I'm all she has left." I sigh. "I'm all she has left…"

The thought scares the hell out of me!

4

Jolene: Hurricane Amy

After what seems like hours passing, the storm subsides enough for the remote vehicle to be lowered into the water. The air inside the cabin is suffocating. Outside, all that lingers are intermittent crashes of thunder and lightning in the distance.

Lieutenant Miller agrees that it's safe for me to go onto the deck. Men shout orders to each other, and searchlights dance on top of the dark waves. I stand quietly, observing the waters from the bow, and feeling helpless, afraid, and grateful to have made it out of the water alive. Emotions churn within, like a storm unleashed in my soul. Each time I hear a splash on the surface, my heart lurches.

The ROV breaks the waterline, and a group of divers gathers a few feet away, swimming toward the cutter with something dragging behind them.

A chill brushes my cheek, like an icy finger tracing my skin. A low, primal moan rises from deep inside me and escapes before I can stop it, raw and uncontrollable.

The man on the deck of the cutter quickly moves his hand across his throat, signaling the divers to stop and wait. They either don't see him, or they ignore his nonverbal command and proceed toward the boat.

Realizing what's about to happen, I raise my hands toward my face to shield my eyes as they haul Wesley's body onto the deck. But before I get them covered, thunder roars and lightning splits the sky, startling me, and illuminating his pallid-looking remains. I scream.

The lieutenant escorts me inside and then excuses himself to return to the deck where he communicates with his crew via a short-wave radio attached to the shoulder of his uniform.

Soon, a handful of men and one woman board the sailboat and snap pictures of random items found around the cabin. They bag and mark artifacts from our personal lives as evidence, including our bedding. Heat rushes to my face as I watch someone grip my satin pillowcase with a pair of tongs and slip it into an evidence bag. Again, I'm left feeling violated, unimportant, but I also wonder if I'm a suspect. *Why are they bagging evidence? Is this now a crime scene? What kind of evidence do they expect to obtain from my pillowcase?*

A few minutes later, the lieutenant slides onto the bench beside me. Compassion fills his eyes. "Mrs. Brown…" he starts.

Jolene's Adonis

I bury my face in my hands, not ready for the details. I want it to be a bad dream. I want to wake up and see that balding, saggy-skinned man with his head on the satin pillowcase beside me. Hell, I would give anything for another pounding from behind. I just want Wesley here, alive.

"Mrs. Brown." His voice softens. "We've recovered what we believe to be your husband's body, based on this picture." He points to the photo. "We'll need someone to officially identify the remains when we reach land." He pauses, his voice softening. "My condolences. But once we're ashore, the local investigators will take over and determine if this was a suicide. We will tow your boat as far as the bay and then a tugboat will take over from there and return you to the marina. I'll remain onboard. Mrs. Brown? Did you hear me? Mrs. Brown?"

Suicide.

The word slices into my soul and rips and shreds the traces of Wesley I treasure on its blood-thirsty path. The man I fell in love with and married would never consider such a cowardly exodus. *My* Wesley would never commit suicide! But the man I must admit I still love—God help me—isn't my Wesley, I reason. He's a mere shadow, a fragment of his former self, not worthy of sharing the same space with *my* Wesley. My thoughts reel, slamming into the memory I had just yesterday from the moment it finally hit me…he changed.

"Mrs. Brown?" The lieutenant's hand covers mine, bringing me back to reality. My cheeks burn as my thoughts return to the evidence bags and our personal items that were carried away by strangers.

Feeling emotionally exhausted, I slump sideways onto the padded bench in the galley and drift in and out of a fitful sleep while the lieutenant steers. Outside, the Coast Guard cutter glides through the now-calm waves, towing us behind it.

Just before we reach the harbor, a tugboat pulls along the starboard side. The commotion rouses me, and I sit up, alert and ready to go home. The tugboat soon takes over and guides *My Knotty Jolene* to the marina where the lieutenant starts the engine and drives into the boat slip. When we're alongside the concrete floating dock that rises and falls on the same level as the boat, I jump out and secure the ropes in the cleats on both ends, just as I've done for years with Wesley at the wheel.

"You're late!" Amy yells from the end of the walkway. She pats her red-soled shoe on the concrete and adjusts her handbag. Sadie, her blonde miniature poodle, whimpers her disapproval at the sudden movement. "Where's Daddy?" Amy demands, ignoring her dog.

"He…" I choke on the words, thinking of his lifeless body being hauled aboard the cutter, bound for the morgue or wherever they take people who die at sea.

I can't call and ask Wesley where they're taking him.

I can never call him again.

Fresh tears flood my eyes and threaten to spill over.

The lieutenant cuts the engine and steps over to join us.

"Who's this?" Amy's face brightens. She extends her hand as if to be kissed and bats her fake eyelashes at the handsome young lieutenant. "I can't resist a man in uniform," she adds with a predatory growl.

"Lieutenant Miller, Miss," he says, accepting her hand and giving it an awkward shake. "Nice to meet you."

"This is Amy." I gesture in Amy's direction and turn to wipe my eyes while Amy's distracted.

"Oh," he says, holding onto her hand and searching her eyes. "You're Wesley Brown's daughter?"

"Yes. I'm Amy Brown. You can call me Amy," she responds. "Where's Daddy? I have plans."

The lieutenant and I lock eyes, and I offer a silent plea.

"This way, Miss Amy," he indulges, and then guides her onto the boat, shutting the cabin door behind them.

I wait near the boat slip, hands wringing, legs unsteady, unsure of what to do. Minutes crawl by. Part of me wants to run, to disappear into my condo, crawl under the soft sheets, and shut the world out. But I can't. Not yet. I have to stay. There's a storm building behind that cabin door, and I know I'll be the one standing in its path.

"*That bitch!*" Amy screeches.

The cabin falls silent for a beat, then Amy lets out a blood-curdling scream. Sadie howls in response, her cry echoing across the deck.

The cabin door bursts open, and Amy storms out, the lieutenant trailing behind her, powerless to stop her. She charges across the boat, gripping the railing as the vessel shifts beneath her, nearly losing hold of Sadie in the process.

The dog glances at me with wide, helpless eyes. I step forward and offer a hand.

Amy slaps it away like I'm nothing more than a bug in her path.

"*You!*" she spats. Her crystal blue eyes brim with unshed tears. "This is *your* fault!"

She hastens down the dock with Sadie bouncing alongside her and disappears into the parking lot. Moments later, the sound of squealing tires reverberates throughout the marina.

5

Jolene: My Knotty Jolene

A surprising wave of reluctance washes over me as I stand on the dock, unwilling to leave the boat and the memories woven into every inch of her. I take a moment to soak it all in.

My Knotty Jolene is breathtaking, especially under full sail. She's a 43-foot cruising vessel, sleek and white, trimmed in warm reddish-brown teakwood that frames her fiberglass deck like jewelry.

Wesley bought her during our engagement. At the time, she sat abandoned for years and was weathered and in desperate need of attention. But she was a bargain, so he paid cash. She's the only thing we ever owned outright, free and clear. Our sweat made her beautiful.

We spent weeks side by side, scraping and sanding, painting and staining, carefully unhooking each sail and sending it off for repair. She became our project. Our escape. And for a little while… our beginning.

The memories come flooding back…

****

"You know what you're getting for your birthday this year?" Wesley teased with a mischievous twinkle.

"I'm afraid to ask," I responded.

"A sewing machine!" he exclaimed.

"A what?" I snorted.

"You, my dear, are going to learn how to sew. You'll save me a fortune on mending and replacing sails."

"How's that a present for me?"

"More money to waste on your designer bags," he said, flicking my orange handbag, which cost more than the boat.

"Hey!" I protested, hugging the bag to my chest.

Wesley pulled me toward him and placed a tender kiss on my lips.

****

I run a finger across my bottom lip, the memory of Wesley's gentle, playful side tugging at me. My eyes lift to the boom, tracing it all the way to the top of the main mast. I can still hear myself screaming the first time he hoisted me up in the bosun's chair to check the rigging. I was convinced the mast would snap in half and fling me straight into the water.

Jolene's Adonis

When he announced we'd spend our honeymoon sailing to Belize, I thought I was doomed. There was something about being on a boat in the middle of the ocean that terrified me. But Wesley was an expert sailor, and all the time we spent together inspecting and restoring every square inch of this boat slowly quieted that fear.

Now, as I glance around, it hits me—there isn't a single corner of *My Knotty Jolene* that doesn't hold a memory of him. A good one. A real one. And for a moment, it almost feels like he's still here.

"I'm going to sell her," I whisper to Lieutenant Miller, who stands silently at my side.

He doesn't hesitate. "Now's not the time to make decisions like that, if you don't mind me speaking frankly, Mrs. Brown."

"I can't spend another minute on this boat," I say, my voice breaking. "She's Wesley's. She'll always be Wesley's. I can't look at her without seeing him." The sob escapes before I can swallow it.

He gently places a hesitant arm around my shoulder, then presses something into my hand. It's a large platinum wedding band.

"This is the only item he had on him," he says softly.

I turn the ring between my fingers, feeling the faint grooves I carved when hammering the soft metal. On the inside, in tiny letters, it reads: *Forever yours, Jolene,* followed by a small engraved heart.

"I made this for him," I murmur, mostly to myself. "In my shop. He never takes… took it off."

"You made it?" he asks, surprised.

"Yeah. I'm a blacksmith," I reply quietly.

"Oh." His gaze shifts to my hands, and his expression softens as he notices the scars on my knuckles and wrists. Realization flickers across his face.

I instinctively fold my arms across my chest, shielding the marks. "You don't think…" I start, the question heavy in my throat.

He raises an eyebrow, but says nothing.

"No! Wesley's a bastard at times, and controlling, but he would never physically harm me. I work with metal and fire. It's a hazard of the job," I explain, though I'm not sure why I should defend the man who constantly disappoints me.

The lieutenant straightens his back. "I didn't mean to imply. I just saw the scars and the ladder, and I couldn't help but wonder if there was more to the story."

"The ladder?" I ask.

"Yes, the ladder. You said that it was lowered when you swam back to the boat. You didn't mention swimming last night, and this morning, your statement was that you slept until he woke you. I'm assuming that your husband didn't use it. So, I'm perplexed as to why the ladder would be lowered," he states.

I shrug. "He lowered it for me, I guess. He knew I would dive in after him, if I saw him." I swallow the gravel in my throat before explaining further. "He's always criticizing me because I don't plan ahead. I plunge in headfirst without thinking of the next step. Stupid, I know. But my only thought was him." I shake my head, trying to erase the memory.

"There you are!" a shrill voice with a slight British accent sings from behind us.

"Oh gawd!" I mutter.

Lieutenant Miller eyes me curiously.

We turn to face a spindly, yet surprisingly formidable-looking woman. Her frail, overly tanned arms host a variety of liver spots and appear to be aged beyond her years. A red visor barely covers sun-bleached, cropped hair, and she's dressed in her usual tennis clothing, down to the standard tennis court approved shoes. Typically, Lisa Hicks struts around the marina in a string bikini and mesh cover-up, unless she's going somewhere. On those occasions, she always has the appearance that she's ready for a match, like today.

To her face, I call her "Lise," which is her nickname amongst the boaters. Behind her back, Wesley and I call her "Hyacinth." Other than a vast difference in body mass, she puts on airs and is just as irritating as the Hyacinth character on the British comedy, *Keeping Up Appearances*. She treats her husband, Larry, just like the character Richard is treated on the show. The similarities between Lisa and Hyacinth, an over-exaggerated, social-climbing snob, are uncanny. The tragic part is that the character in the show was designed to entertain and make people laugh at the absurdity of her over-zealous lust for attention. There's nothing entertaining about Lisa.

"There you are!" Lisa repeats. "Amy was looking for you! That girl gets cuter every time I see her! What a stunner!" she announces, flashing the Lieutenant her best smile.

"She found me," I respond, emotionless.

"Good," Lisa says, searching over my shoulder. "Where's that handsome bloke of yours? I have news!" she sings.

I feel my face fall, but the words won't come. I can't bring myself to say it out loud—that Wesley is gone forever.

I thought it would be obvious. My disheveled hair, my red, swollen eyes. Surely anyone could see the grief clinging to me. I must look like I've been torn apart.

But this is Lisa. Self-absorbed as ever. She doesn't notice that anything's wrong.

And I won't be the one to tell her.

I can't tell anyone.

Not today.

"I'll wait in the parking lot until you're ready to leave. Someone will escort you to the station," Lieutenant Miller whispers before taking Lisa's arm and leading her away.

Lisa peers up at him and beams, lacing her fingers across his bicep, and giving it a squeeze. "I'll tell him later!" she calls over a shoulder as she's led down the dock.

With one final look at the boat, I say goodbye to all the memories it holds, and move at a snail's pace past the other docked boats, reluctant to meet up with the lieutenant. *I know he's just doing his job, but I don't feel like reliving Wesley's death again.*

Lieutenant Miller waits patiently at the gate leading to the parking lot. Thankfully, Lisa is nowhere in sight.

He guides me into the passenger seat of an unmarked police car, then introduces me to the undercover officer behind the wheel. With a brief, almost apologetic wave, he steps back as we pull onto the highway.

We ride in silence for two miles before reaching a modest, nondescript police station.

For the next few hours, I recount the details leading up to the Coast Guard's arrival. The officer listens silently, taking notes but rarely interrupts. I share the same timeline I gave to Lieutenant Miller. Every moment I can remember. Every movement Wesley made. Every word we exchanged.

No one says it outright, but I feel it lingering in the air: suspicion.

They're trying to figure out if I'm lying.

When I finally stop talking, the officer gives a stiff nod. "We'll be in touch if we need anything else."

I'm escorted out and driven home in silence.

When the patrol car pulls up in front of the building, I step out slowly, my legs stiff from sitting so long. I stare up at the place I shared with Wesley.

Our condominium crowns the top floor. It's a sleek glass box with a 180° view of the Gulf of Mexico. From here, the water wraps around us.

The island is just a thin strip of land, and just one mile from bay to sea. From our penthouse on the

20th floor, it feels like I'm floating in the middle of nowhere.

I used to love it here.

But Wesley's gone.

I push open the door and step into the stone-floored foyer, nodding at the night watchman on duty. Without a word, I enter the glass elevator, insert my key into the panel, and press PH.

As the elevator rises, trepidation tightens in my chest. With each ding announcing another floor passed, the weight of what waits above grows heavier.

The elevator comes to a gentle halt, and the doors slide open, but I can't make myself step forward. My feet stay planted, just shy of the plush carpet that spills into the living room.

The thought of spending the night without Wesley is unbearable. It drags the tragedy of his death back to the surface, sharp and fresh.

I just want to forget.

I pour myself a glass of red wine, skip changing out of my wrinkled clothes, and sink into the couch. Pulling a fleece throw over my body, I curl up and drink, hoping to dull everything.

The wine blurs the edges of my mind, and eventually, I drift into a heavy sleep. I dream of

Wesley—his laugh, his smile—until the warmth fades.

At dawn, I jolt awake from a nightmare. He was there, tugging at my wrist, trying to pull me into the unknown. His eyes were lifeless, hollow.

And he wouldn't let go.

6

Jolene: Awakening

The days after Wesley's death pass in a blur. Flashes of a life I no longer recognize. Everything feels foreign, like I've stepped into someone else's nightmare. My mind is a ticking time bomb, and each new revelation inches me closer to detonation.

"Suicide," the coroner says.

Tick.

"Your insurance policy doesn't cover suicide," the agent tells me.

Tick.

"I'm sorry, Mrs. Brown. You only have $1,200 in your account," says the bank teller.

Tick.

"Your savings and investment accounts were closed weeks ago."

Tick.

"Your bonds have been cashed."

Tick.

"Your husband still had a mortgage on the condo. He prepaid for two more months. After that, it's yours to cover."

Tick.

"The vehicles are leased in your husband's name. You'll need to either take over the lease or pay the balloon balance and register them yourself."

Tick.

"Mrs. Brown, your husband closed his business months ago. It no longer exists."

Tick.

I snap.

My heart races, my chest burns, and a pressure rises in my throat like I'm going to scream, or break. I want to hit something. Anything. Wesley's face flashes in my mind and I growl at the empty space between me and the funeral director like it's his fault.

"Ma'am, can I get you something?" the man behind the mahogany desk asks, his voice shaking.

"Five thousand is the lowest you can go?" I say, trying to hold it together. "Can't you do it for less? I have nothing." My voice breaks. "He left me with nothing, that bastard! I've lost everything. He didn't even tell me he lost his business." I laugh bitterly.

"All I have left is his dumb boat. Do you take boats as payment?"

He blinks, stunned. "No, I'm sorry. We need payment upfront. We accept life insurance, if that's available."

I let out a short, sharp laugh, half-hysteria, half-spite. "You're a comedian, Mr. Reynolds? Has anyone ever told you that?"

He clears his throat. "The best I can do is a simple graveside service and our most affordable casket. $2,500. I really can't go any lower. I can also allow one family car for transportation from your home to the cemetery."

He slides a blank form toward me. "Please write down the pickup address. I'll make the arrangements."

"That's fine," I mutter, defeated. "I'll get the money to you by tomorrow."

I sign the paperwork and scribble down Amy's current address where she's staying with friends. She'll expect limo service, of course.

But there isn't a car on earth big enough for the two of us.

I drop the top on my red Mustang convertible and press the gas, pushing it as fast as it'll go. I've driven this stretch of highway a hundred times, the narrow ribbon of road between Port Aransas and the more developed end of the island just before the causeway into Corpus Christi. But today feels different.

This is my last ride. And I'm going to enjoy every second of it.

Spanish-style houses with stucco walls and red tile roofs blur past me. Towering condominium complexes rise between the scattered single-family homes, offering maintenance-free living for what the locals call "snowbirds." Just like the name suggests, they migrate south before the first snowfall, arriving in flocks and filling the island for the winter.

I pass winding canals that snake behind the houses, leading out to the Gulf. I can still picture the way the water sparkled at Christmastime when Wesley and I visited friends along the canals to watch the parade of boats. Kids stood on their docks, bundled in hoodies and holiday pajamas, waving as boaters passed by, tossing candy like confetti. Santa always rode in the final boat, closing the show and officially ringing in the season.

Christmas will never be the same without Wesley.

When I reach Jessica's neighborhood, I slam on the brakes a little too hard. The tires squeal, and the Mustang jerks forward before settling into a calmer roll. I ease up, forcing myself to drive the speed limit.

If there's one person I can trust, it's Jessica.

Jolene's Adonis

We met not long after Wesley and I bought the condo. She and I couldn't be more different, but somehow it works. I'm fire, always burning, always hungry for more. Jessica? She's earth. Grounded. Nurturing. The kind of steady I used to think I didn't need. But today, I need her more than anyone.

I stop in front of Jessica's expansive house and take a long breath. The drive cooled my nerves, smoothed the jagged edges of my rage. There's just something about speeding down the road with the wind whipping through my hair and the stereo cranked high that makes me feel alive.

Damn, I'm going to miss that car.

Jessica meets me at the door with a warm hug and a smile, one that quickly fades as I unravel the mess Wesley left behind.

"Ask your parents for the money," she suggests gently after listening to everything.

I groan, collapsing onto her sofa like a sullen teenager. "They'll make me move back home. I swear, my head's going to explode. I can't go back there, Jessica. I just can't."

Her green eyes flash with concern. "Then move in with us. George won't mind. He adores you."

I reach out and brush her red hair away from her face, then tilt her chin so our eyes meet. "Jessica, you've been a great friend, and I love you for that. But I can't live with you." I wave a hand around at her immaculate, picture-perfect home. "You're too perfect. I work with grease, metal, and grime. I'd drive you absolutely insane."

"Perfect? Me? Bah!" she scoffs, then frowns. "I'm worried about you."

"I'll be okay. I just need enough to get through the funeral and stay afloat for a little while. Then I can throw myself into my work. At least I still have that." I sit up straighter, needing her to understand. "Wesley leased the storefront in my name, so as long as I can pay rent, it's safe. But there's a no-occupancy clause, so I can't live there.

"And as far as I know, the bank can't take the boat. If I sell it, they might be able to go after the proceeds, and then I'll have nothing. So I've thought it through. I have sixty days left at the condo. After that, I'll live on the boat for a while, ride my bike to the shop, and earn what I can. It's temporary. Just until I get back on my feet."

I stand and pace in front of the wide window that overlooks the canal. My chest tightens as I speak. "If it weren't for Amy, I'd cremate the bastard and be done with it. But she loves him… and so do I." I pause and glare out at the water. "Damn him."

I turn back to Jessica, my voice steadier now. "I'm not asking for a handout. Just let me borrow the money. I'll pay you back, with interest."

"Anything for you," Jessica says, her voice softening. "But please, consider my offer. My door's always open."

7

Orlando: Entanglements

I turn onto the desolate two-lane highway that runs across the narrow strip of land between the bay and the Gulf. I've driven it before, but not like this.

I always feared this day would come—being called to clean up after Wesley. My partner. My brother in everything but blood. For months now, he's been pulling away. He stopped sharing information, stopped looping me in on the case we started together. That only meant one thing: he was in danger. And he didn't want to drag me down with him.

But I felt it. I *always* feel it. That pit in my stomach has been twisting like a hangover from cheap draft beer for months. I knew something was coming. We both did.

The men we dealt with don't forgive. They wait. Then they hit back. Wesley knew it too. He was smart—smart enough to win a few battles, but also smart enough to know you can only win so many before the tide turns.

So why the hell did he go in alone? No backup. No warning. Just gone.

I tried to get him to open up, to let me help. But Wesley could be a mule-headed jackass when he wanted to be. And this… this was the result.

I drift onto the shoulder, letting a line of cars pass. It's the custom out here.

I curse under my breath. "Damn you, Wesley."

Old superstition says not to speak ill of the dead, but I figure I've earned the right. He was my partner. My responsibility in a lot of ways. I'll talk about that stubborn fool however I damn well please.

He was older than me, had more years on the job, but I always approached things with caution. Methodically. I kept my personal life sealed off from the work. No attachments. No distractions. Never married. Never seriously dated. It wasn't worth the risk.

Didn't matter how much I craved a woman's touch or the comfort of warm skin next to mine, I'd never drag someone into this life. I saw too much. I *know* what happens to soft targets.

But Wesley? He fell for a pretty young thing, not much older than his own daughter, and married her. Just like that, he cracked the already fragile relationship with his kid and created a whole new liability in his wife.

I tried to understand it. What could possibly be worth the risk? He knew who we were dealing with—men who don't blink before putting a bullet in a kid or a woman if it sends a message. People with no conscience. No lines. They go after what you love most. And he gave them a second bullseye.

I spent years protecting his daughter. Whenever he went dark on overseas missions, I watched over her myself or arranged someone to do it. She's just as stubborn as him. Doesn't take orders well. Grew up seeing us as glorified babysitters, uncles, nannies. She didn't even know what her father really did until she turned eighteen.

Even then, she still ran off. Raves. Parties. Massive crowds where no amount of protection could keep her safe if someone marked her.

And then Wesley went and married someone else. Didn't even introduce her to the team. No uncles. No protection. Just shadows watching her from a distance whenever he was active. But distance isn't safety. Not in our world.

Every time he worked a case, *both* of them were at risk. Double the exposure. Double the effort. I never understood why he took that chance.

But maybe today, I'll finally get a look at the woman he risked everything for. The woman he kept hidden, even from me.

Jolene's Adonis

I think of that old phrase—*Over my dead body.* I guess that's what it took. Because now, finally, I'm about to see the woman Wesley married.

And he had to die for it to happen.

I ease the dark-colored rental car into the small cemetery and park at the end of a long line of vehicles. From here, I can see a crowd gathered beneath a cloth tent, the casket perched on a mechanical lift.

I wish I could get closer. Just one last look at Wesley, my partner, my mentor, and my friend. But I can't risk it. Not with all these people as witnesses. If Amy sees me, the whole thing unravels. She'll blow my cover without even realizing it.

I need to be patient. Calculated. If I want to find out what really happened to Wesley, I can't be *me*. Not here. I have to go undercover. I need a plan.

I slip out of the car and make my way through the rows of headstones, finally kneeling beside a mausoleum near a double tombstone. I rest one hand on the cold granite, pretending I'm visiting a long-lost loved one, my head bowed just enough to go unnoticed.

I spot Amy right away. Dramatic. As always. Her movements are big, almost theatrical, but there's something in the way she clutches her arms that makes her look lost. Wesley may have had others step in as caretakers, but he was the only true parent in her life. She loved him fiercely. That bond was unshakable.

It's been years since I saw them together. After he got married, Wesley and I only met in secret. His wife was a mystery, but Amy? Amy remained at the center of his heart. She's a goddaughter to me. I can't even begin to imagine what this is doing to her.

I continue scanning the cemetery, letting my eyes shift naturally from one mourner to the next. A few feet away, a tall blonde dabs at her face with a handkerchief. I can't tell from here if the tears are real or just part of the performance.

Behind the group, two men stand back from the others, arms folded, eyes sharp. They're surveying the scene, quiet but alert. Plainclothes officers, no doubt. I'd bet money they're local and stationed here by the chief. I made a few calls after the death was ruled a suicide. I probably stirred the pot more than I meant to.

But they won't interfere.

They can't.

I'll get to the truth myself.

No matter what it takes.

8

Jolene: The Plunge into Darkness

The details of the funeral blur together in a haze. I stand awkwardly in a black lace dress, staring blankly at the casket, trying not to think about what comes next.

My soul feels something like freedom for the first time in years, but my heart grieves for the only man I've ever truly loved. Or thought I loved. He's a stranger now.

At what point did everything between us twist into something unrecognizable? We had the condo, the boat, the cars, my business. Wesley took care of everything. I never thought I needed to worry. Never questioned that he had it all under control.

And yet… here I am.

As gutted as I feel, I can't watch them lower him into the ground. I just can't. I quietly ask the director to wait until everyone's gone before finishing the burial.

Mourners pass by, murmuring condolences. Amy and I stand side by side, though it feels like there's an ocean between us. She mumbles responses, clearly in shock. I nod at the outstretched hands, shake the ones offered, but I don't register the words. My eyes stay locked on the casket.

I keep thinking if I stare hard enough, I'll see through it. I'll find Wesley in there somewhere, and he'll explain all of this, like why he left me this way, and why he kept so much from me. He knew I had nothing to fall back on. He knew. And he still left.

"Jolene, are you sure you don't want to come home with us?"

My mom's voice breaks through the fog, and she steps between me and the casket, blocking my line of sight. Her lips are pursed in that way that says she expects me to obey without argument.

Behind her, my dad stands silent, holding his Sunday hat in his rough, calloused hands. He hasn't said more than two words to me since Wesley died. But his expression says enough. Disappointment, maybe. Or grief. Maybe both.

"I'll be fine," I tell them, though it hurts to say it. The lie sits like lead in my chest. I've never lied to them before. And I'm sure they know I'm lying now. But I can't go back to the farm. I just… can't.

Mom sighs, then hugs me quickly… tightly… and makes me promise to call if I need anything. Dad gives me a sideways hug and presses a kiss to my forehead before they walk away.

As they climb into their truck, regret swells inside me. It would be so much easier to just go back. Life would be simpler. Safer.

But no.

It's time I stand on my own two feet. Time I stop depending on anyone else, so I never feel this helpless again.

My gaze snaps back to the casket and the son of a bitch lying inside it. The blur of mouths moving in sympathy around me becomes a stream of noise I can't hear. Soft words, gentle hands, meaningless comfort. I'm hugged, pulled in, touched, but I don't feel any of it.

Eventually, the crowd thins, and only Amy and I remain.

"Daddy didn't deserve this," she says coldly, not even glancing my way.

"Nobody does," I reply, eyes still locked on the casket, my heart molten and burning in my chest where something softer used to live.

Amy steps into my space, blocking my view and forcing me to look at her. Her mascara and eyeliner are smudged into a raccoon mess around her overly animated blue eyes. Her jet-black hair is pulled into a tight bun at the nape of her neck, and a lace birdcage veil hangs just above her bangs, dipping slightly below one of her perfectly arched brows.

"Did you have to put him in the cheapest fucking casket?" she hisses, eyes gleaming. "Trying to save money for a boob job or to lift your saggy old ass?"

She jabs her finger hard into my chest.

"This is your fault! You'll pay for this! And you won't get a dime from his estate or his life insurance. I'll make damn sure of it. You'll be stuck with your saggy tits and ass, bitch."

She draws out the word like she's savoring it, then spits it out like poison.

I clench my fists, my nails digging into my palms. Every cell in my body screams to lash back, to put her in her place, but I don't. I can't. Not here. Not now.

The age gap between us isn't wide, but I take my role as her stepmother to heart. It was never simple, but I tried. And even now, with her fury aimed squarely at me, this isn't the moment to defend myself. This isn't the time to set her straight.

So, I drop my gaze and hold it down, working to control the volcano threatening to erupt inside my chest. Let her have her moment. Let her think she won.

"You'll get nothing!" she screams over her shoulder as she storms toward the family car.

Jolene's Adonis

I exhale slowly and turn away, my legs heavy as I walk toward Jessica, who's waiting by her SUV.

"What was *that* about?" she asks, eyes narrowing.

I shake my head. "You know… Daddy's girl is in for a rude awakening," I say, a flicker of guilt tugging at me for staying silent through Amy's verbal assault. Stepmom or not, I didn't deserve that.

"Karma's coming," I mutter, opening the passenger door. "Let's go."

9

Orlando: Goodbye Brother

I shake off the awkward tension between Amy and the blonde. I only caught fragments of their argument, sharp and confusing, but I fight the urge to step in. It's not my place. Not yet. I stay still, watching, waiting, until the last of the mourners climb into their cars and drive away. Then I approach the casket and nod to the funeral attendant standing a few feet away, his hands clasped in front of him like a soldier at rest.

"Hi. I'm late. Missed the service," I say. "Do you mind lifting the lid so I can say goodbye?"

He eyes me carefully. "Are you a relative?"

"You could say that," I answer. "He was my business partner. My brother."

The man nods and gently removes the flowers from the casket before lifting the lid. Then he steps back to give me space.

I move in slowly and look down. Wesley's dressed in a dark suit and tie, with his face covered in layers of makeup. I wonder why the funeral was closed-casket. On the surface, he looks… fine. Bloated, sure, but like he's just sleeping.

I lean in as if I'm reaching for his hand, but instead, I brush my thumb across his neck, wiping at the heavy makeup. There they are…faint red marks dragging across his skin. Not from drowning. No way.

"You asshole," I mutter, just under my breath. "You got in over your head."

Then, louder, for the benefit of the attendant still nearby, I say, "I'll miss you, brother."

A car engine rumbles in the distance and my instincts flare. I gently lower the lid, nod to the attendant, and replace the flowers before slipping away into the rows of headstones.

This isn't over. My investigation's just begun. And I won't stop until I know what really happened.

10

Jolene: A new chapter

Time creeps by as I stumble through my new reality without Wesley. I lose track of the weeks, locking myself away, ignoring the world while I deflect daily calls from my parents and friends. They're desperate to check in, to poke through the cocoon I've built around myself.

"I'm fine. I don't need anything," I say for the hundredth time, the words falling out of my mouth like lines from a script I no longer believe. Each call is the same, and I've become a glorified switchboard operator. My voice steady, polite, and automatic. I'm not part of the conversation anymore. I'm just the middleman, the hollow voice between worried loved ones and the version of me they hope still exists.

It's like I've been reduced to a headset and a blinking red light, trapped in an endless loop. *Thank you for calling. Please hold for the illusion of stability. How may I deflect your concern today?*

Somewhere beneath it all, I know they mean well. But I don't have the bandwidth to let anyone in. Not yet. Maybe not ever.

Jolene's Adonis

Most days I sit curled on the couch in the penthouse, surrounded by half-empty bottles of wine and tear-streaked photo albums. I flip through pages that feel like fiction now, drinking away the ghosts of my old life. "I'm fine. I'm fine. I'm fine." I say it like a mantra. A lie. A performance worthy of an Oscar.

For years, I was Wesley's wife. But who am I now? Just Jolene? The name feels hollow, empty of meaning or place.

My upbringing instilled in me the belief that a woman's purpose was to marry and serve her husband. That was the plan. The path. God's will, they said. I stopped believing in God the day I left the farm, but the rules I learned from my community still echo through me, like a hymn I can't forget.

When I said *"I do,"* I thought I was stepping into something solid, something lasting. But now it's all unraveled. The marriage, the man, and the promises. They're gone.

And I'm not just grieving Wesley. I'm grieving the version of life I was taught to expect. The one I never questioned until it was too late.

Now, I don't know who I am or what kind of life I'm supposed to build from these ashes.

I pack the last of my things into Jessica's SUV and glance one last time at the boxes labeled for storage. The movers will come in the morning. What doesn't fit on the boat stays in limbo until I figure out what's next.

At the front desk, I hand the condo key to the doorman without a word. Then I hop on my bike and pedal toward the marina, Jessica trailing behind me in her SUV like a shadow I'm not ready to lose.

At the marina shop, we grab one of the big, clunky pushcarts—basically a plastic trough on wheels—and load it up. Together, we haul everything to *My Knotty Jolene*, unloading the contents onto the deck in a haphazard pile.

"Are you sure you'll be okay?" Jessica asks, rummaging through her oversized bag for her keys.

"I'm fine. Go!" I say, nudging her gently off the boat with a small grin I barely feel.

She blows me a kiss and heads down the dock, fading from view like the last remnant of the life I just left behind.

I sink into one of the cushioned seats near the helm, letting the silence settle over me. A few minutes pass before I drag myself upright, toss my keys, phone, wallet, a bottle of water, and an apple into my messenger bag, and hop back on my bike.

Time to ride to the store. Time to pretend again. Time to keep moving.

Jolene's Adonis

I enjoy the sounds, smells, and scenery during the one-mile bike ride from the marina to the studio. I used to make the ride often from the condo, which was even farther away. It gives me time to clear my head and shift into artisan mode. It also helps me stay in shape.

Clouds drift across a powder-blue sky, and a cool Gulf breeze carries the lingering scent of pink evening primrose through the late morning air. Locals call them "pink buttercups." I just call them heaven. I inhale deeply, savoring the sweetness. Once, it electrified me. Now, it grounds me.

Seagulls cry in the distance, begging anglers for scraps from their bait buckets. Waves lap onto the shore and roll back into the hazy blue depths. It's January. Tourist season hasn't begun, so the sand-lined streets are still quiet and clean.

Here in the small coastal Texas town, most businesses rely on the busy tourist season—from March through late August—to carry them in the slow winter months. This winter has been especially hard on my business. I'm not sure why.

I lean to the right as I round the last corner, and the studio comes into view. The sign above the door reads, "Jolene's Treasures." Wesley painted that sign. I'll never forget how proud he was the day he gave me the keys and the lease to the store.

The bell above the door chimes as I roll my bike over the threshold and into the studio. Metal sculptures inspired by the sea decorate the left wall. Waves, fish, and seashells. My inspiration from days past is clear. In the corners, glass display cases hold my metal jewelry—earrings, rings, belts, bracelets, and cuffs. Each piece is uniquely designed and forged in the back of my shop. To the right are my newest pieces, the ones that customers look at and giggle. Though I'm still not sure why. When I made them, I let the metal speak to me. They're abstract. Modern. Enigmatic. I guess when every other store in town sells starfish and sharks, my conceptual art just seems too weird.

During the off-season, I spend most of my time creating. I work long hours to fill the shelves and cases before the tourists arrive. I can't afford to hire help, so I take clients by appointment only in the winter. That way, I have the focused time I need to design and forge without interruptions.

I roll my bike into the back room and lean it against the wall. My workbench is just as I left it, with a partially hammered bracelet still clamped in the vise. I crank up Alanis Morissette and belt out the chorus, raw and jagged, pounding the metal in rhythm. Tears mix with sweat and drip down my cheeks onto the table. Movement in the corner catches my eye. I pause mid-lyric.

The most beautiful and exotic woman I ever saw strolls toward me, with a well-dressed man following closely behind. I quickly turn off the stereo and wipe my eyes with the back of my sleeve.

The woman extends a graceful hand in my direction and asks, "Open?" Her Spanish accent is thick and musical.

"Sorry, yes. I am," I say, mentally kicking myself. *Dummy, you forgot to lock the door.*

She holds something in her other hand. A leash? A tinkling sound echoes across the concrete floor. I follow the noise to its source.

The man is wearing a black vinyl spiked dog collar. A delicate silver chain connects the collar to the woman's hand.

What the hell...

11

Orlando: Surveillance

I pull into my regular spot a couple hundred feet away from Jolene's Treasures, scanning for anything out of the ordinary. I'm late. Since the funeral, I've tailed Wesley's widow through her predictable routine. Now that she no longer lives at the condo, her habits will shift. I welcome the change.

Honestly, I'm feeling bored, and maybe even a little sympathetic, watching the dull, lonely life Jolene seems to lead.

I want to watch her every move, so I slipped the daytime doorman a hefty bribe to get into her condo and installed hidden cameras. So far, I haven't figured out how to see inside her store. I can't risk interacting with her. Not yet.

When I set up the surveillance, I wasn't sure what I expected. Hell, I half thought I'd catch her with a boyfriend, or at least out partying every night, celebrating her new single life. Isn't that what people do when they free themselves from an unhappy marriage through deadly means? A sudden death, followed by excessive spending or wild behavior, tends to trigger suspicion. Some widows blow through life insurance money on designer bags and luxury vacations. Some start partying, drinking, or even move in their lovers within days, passing them off as friends or security blankets.

But not this girl.

I don't know what kind of life Wesley and Jolene shared before he died, but I can't imagine it was anything like the sad, quiet one she lives now.

She's either calculated in her reaction, or she's innocent. Instead of doing anything that might raise suspicion, she interacts with no one except one friend. She bikes to her shop, returns home before dark, packs boxes while crying, and eventually passes out on the sofa after a few glasses of wine.

What I've seen of her life is, frankly, pathetic. Is she really grieving, or just putting on a show to avoid suspicion?

Even when I catch her crying alone, I can't tell. Is she mourning Wesley, or is she mourning the loss of her charmed life? I know she's broke. Wesley left her with nothing but debt. Still, something doesn't add up. Could she have a motive that wasn't financial?

I want answers. So far, my instincts are nudging me away from suspecting her as a cold-blooded killer. She's starting to look more like a naïve introvert—someone who didn't have a clue what was happening around her.

Now that she's moved onto the boat, I'm hoping her new environment sheds some light. Marina life is wide open with people who work outdoors, fish, and socialize. She can't hide anymore.

12

Jolene:

Mistress Selena and her pet

The exotic woman moves around the metal displays with such confident ease she seems even more mysterious. The man with her is so in sync, every step like a meticulously choreographed ballet. They're both wearing Gucci. He's dressed for a day at the country club. She's ready for a night at the Met. The sight of them is hypnotic… and, honestly, tantalizing.

I have an eye for fashion and instantly start flipping through the mental catalog of designers and collections stored in my brain. I call it my superpower, though I'm not sure it's useful to anyone but me. I just love spotting a label and testing myself to see if I can name it.

As a kid, while my friends memorized Bible verses, I studied seasons and runway collections. I dreamed of owning something designer one day, so I paid attention to the subtle details and signature styles of every major brand like scripture.

After I married Wesley, that dream finally came true. And once I had the clothes in my hands, on my body, I only became more obsessed with the craftsmanship, the artistry, and the pure imagination behind every piece.

"We don't get many tourists this time of year," I call out from behind the small check-out counter, noticing the woman's interest in one of my latest creations. I don't approach her because I'm not one to hover. I prefer to observe from a distance, but to say I'm curious about this woman would be the understatement of the year.

"I'm not your average tourist," she purrs, her voice husky and low.

The man avoids my gaze completely. His eyes stay glued to her Christian Louboutin lace-and-satin knee-high boots. I can't blame him. They're like exotic tattoos wrapped around her long, tan legs. Siren-red toenails peek out from the open toe. The black lace is sculpted into a delicate floral pattern that clings to her skin like a second, sexier layer. I saw pictures of a celebrity wearing those boots on a red carpet a few weeks ago and nearly fainted. In person, they're breathtaking.

She fingers a bronze sculpture and raises a heavily penciled brow. "This is phallic, no?"

Heat rushes to my cheeks. I tilt my head and try to see it from her perspective. "Um… I guess it is.

Though that wasn't the intention." I chuckle nervously.

"No?" she asks, sliding her hand slowly up and down the sculpture while biting her lip. Her companion shifts uncomfortably beside her.

"No," I repeat, swallowing hard and fighting off a fresh wave of tears as I scan the rest of the display. Oh my gawd… they *all* look phallic. How the hell did I not see that? I must've been so distracted while sculpting and crying over Wesley, over our lost intimacy, over everything. Then he died. Of course I wasn't paying attention to form. Just function. Just survival.

"How much?" she asks.

"Huh?"

"How much for this beautiful cock?" she says, still stroking it.

Well, shit! That's why no one's shown interest in this collection. Now it all makes sense. Was I that lonely? That desperate? What the hell is wrong with me?

I inhale slowly. I still have to support myself and Amy. My voice comes out hoarse. "Fifteen hundred?"

"I'll take it!" she replies.

"You will?" I blink.

She snaps her fingers and the man hands her a neat stack of cash before bowing to her. "Yes, Mistress."

She glides toward me and fans fifteen $100 bills on the counter.

"Th…thank you," I stammer.

"I don't want to take it now. Please deliver it to my hotel," she says.

"Sure! Where are you staying?"

"The Surfside Suites off the main highway. Room 212." Her English is now flawless, but her accent is faintly Spanish… or maybe French?

"I'll have it there in the morning." I nod, trying not to dwell on the shifting accent and instead picturing my overdue bills. Mentally, I check one off the list. One down. Twenty to go.

Her scent wafts toward me. It's a blend of forest, sea, and space. It draws me in. "What scent are you wearing? If you don't mind me asking."

"*Eau des Merveilles,* of course." Her voice now has a French lilt.

"It's lovely."

Her dark brown eyes lock with mine. "You're sad, *cara mia,*" she says gently.

"I am." I throw up my hands. "My husband killed himself. I'm broke. I lost my condo. I lost my car. I lost everything!" I cover my face, mumbling, "I'm sorry. I shouldn't be telling you this. I just…" The tears spill out. I can't stop them. *Don't get personal with clients,* Wesley used to say. I can almost see him standing in the doorway now, wagging his damn finger.

"I want to buy a drink for you. We'll talk," she offers, handing me a monogrammed handkerchief.

"Okay," I say, swiping at my eyes with my sleeve. "I'm Jolene," I sniffle, glaring at the hallucination of Wesley and mouthing, *Go away.* I extend my hand to her.

"I'm pleased to meet you, Jolene." Her gaze softens. "You can call me Mistress Selena. This is my… pet." She gestures to the man beside her. "Just call him Pet."

I stick out my hand, and Pet looks to his mistress.

"You may greet her," she tells him.

"Thank you, Mistress." He bows, then gives my hand a warm shake, still avoiding my eyes.

I'm beyond intrigued.

They step outside while I finish closing the studio. I flip off the lights, tuck the bills into my bag, and throw it over my shoulder.

J. Jaden

What the fuck am I doing? These people aren't locals. Hell, they're strange. And I just agreed to get in a car with them? Have I officially lost my mind?

I take a deep breath and step outside, locking the door behind me.

A long black sedan waits at the curb, its windows tinted so dark I can't see a thing inside. A stocky man in a chauffeur's cap steps out and opens the rear door.

There they are… those incredible boots and the long legs that wear them.

What the hell. You only live once, right?

I shrug and slide into the seat.

13

Orlando: Change

The door to Jolene's store creaks open, snapping me out of the hypnotic rhythm of surveillance. I lift the camera from my lap, already zoomed in and ready. Reflex. Habit. Comfort.

I live for this. For watching from the shadows. For catching people when they think no one's looking. I don't need accolades or medals, just the rush of putting the pieces together before anyone else even sees the puzzle. Most guys in the agency hate stakeouts. I crave them. The stillness. The silence. The way a single movement—just one wrong twitch—flips the entire narrative.

And now… this.

A couple walks out of Jolene's shop like they're stepping off a Milan runway. She's wearing expensive clothes. The man? Collared. I blink and adjust the lens again, but no, I'm not imagining it. The collar glints in the low afternoon sun. And she's got him on a leash. A fucking leash.

I sit up straighter. My back protests. I've spent too much time in this seat the past few weeks, but I ignore it.

"This is new," I murmur, voice low.

The man follows silently, head lowered, movements obedient. The woman's heels click like a metronome on concrete, her posture proud. Confident. Commanding. They don't just walk. They *own* the sidewalk.

And then there she is. Jolene.

She steps out of the store and locks the door like she's just closing up after a quiet workday. She doesn't flinch. Doesn't look around. Doesn't hesitate. She walks straight to the same sleek, black sedan and climbs into the back like she belongs there.

My breath catches. I don't even realize I'm gripping the steering wheel until the leather creaks under my fingers.

"Here we go," I say, a quiet thrill buzzing under my skin.

I slide the car into gear and follow. Not too close. Never too close. Distance is key. Let them feel safe. Let them think no one's watching.

The truth is, I've been watching Jolene for too long.

The truth is, I'm hooked.

Jolene's Adonis

Not romantically. I'm not that reckless. No. This is the purest form of obsession. Watching someone try to be normal when I *know* they're not. Waiting for the mask to slip.

And tonight, it just did.

There's more to Jolene than grief and gallery talk. She's not just the sad widow trying to make ends meet with abstract bronzes and scented candles. That was camouflage. Clever camouflage, too. The best kind. Slow, subtle, and non-threatening. But this version? The one who follows a dominatrix and her collared boy into a blacked-out car like it's a goddamn limo ride to a secret underworld?

That's the Jolene I've been waiting to see.

I sink into my seat, adjusting my mirrors as I tail them. Headlights off. Engine quiet. Just another car on the highway, nothing to see here.

But I see everything.

And tonight, I will get closer.

14

Jolene: BDSM

The car stops just a few blocks from my studio, in front of a local dive. I release the breath I didn't realize I held during the three-minute ride and crawl out of the backseat. I'm wearing a long-sleeve t-shirt and denim shorts. I'm casual, maybe even underdressed, but definitely more appropriate for a place literally called *Bar* than the pair standing beside me.

The building is off-white cinder block, its windows spray-painted black like it's hiding from the world. I've passed it dozens of times, always wondering what it looks like inside. Turns out, it's exactly what I expected. The air is stale with years of cigarette smoke and spilled liquor baked into the floors and walls. A couple of guys are playing pool, and a large man with more gut than neck is slouched behind the bar, pouring drinks with the enthusiasm of a corpse.

We slide into a small booth tucked in a dark corner. Mistress Selena unhooks the leash from her companion and gives him our drink order like she's ordering room service. He bows slightly and thanks her before heading to the bar.

I watch as he slides a hundred-dollar bill across the counter. The bartender raises an eyebrow, then grins—wide, toothless, and vaguely unhinged.

Trying to break the awkward silence between us, I lean forward. "Where are you from?" I ask, forcing a casual tone. "Your accent… is it Spanish? French? South Texas?" I laugh, mostly at myself. "I can't seem to place it."

Selena throws her head back and laughs. It's rich and melodic, like she's genuinely amused. "The accent," she purrs, dragging the word out like a secret. "I was born in Spain. Lived in France for a while. I moved to America a few years ago." She reaches into a tiny, beaded bag, pulls out a cigarette, lights it, and exhales a perfect ring of smoke like it's part of her DNA.

"I see," I say, already feeling like a fool for asking.

"Men," she says, taking another drag. "They love it. The accent. It's almost an aphrodisiac. The thicker it is, the less English I seem to know, the more irresistible I become."

"You don't need any help in that department," I blurt. *Crap! Did I say that out loud?*

Her smirk says yes. I want to melt into the floor.

J. Jaden

Gawd, I'm such a dork. I complain all the time about small-minded locals who don't understand my art, and here I am, acting like a square in front of the one woman who not only bought my work, but clearly gets it. Just drink the drink, Jolene. Smile, nod, shut up.

Except I never do as I should.

A few minutes pass before curiosity gets the better of me. I nod toward the man she calls *Pet.* "So… what's this?"

She turns to look at him, smiling with what I can only describe as pride. "He's my sub."

"Your… what now?"

"My submissive. BDSM. I'm his dom. He's my sub," she explains smoothly, as if she's describing a recipe.

I blink. "I don't… understand."

Pet returns with a small tray, setting a shot in front of me—lime wedge balanced neatly on the rim—followed by three more and a bottle of water. Then, with quiet reverence, he lifts his chin so Mistress Selena can reattach the leash. A faint smile lingers on his lips the entire time.

I toss back the shot. Fast. Clumsy. The tequila scorches my throat, and I nearly choke on the lime. "First one's always the kicker," I cough, trying to laugh it off.

Jolene's Adonis

Jesus, Jolene. Pull it together.

Selena tosses back a shot like it's water. Pet puts a sliver of lime in his mouth. Without missing a beat, she leans in, sucks the lime from between his lips, and drops it into her empty glass. No one else in the bar even notices.

I do.

"Let me tell you a story," she says, reclaiming her slight Spanish accent as she settles back in the booth. Her eyes find mine, warm and mischievous.

The room tilts slightly. I steeple my fingers under my chin, elbows on the table, determined to listen.

"As a child, I lived in a small village in Spain with my older siblings. My parents died when I was young. Five children left to survive on our own." Her tone is soft, nostalgic, but never pitying. "We learned to work hard. To appreciate everything life gave us. But I wanted more than survival. I wanted experience."

I nod, too enthralled to interrupt.

"When I turned eighteen, I got invited to a party in Madrid. They told me to dress sexy. So, I bought the cheapest little corset I could find, some go-go boots, fishnets… and put my hair in pigtails." She lifts her hands and pretends to fix her hair, a small, knowing grin spreading across her face. "I went alone. While waiting outside, I met a man, his wife, and his girlfriend. That's when I knew this wasn't an ordinary party. It was my first introduction to the fetish world… and I was hooked."

She downs another shot with practiced ease. I take mine too fast and gag on the lime again.

"I started going to more parties," she continues. "Eventually, I met a wonderful French dom. He had years of experience. He taught me everything I know."

She pauses, glancing at Pet as he watches her with quiet devotion. Then, as if it's nothing, she leans in and kisses his cheek.

"And then," she says, brushing an invisible thread off her blouse, "I met a man who was a switch."

"Switch?" I ask, my curiosity now fully aroused.

"A switch is both dominant and submissive," Mistress Selena says, her voice as smooth as ever. "Some days, I'd be dominant to him, and on other days, he'd be dominant to me."

I nod, toss back another shot. No lime this time. I turn my full attention to her, fully caught in the current of her story.

"Our relationship became a struggle for domination," she continues, eyes glinting. "He'd tell me, 'I really want to tie you up tonight and whip you.'

And I'd say, 'No. I'm going to tie *you* up and fuck *you* in the ass tonight.'"

My eyes go wide before I can stop them.

"That's when I realized I'm not submissive at all," she says, giving Pet's chain a little shake. "I'm what you call an exhibitionist." She leans in and licks the contours of his mouth, slow and deliberate.

Pet squirms under her touch and nods obediently, lips still glistening.

"You get paid?" I slur, trying to keep up.

"Yes! Wealthy men like Pet get tired of always being in charge. Sometimes they just want to be told what to do. And they're willing to pay for it… a lot." She throws back another shot, then sucks the lime from Pet's mouth again before turning her attention to me. "I like you, Jolene. I see a younger version of myself in you. You're artistic. You're not prudish. You could turn that studio of yours into one hell of a dungeon."

I laugh. Or maybe choke. I'm not sure. "How? Wesley would *never* let me…" I stop. "Shit."

The words land like stones in my gut.

I look down at the empty glass in my hand. "I guess it doesn't really matter what Wesley wants anymore… does it?"

I slam the final shot glass down on the table and turn to Mistress Selena, pointing toward the chain. "Lessons?" I scoff, trying to sound skeptical. "I'd never do anything like *that*. No offense."

"None taken. It's not for everyone." She strokes Pet's chin, her voice turning soft, almost affectionate. "But Pet and I don't have a place to play in this small, drab town. There aren't any swingers or exhibitionists that I know. We could come by tomorrow, play with your equipment. I'll show you a few things. We'll pay you well for the space. Won't we, Pet?"

He nods eagerly.

Their voices fade in and out as the room wobbles at the edges. I try to keep my focus, but everything feels soft and distant. My head dips from where it's propped on my fingers and nearly crashes into the table. I jerk it back up just in time.

Mistress Selena leans closer, her tone final but gentle. "We'll talk tomorrow," she says. "Tonight, you rest."

15

Orlando: The plan

I park near the southern corner of the building, where shadows swallow the back end of the lot. It's quiet here—secluded. Easy to slip in unnoticed.

I walk into the bar and scan the room. Low light. Stale air. The usual dive décor: neon beer signs, cracked vinyl booths, and the faint buzz of a jukebox that hasn't been touched since the Cold War was still hot in Langley briefing rooms. We updated our files. This place didn't.

Then I see her.

Jolene.

She's tucked into a booth in the far corner, seated with the same couple I saw at her shop—the woman with the stilettos and the man in the collar. I take a seat at the bar, choosing a stool that gives me a clean line of sight without being obvious.

Raising two fingers toward the bartender, I wait for his attention.

When he finally shuffles over, I say, "A shot of whiskey. Neat."

He grunts and reaches for a dusty, unmarked bottle on the middle glass shelf.

"No. Not that one," I interrupt, stopping him mid-reach. "Take it from the bottle under the counter. The one marked Jack Daniels. And bring it over here to pour it."

He pauses. Glares. But he complies, reaching under the bar and pulling out a sealed bottle of Jack. He cracks it open and pours the amber liquid into a glass, sliding it in front of me.

"That'll be five dollars."

I pull a twenty from my wallet and place it on the counter, then nod toward the corner booth. "What's the story on them?"

He lifts an eyebrow, eyes dropping to my open wallet.

Of course. Greedy bastard.

I pull another twenty and place it on top of the first.

Now he moves. He snatches the bills and shoves them into his pocket. "Don't know who they are. Never seen any of 'em before tonight. But the man's real strange. Fancy clothes, but he's wearin' a dog collar. Hot chick's got him on a chain. They're slammin' back tequila like it's water. That's all I got." He throws up his hands and shuffles off.

I shake my head. Got played anyway. I could've figured out most of that myself, minus the fact that it's their first time in here. Guess that's worth twenty bucks. Maybe.

Lucky for him I'm not in the mood to make a scene. Otherwise, I'd retrieve my $35, plus interest.

I knock back the whiskey. Clean burn. Good choice. Then I glance over at them.

They're deep in conversation. The shot glasses stacked in front of them tell me the bartender wasn't lying about the tequila. They're getting hammered.

But what the hell is Jolene doing with people like that? What kind of grieving widow hangs out with strangers in collars and chains?

I've watched her long enough to know she doesn't move without purpose. This isn't coincidence. This is a choice.

And that means I've got more to learn.

Wesley's widow is still hiding something. Probably a lot of things.

I tap the rim of my glass once, slow and deliberate.

Time for phase two.

Contact.

I stand up and head toward the door, glancing once over my shoulder to make sure the threesome is still engaged and hasn't noticed me. They're laughing, drinking, leaning in close. No sign I've been made.

Good.

I step out into the night, moving quickly, but not suspiciously through the parking lot and back to my car.

As I drive the short stretch to the commercial fishing pier where I docked my rented boat earlier this week, I mentally catalog everything I've just observed. It's the closest encounter I've had to date with my target.

- ✓ She left the store in a chauffeur-driven car with a strange couple who might be into some kind of bondage.

- ✓ The man with her looked wealthy. Tailored suit, definitely not off the rack. And definitely not from Sears.

- ✓ The woman dressed provocatively—sultry, calculated—but didn't have the vibe of a working girl.

- ✓ They seemed new to town. The bartender didn't recognize any of them, not even Jolene. Which either means she's been laying low... or he only knows the locals who hang out at that place.

- ✓ Jolene was comfortable. Too comfortable. Guard down. Drinking heavily. Looked close to passing out by the time I left. Maybe they're friends from out of town. Maybe they came to check on her.

I'm not sure yet. But the puzzle just got a hell of a lot more interesting.

When I pull into the pier lot, I park the car in a well-lit space near the docks with high visibility to deter theft. The car's a rental, nothing flashy, but I don't take chances. I've kept tabs on local crime logs. Around here, even boring cars left overnight can get stripped of hubcaps, catalytic converters, batteries, and even license plates. Nothing's off limits.

Call it a side effect of the job, but I always plan every move before I make it. Earlier in the week, I checked the trolley schedule. It runs from the marina to the docks. In the morning, I'll take it back and retrieve the car so I can resume daytime surveillance without raising eyebrows. For now, the next phase.

I jog toward the boat and climb aboard. The engine fires up without hesitation. I untie the dock lines and head out toward the bay.

On land, the distance between the pier and the upscale marina where *My Knotty Jolene* is docked is nothing—five, maybe ten minutes by car. But by water? It's a different game.

Instead of a straight shot, I have to ease past the cluster of commercial fishing boats at the public access docks, then circle inward toward the bay. Not outward to open water, but *inward*, winding around sleepy waterfront neighborhoods with private slips and dead-end canals. Then into the marina itself, easing past rows of expensive docked vessels until I reach my assigned slip.

Which just happens to be a few feet away from Jolene's. Exactly where I need to be.

It's a quiet, moonlit night. Nets hang from the rigs of dozens of commercial fishing boats like ghost limbs, their cabins dark and still—inhabited now only by the memories of fishermen swallowed by the deep. I idle past slowly, careful not to create a wake that could knock the boats against the docks and cause damage. On any other night, this would be a peaceful cruise. But tonight, I'm in a hurry. I need to reach the marina before Jolene succumbs entirely to the tequila.

I keep my speed low, but my mind moves fast, working through my next steps. The encounter tonight changed the game.

I think back to another case. It was years ago now. Serguei. My first contact in Belarus. The man jogged five miles a day, lifted weights like a bodybuilder, and stuck to a plant-based diet like his life depended on it. He was forty-two, built like a tank, and carried only twelve percent body fat. No risk factors. No warning signs. No clinical reason to die of a heart attack.

But he did.

The higher-ups accepted the Belarusian government's official explanation. I didn't. I dug deeper. Months of quiet investigation, secret meetings, and back-alley trades, in cities tourists will never find on a map, eventually uncovered the truth: spy dust.

A newly developed strain of nitrophenyl pentadienal. Undetectable, clingy, and color-coded. The Russian answer to surveillance. I learned the hard way that when the SVR suspects someone, like an American, someone like me, they secretly coat them with the dust. If it transfers to someone else, let's say a Russian they already suspect of treason, through even the slightest touch, the mark is made. A flag. A signal. A target.

In training, they teach us to avoid physical contact at all costs. But in the chaos of an extraction gone wrong, I grabbed Serguei's shoulder. I brushed against his back. And I signed his death warrant. Once detected, Russian counterintelligence moved in and executed him via potassium chloride to mimic a heart attack.

My mistake cost a man his life. It was my first brutal reminder that precision isn't a luxury in this line of work. It's the only thing that matters.

Wesley didn't kill himself. I know it the same way I knew something was wrong with Serguei's case. Once the scent of deception hits my gut, it clamps down and doesn't let go until the truth spills out.

I steer closer to the marina now, easing through the narrow canal that winds past neighborhoods with private boat slips and manicured hedges hiding God knows what. From the moment Jolene's doorman let it slip she was moving onto her boat, I knew I could make contact as a friendly neighbor, posing as someone established, trustworthy. Maybe a seasoned sailor.

But I waited.

I needed her broken open. Needed to see what emerged from her grief cocoon. Tonight, she's cracked just enough to glimpse what might be underneath.

I've dealt with widows in the past. In this business, you meet too many. I've earned their trust, let them lean on me, let them cry. Eventually, they always slip. They let something out… something small. Something seemingly insignificant. A careless phrase. A stray look. A missing memory that doesn't quite add up. Some of them try to seduce me. Most think they're smarter than they are.

But I don't miss details. I collect them. I cache them away like emergency rations. And when winter comes—when the cold reality hits and their lies finally crumble—I'm ready.

Some of those winters have been especially brutal. In a few cases, I've handed prosecutors enough evidence to bury the person sitting across from me. It's not my job to deliver convictions, but when it's one of ours that gets taken down, I go above and beyond. I wrap the truth in a bow and deliver it with a big *Fuck You* to the ones who thought they could get away with it.

I'm the nightmare of every killer who thinks wearing a veil makes them innocent.

And this time, it's personal.

I round the final bend into the marina. My boat's assigned slip is just a few feet from hers. Coincidence, if she ever asks. But everything I do is deliberate.

Wesley wasn't just my partner. He was my mentor. The closest thing I ever had to a father. He took me in when I was green, raw, and eager to prove myself. He taught me how to navigate the game without getting killed. Always called me his little brother, even though I saw him as more. Amy used to call me Uncle. Wesley laughed about it. He said it made him feel younger. I teased him, like we were equals.

But we weren't. Not really.

I fight the tightness building in my chest, the memories of Serguei and Wesley crashing into each other like waves against the hull. My jaw clenches.

I won't take another assignment until I know what happened. Until I untangle the mess that took Wesley away. I owe him that much.

And Jolene, whether she knows it or not, is holding the key.

16

Jolene: Adonis

I stumble out of the bar and into Selena and Pet's waiting car, slurring out directions to the marina. The man in the chauffeur's cap helps me out of the back seat when we arrive and guides me, not-so-gently, down the dock.

Amy's waiting on the deck of the boat, clutching Sadie's carrying bag in one hand while digging through my belongings with the other. The boxes I stacked so carefully earlier are now torn open, clothes and toiletries spilling out like confessions.

"Replaced him already, did ya?" Amy snaps. "Couldn't you wait until his coffin's cold in the ground?"

I sway, trying to focus, and point toward the man. "He was just... helping me."

The words come out thick and tangled.

"So desperate, you had to date the help?" She rests one hand on her bony hip and tosses her hair. "I could care less what you do. I just want to know what the hell is going on. I went by the condo and the doorman wouldn't let me in. He said you moved out and were living here. Why? What's all your crap doing on the boat?"

The man helps me step onto the deck, then disappears down the dock without a word. I watch him go, wishing he'd take this moment with him.

"I... I..." I start, but I can't get it out.

I want to tell her that her father was a low-down, dirty, lying bastard who left me broke and pissed off, that nothing she believes about him is real. But I can't. Even now, even like this—stumbling, sloppy, gutted—I can't be the one to destroy her version of him.

Instead, I zip my lips with my fingers. Literally. Thumb to forefinger, across my mouth, sealed shut.

Amy rolls her eyes. "If you're not going to tell me what's going on, then at least give me my rent money. My roommates need it."

She sticks her hand in my face, palm up, and wiggles her fingers expectantly. Sadie lets out a soft whimper at the sudden movement.

"I have it!" I shout, louder than intended, and start digging through my bag. I pull out the thick stack of bills Mistress Selena gave me and slap them into Amy's palm with a dramatic flourish. My smile is sloppy, but triumphant.

Jolene's Adonis

"Hmmm," Amy mutters, flipping through the crisp bills. "I have other expenses, you know. Since my car got towed, I'm paying friends to drive me around. And I'm visiting Daddy's attorney tomorrow to get everything settled so I don't have to see your ugly face ever again."

She places a protective hand over Sadie's bag as she hops off the boat and stomps down the dock, vanishing into the night and leaving me alone with a scattered mess of half-packed boxes and a quiet that rings louder than any goodbye.

I lean against the railing and watch her go. Then I smile.

That little hand on Sadie's bag. That wasn't for show. She didn't think I saw it, but I did. She's protective when no one's looking. That tough girl act? It might just be that—an act. A cracked shell.

I sigh and sink down onto one of the padded benches near the helm. The cushions are soft and sun-warmed. I stare up at the night sky. *That's it, then.* She'll find out tomorrow. I won't have to be the one to say it. I smack my hands together as if I'm dusting off the responsibility, but there's still a small, tight tug in my chest right in the spot where Amy lives.

I release another sigh and stretch out across the bench, folding my hands beneath my head like a makeshift pillow. The stars above blur and glide into one another, twinkling just for me in some personal little performance. It's beautiful. Breathtaking.

Then the boat starts to pitch and sway against the dock fenders, and an unmistakable engine rumble ruins the show.

I push myself up on my elbows just in time to see a sailboat, smaller than *My Knotty Jolene*, slide into the slip beside mine. A tan, shirtless man with lean muscles and a sculpted torso jumps onto the dock, ties off his boat like it's second nature, then slips back inside to kill the engine.

I don't even register that he's approached until I look up and see him standing over me.

Dark, wavy hair. Walnut eyes. Chiseled everything.

The world tilts.

"Adonis?" I whisper, just before it all fades to black.

17

Orlando: Jolene

I settle onto the padded bench across from her, kick up my feet, and lean back, keeping my eyes on Jolene.

The marina is quiet. The boats in the surrounding slips rock gently against their buoys, creating a rhythmic swish-swash that lulls everything into stillness. I get it now—why Wesley loved this life. Out here, it feels like another world. An escape. It's open, yes, but somehow still private. Safe, even. Like nothing bad could ever happen when you're surrounded by nothing but water, stars, and soft movement.

It's disarming.

Maybe that's what happened to Wesley. Maybe he felt too safe, too calm, just long enough for someone to catch him off guard. Was it her? Did Jolene lower his defenses? Did he trust her so much that he missed the warning signs?

Too many questions. Not enough answers.

Jolene stirs, rolling onto her side and curling into the back cushion with a low moan. Her body tenses, then relaxes again. She's dreaming.

I wonder what she sees. Who *Adonis* is. I caught the name when she whispered it before passing out. A man from her past? A code word? A slip? I file it away. I want to know what makes her tick, what she's hiding under all that guarded grief and tequila haze.

I stand quietly and rummage through one of the nearby boxes. I stop myself from digging too deeply but look just enough to find a small blanket and drape it over her gently. She doesn't stir.

The urge to search through her things hits hard. But I resist. Not because I'm feeling noble, but because it's not the right time. Not yet. I can't risk getting caught snooping. If one of the marina neighbors sees me, or if she wakes up and senses something's off, I lose my advantage. I need her to trust me first. Besides, I probably know the contents of the boxes better than she.

I hop back onto the dock and step into my own boat, which is nestled just a few feet away from hers. I ease onto the bench at the helm and recline, keeping her in my line of sight.

I watch her sleep.

Dozing off intermittently, I pass the long hours thinking, refining the plan, and sharpening it. In the morning, I'll introduce myself. Be helpful. Memorable. I'll insert myself into her life, subtly, slowly. No pressure. No threat.

Normally, I'd turn up the charm. Just enough to make her lean in. Just enough to let her think it's her idea. I'm good at that. Hell, I've done it in a dozen languages. Women spill their secrets eventually. Most want to. They just need someone who makes them feel seen.

But this one? She's Wesley's widow.

So I adjust.

I'll treat her like the sister I never had—cordial, caring, and above all, platonic. She'll see me as someone safe. Someone steady. Someone to lean on.

In time, she'll let me in.

And once I'm in, I'll find out what she knows about Wesley's death.

Still, despite myself, my eyes linger. Pouting lips. That slight upturned nose. Soft, rounded cheeks that look untouched by age or city life. There's something wild about her. Something untamed, like she's holding back a storm behind that fragile sleep.

I understand now. Why Wesley was drawn to her. Why he might have let his guard down.

J. Jaden

She's beautiful.

Dangerously so.

How dangerous?

I intend to find out.

18

Jolene: The morning after

Lisa's shrill voice jerks me awake. "Mind the bags, Larry! You're creasing them!"

"Ouch," I mumble toward the hazy blue sky. My eyelids feel like sandpaper when I try to blink. My head throbs.

"Jolene?" Lisa calls out in my direction.

Shit. I forgot this part of living at the marina. Wesley used to joke that every time he sneezed, Lisa showed up within seconds holding a tissue. "Blood-sucking old bat," he'd say through gritted teeth then flash his brightest grin and wave as she climbed back onto her boat after "checking on the noise."

There goes my privacy.

There's no such thing as privacy at the marina. Not with Lisa as a neighbor. Wesley and I used to motor past the jetty just to have sex without worrying she'd overhear. We even considered switching docks, but honestly, there's a Lisa on every pier. We figured it was better to deal with the devil we knew than anchor somewhere else and get a worse version. Living in close quarters doesn't begin to cover it.

"Larry! Hold on a tick. I heard something." Her footsteps echo closer. "Bloody hell, Larry! I *told* you not to crease that bag! Is it really that difficult to carry two handbags without mucking it up? Just stand there and try not to ruin anything else."

Great. She's almost on top of me now.

"Jolene?" she calls again.

I slam my eyes shut and hope she thinks I'm asleep and leaves.

"Well, hello there! And who might you be?" she asks.

What?

A deep male voice answers, "I'm your new neighbor. My boat's just over there."

Lisa giggles—of course she does—and her accent thickens. "Lovely to meet you, neighbor. And what brings you round here, then?"

I crack one eye open. Lisa's standing right next to my boat, smiling like she's seventeen again. A man I don't recognize leans against the cabin casually. He's tall... so tall, the top of the cabin barely hits his hips. My gaze drops to his khaki shorts and those dark tan legs. Wavy brown hair falls across his forehead, and when he smiles at Lisa's flirting, he flashes perfect white teeth. That mouth... damn.

"I just arrived last night," he says. "This young lady collapsed. I came to check on her."

This young lady? Oh, give me a break.

"Poor dear," Lisa whispers in that shrill, snotty voice she reserves for pretend discretion. The one that carries across the entire marina. "Her husband topped himself, you know. Tragic, really. I believe she's living on the boat now. Or so I've heard." She cups her hand like she's spilling royal gossip. "He was ever so much older. Married him for money, that's what people are saying."

You nosy, judgmental cow.

"I see," the man replies, smooth as silk. "They're usually right."

Then he flashes her another one of those smiles that could unbutton a nun.

Lisa giggles again. It's a full-on, breathy, private-school crush giggle. "I'm Lisa, by the way. Friends call me *Lise*. That's Larry over there. Yes, the one holding my bags. And you are?"

"Orlando," he says. "Pleasure to meet you, Lise. Larry." He offers a friendly wave across the dock.

Orlando. Interesting. He looks Hispanic, maybe Mexican? But he speaks flawless English. No accent. *Huh.* Intriguing.

Lisa glances at her watch and gasps. "Oh heavens, I'm running late! I've made the finals in ladies' tennis at the club. Match is today. You really *must* come watch. Wesley used to attend some of my matches. Such a shame, really." She shakes her head with a delicate sigh, lips curled in a pitying little smirk. "Anyway, it's the club right at the edge of Padre. Just tell them you're with me."

Her voice trails off as she barks more orders at poor Larry.

"I might see you there!" Orlando calls out, then turns and faces me directly.

I snap my eye shut and try to even out my breathing.

Married him for money? Really, Lisa? Thanks for having my back. Just leave me here with a strange man while you run off to play tennis. Classy.

The heat rises under my skin—anger, betrayal, and the old resentment Wesley left behind, all bubbling back up like swamp sludge.

"She's gone," the man says, stepping closer. "I know you're awake."

Damn it. I peek at him through one squinted eye. "They're usually right?" I shoot back. "Who are you to make that distinction?"

He raises both hands in mock defense. "Calm down. I was only humoring her."

"Calm down? Like hell I will! I don't even know you. What the hell are you doing on my boat?" I push myself upright with a groan and drop my head into my hands. "Oh gawd. How much did I drink?"

"Here." He reaches behind him on the cabin roof and retrieves a tall glass filled with some red, foamy concoction. He shoves it toward me.

The stench hits me like a brick wall. "No, thank you." I wrinkle my nose and wave it away.

"It's an old family recipe. Guaranteed to cure your hangover…"

"How do I know it's not poison?" I narrow my eyes at him. "And how do I know you're not some psycho pervert who gets his kicks from unconscious women?"

I don't know him. I have no idea what happened after I passed out. But I'm fully dressed, everything feels… normal. No signs of anything untoward. Still, the whole thing makes my skin prickle. He's the perfect outlet for my anxiety, and unfortunately, also stupidly attractive.…On second thought, maybe I wouldn't mind being taken advantage of. Ugh.

I shake the wicked thoughts from my head.

"That was unnecessary," I blurt out. "I know you didn't…"

He raises a hand to cut me off. "Say no more. You've been through a lot." His voice is gentle, and something in his eyes tugs at my memory. "Here. You'll just have to trust me."

I stare into his eyes, trying to place the familiarity. He nudges the glass back into my hands.

"Drink," he orders.

Well… it can't get worse. And I did insult the guy. Honestly, I feel like I'm living on borrowed time anyway. That's what the grief counselor said after Katie died. Part of the process.

I pinch my nose, tip the glass, and gag as the vile liquid slides down my throat. "What the hell is this?"

"A touch of the hair of the dog that bit you," he says, smiling. "Fresh-squeezed tomato juice, Tabasco, Worcestershire sauce, and a clove of garlic."

I force down the last drop and stick out my tongue in protest. It tastes like death.

"Better?" he asks.

I shake my head and shove the empty glass at him.

He pulls a disposable coffee cup from behind his back, grinning. "Would you prefer this?"

"Oh gawd, yes," I say, reaching for it. "Please."

"Here you go."

The moment I wrap my hands around the cup, I inhale the scent. Hazelnut. I raise an eyebrow.

"The chef told me what you like," he says.

Chef John. My hero. He's cooked at the marina's restaurant for years. James Beard award. Three Michelin stars. People always ask why he works here, and he always says, "Where else can I cook for and satisfy palates from every part of the world?"

He's not wrong. The marina might be small, but with its concrete floating docks, pool, hot tub, grocery store, laundry, showers, and five-star food, it's a magnet for the rich and the restless... people like Lisa and Larry.

"Thank you," I say, feeling more like a functioning human. "And thanks for checking on me. I don't usually drink like that. And I *never* drink tequila. Wine's my poison of choice." I manage a laugh.

"It's my pleasure," he says, locking eyes with me. They're so damn intimate. "You scared me last night. Anyway, I'll go. Looks like you've got things to do."

He gestures to the chaos strewn across my deck, then hops onto the dock. Before walking off, he turns back. "You are Jolene?"

"Crap!" I smack my forehead. At least the pounding has subsided. "Yes, I'm Jolene. You're… Orlando?"

He gives me a playful bow. "At your service."

I can't help but smile. "Thank you, Orlando!" I call after him as he climbs aboard his boat.

I glance around at the mess, then yank my phone from my bag. *Shit.* Less than thirty minutes to get to the store and I have *no* idea how I'm getting there. I didn't check the trolley schedule. My bike's not here. And during the winter months, I usually open by appointment only, but lately, money's tight. I need to open and stick to regular hours.

I rummage through a box of clothes, yank out a navy and white striped tank and a pair of faded denim shorts, and race into the cabin. I throw them on, drag a brush through my hair, tie it in a high ponytail, brush my teeth, and splash water on my face. No time for makeup.

"Oh well, this'll have to do," I mutter to the mirror. I grab my kicks and toss a pair of white stilettos into my bag, just in case. "A girl's gotta have her heels, mascara, and lipstick. That's all she needs!" Jessica's words ring in my ears.

I shove my makeup case into the already overstuffed bag, leap off the boat, and sprint down the dock with coffee in one hand, adrenaline in the other.

A sleek black sedan idles in the parking lot. The same chauffeur from last night steps out and opens the rear door.

"I'm told you need a ride, madam," he says with a slight bow.

I narrow my eyes. "By whom?" I take a cautious sip of the glorious, steaming coffee.

"Mistress Selena," he replies. "She said you left your bike at your store. I'm to deliver you there and then pick up Mistress Selena and her gentleman companion. They'll join you in an hour."

"For what?" The night before is a tequila-soaked blur, but I know there's something I'm forgetting.

He shrugs. "I'm not sure, madam."

I don't have time to argue. "Thank you," I mutter and slide into the blissfully cool seat.

As I lean back, finally catching my breath, I realize something. My headache's gone. No more nausea. *Huh. Maybe that awful drink really did work after all.*

19

Orlando: Trolleys

I keep myself busy adjusting the aft lines, stealing a glance over my shoulder as Jolene disappears around the corner of the marina. I don't want to look too interested. Not yet. No one should suspect me of watching her, especially not one of the live-aboards. There's always someone watching in places like this.

I don't know who keeps tabs on everyone here, but the bony, over-accessorized woman with the piercing voice is a safe bet. What was her name again? Leslie? Lilly? No… Lisa. That's it. Lisa. She's exactly the type to keep a mental spreadsheet on every soul who docks here, like it's her civic duty.

I make a mental note: Lisa might be a problem.

She's what the guys in training used to call a *shlyukha*. A slut. One of the first Russian words I learned during agent training. Women like her are always scanning for new conquests, especially when they catch the scent of fresh testosterone. Like wild topi antelope in heat—sniffing the air, stalking the source, and fighting off competition mid-thrust to get what they want. There's a twisted kind of power in it. They're predators. Top of their little sexual food chain.

And Lisa? She wears that dominance like a perfume. Too bad it clashes with everything else about her.

I don't find her attractive. Not even a little. Her confidence is inflated beyond her frame. I prefer humility and curves. A woman who blushes when you compliment her, who fills out a bikini like it's made for her. Someone real. Not polished and posing.

I glance again toward the marina entrance. No sign of Jolene.

Right. Back to work.

I drop the rope, hop onboard, and grab what I need, taking quick inventory of the time. This operation is rough. Tight timeline. Little prep. No recon. I feel like I'm flying blind. Wesley's death came too fast, and there wasn't time to build cover from the ground up. I had to slide in quickly and quietly, just another sailor living aboard his boat. A man with the ocean as his compass. Just some sun-kissed nobody with salt in his hair, pretending he has nothing to do but relax and ride the tide.

Joe Schmo.

That's who I'm playing. No profile. No threat. Just another guy with tan lines and a post-card worthy lifestyle.

The trick is to vanish. I've lived long enough in the shadows to know how to disappear without actually leaving. Especially here. Men at the marina wear smiles like armor. Behind the mirrored sunglasses and calloused hands, they reek of loneliness. They tell the same stories. Drink the same cheap beer. Search the same bars for someone who won't look too closely at the wreckage inside.

Not me. I know how to keep it buried. My career depends on it.

I walk the dock at a steady pace with measured steps and a casual stride. Not too fast. Not too slow. I've got to catch the next trolley, but I can't look like I care. Off-marina, I fade even further into the backdrop. Background noise. Invisible. I've been trained to observe without being observed.

And I need to keep my eyes on Jolene. See if she's what Lisa painted her to be. A callous gold-digger. Or something else entirely.

The parking lot comes into view just as the red "trolley"—which looks more like a stubby bus than anything resembling a streetcar—pulls up to the covered bench marked *9*. The word *TROLLEY* is slapped in thick paint across the front, like it's hoping the label will make it charming.

The doors wheeze open, and I step onboard, digging around in my pocket for loose change. I drop the coins into the metal box with a dull clatter and flash the driver an apologetic smile.

"No pass today?" he asks.

"Not yet," I reply, keeping my tone light.

He waves me through. "Have a seat."

I head for the middle of the bus and pick the most open spot. No one too close. No way to block me from exiting. I settle in as the bus lurches forward.

The marina's stop is almost at the end of the line. Stop 9. I'm heading to Stop 5, where I left my rental car. Half the loop. Thirty minutes, give or take. The trolley winds through the quieter parts of the island, and past RV parks, condos, and beach access points. A fisherman and a kid hop off with their gear. A woman with a sunhat boards with a tired pug in her arms.

We pass through the small town center. Post office. Surf shop. The bakery. And then, there it is.

Jolene's Treasures.

The storefront looks closed. Deserted. Good. I haven't missed anything.

Two more stops, and I'll be at the marina where my car's stashed. Another tightrope walk. But that's the job. Disappear in plain sight. Watch without blinking. Wait for a crack in the mask.

It's a delicate dance.

And it's the only dance I know.

20

Jolene: The cock

As I wrap Mistress Selena's merchandise, I think back to the way she handled it with such pleasure.

"A cock," she said, so matter-of-fact.

How did I not realize? I thought they looked like eels or something you'd pull from the Gulf of Mexico with a shrimp net. But now, with fresh eyes, I scan the display. At least ten pieces that could pass as phallic. *Huh.*

If I could find the right market for this kind of art, my money problems might just disappear... at least temporarily.

Note to self: Ask Mistress Selena where she finds customers who appreciate my—*ahem*—creations. She seems to be well-connected in that little-known world. A world I used to find vaguely amusing. Now? I'm listening.

The bell above the door jingles.

Selena and Pet glide inside. The chain that attached him to her wrist yesterday is gone. If not for the fact they're draped in Christian Dior, they could almost pass as normal.

Almost.

I spot the beaded floral detail from the fall runway collection—definitely Dior—but now that they're closer, I can make out Selena's nipples through the sheer panel of her dress. Full breasts framed by a fabric dip that plunges from the shoulder to just shy of her navel. From the back, or even the side, it's elegant, feminine, and dramatic. But from the front? It's straight off a Paris catwalk. Not exactly what you expect to see in small-town Texas. Or in my store.

She did say she was an exhibitionist. I bet she already raised a few eyebrows before noon.

"I was going to deliver this to you," I say, placing the sculpture in a large logo bag. "Not that I mind the visit. And... thank you for last night. I needed it. Even if I can't remember much. Oh, and thank you for the ride this morning."

Pet takes the bag and heads back outside toward the waiting car.

Selena steps up to the counter, and suddenly, I have no idea where to look.

Oh gawd. Do I look at her face? Her gorgeous dress? Her nipples? No, not there. Her hair? Her lips?

Now I get it! I finally understand why guys always look so awkward around cleavage. Being face-to-face with fully exposed nipples through barely-there fabric is... distracting. And confusing.

"You don't remember my offer?" she asks, clearly amused at my discomfort.

"What offer?" I force my eyes to lock on hers. *Safe zone. Just stay there. Don't blink.*

She pulls a thick stack of hundreds from her Dior clutch and sets it on the counter.

"The offer to use your playroom, or workroom, if you prefer."

Playroom? Wait... She told me a story. I remember that. About what she does. Why she does it. And the money. Oh gawd, the money. She offered to teach me. I said no.

But then... then what?

My eyes drop to the cash. I swallow hard.

She's my only real customer this month. Hell, this winter. Wesley's gone. So is the financial cushion he provided while I "followed my artistic vision." I'm barely scraping by now. And winter isn't even over yet.

But I can't cross that line. I can't become... *that.* I can't even let myself say the word. I'd never be *that* desperate.

"I can't," I say quickly, shaking my head like it might fling the temptation out of my skull.

Selena laughs lightly. "You don't have to *do* anything. We just want to rent your space. You're welcome to watch, of course. It's always more exciting with an audience."

I glance, accidentally, at one of her nipples again and snap my eyes back to her face. "What will you be doing, exactly? I mean, I *can* guess, but... I don't want to watch you have sex. I'm not into that. Honestly, I'd rather leave and let you two do whatever it is you're into. I'll come back when you're done. No offense. It's just not for me."

She waves her hand like I'm a child being cute. "Not offensive at all. I was like you once. I didn't think I'd ever be interested either. Besides, we don't have sex. He's not my lover. He's a client. And no, I don't consider myself a prostitute."

"I didn't mean..."

Another wave of the hand, silencing me. "I don't have sex for money. At least not the way you're imagining it." She gives me a wicked wink. "We even have separate hotel rooms. Like I said, he's a client, and he likes you."

My jaw drops. "Me? No. Never. I mean... I'm confused. Your story..."

"My *story* was about lovers. That's different. This is business. Trust me, you'll enjoy it. It's not about sex. It's deeper. Sensual. If it makes you uncomfortable, you can leave and still keep the money."

"But the chain... the lime... I mean..."

"Yesterday, I walked him on a leash. Today, I'm exposing myself in public and loving every second of the shock it causes. *That* is his fetish. The stares. The gasps. That's what gets him off."

Right on cue, Pet opens the door and walks back in, holding two Louis Vuitton shoulder bags. He hands one to Selena.

"You'll see," she says with a smirk, her tone smooth and assured. "Trust me."

Trust me. Why is everyone saying that lately? Trust is exactly what destroyed me. I trusted Wesley. Look how that ended.

Selena glances around. "Where can I get dressed?"

I blink. "Wait...this isn't what you're wearing?"

She smiles like I just told a charming joke.

Pet catches my eyes and stares. His irises are crystal blue, calm, curious, and maybe a little dangerous. He's stunning, really. Too polished. The type of man who's never known struggle, never had to stretch a dollar. His blond hair is perfectly styled, eyebrows trimmed like a GQ model. His frame is lean, athletic, practiced. Almost... too practiced.

That's when I notice the bulge in his tailored Dior pants.

I drop my eyes to the floor, skin burning with unease.

Selena tracks the interaction and smiles like the Cheshire cat just caught its favorite toy on a string.

"No," she says, voice like silk. "This is just my everyday wear. I have to change."

I blink, wondering if I'm still dreaming. *It's too much.* Maybe I'm still back on the boat, sprawled across the cushions in the sun, and this is just some weird, vivid dream… or a tequila-induced hallucination.

Without saying much, I lead them through the workshop door beside the sales counter. My eyes stay glued to the floor as we walk. I motion toward the small private restroom in the back corner. Pet looks at me, waiting.

"There's only one restroom," I say, clearing my throat. "You can wait or join her. Your choice. I'll be out front, just locking up and taking care of some business."

Before either of them responds, I slip out. I double-check the front lock, flip the "closed" sign, and turn off the showroom lights. Then I crouch behind the counter, pretending to dig through a box of unopened mail, but really just trying to ground myself. Trying to forget what's happening just a few feet away in the workroom.

My store's small. If not for the thin wall between the two rooms, we'd practically be within spitting distance.

If I stay quiet enough, maybe she'll get so involved she'll forget I'm even here.

That's the hope.

Then, a squeal. Metal on metal, like a chain being pulled through a vice.

Then silence.

Another squeal.

Silence again.

I freeze.

My mind races. *Should I leave? I don't know them. Just met them. And they're unlike anyone I've ever encountered in my life.*

Am I in danger?

My gut says no.

Even if I leave, where will I go? Back to the marina? What will I do there? I still have work to finish, and at some point, I'll need to be back here.

I stay.

But I can't focus. My mind keeps drifting to what's happening in the backroom. A sexual act is happening *right now*, and I haven't been touched since Wesley died. I'm lonely. Starved for connection. For skin.

Maybe just a peek.

I push myself up from the floor and tiptoe toward the workshop door. I crack it open, just enough to see inside.

Oh.

Now I understand why she calls herself *Mistress*.

Selena is dressed in a black jumpsuit that surprisingly covers more than the sheer Dior dress she wore earlier. A mask covers the upper half of her face, with slits cut for her eyes. In one hand, she holds a riding crop. It's silver-tipped on one end, frayed on the other.

Pet is nearly naked, wearing only a black thong. His private parts are mercifully covered. His wrists are wrapped in small chains with one connected to the heavy steel worktable, the other to a nail in the wall. His legs are spread wide, arms stretched open, head bowed in submission. His body looks relaxed, almost limp in the restraints.

And yet… his bulge throbs against the fabric.

"Yes, Mistress," he says, lifting his head.

His eyes find mine again, and they *burn*.

Selena doesn't miss a beat. She turns her head slightly, her gaze searching the dark space around the door. "You don't have to hide," she says calmly. Then she gestures toward the small sofa against the far wall. "We haven't even started yet."

That's it. I've lost my mind.

I want to say no. I *should* say no. But I won't be able to focus if I go back to the mail. Not while this is happening in my workspace.

I sigh. A sigh of surrender.

Slowly, I push the door open wider, step into the dark room, and let it close behind me, shutting out the natural light from the windows.

Candles flicker on top of the worktable and two thick pillars blaze on the floor in front of Pet. The scent of fresh-cut flowers hangs in the air, blending with the usual metallic tang of the shop. It's strangely… pleasant.

I take cautious steps toward the sofa, unable to tear my eyes away from him.

Why now? Why is he looking at me like that?

"What is *My Knotty Jolene*?" Selena's voice startles me, and I nearly collapse onto the dusty cushion.

"Pardon me?"

"Your boat. Why the name?"

I frown. "How do you know the name of my boat?"

She trails the handle of her whip down Pet's cheek. "The driver told me. He said your boat's named *My Knotty Jolene.* Why?"

I let out a nervous laugh. "Oh, that… It was a private joke. Between Wesley and me. He liked to be blindfolded. So did I."

My voice falters. The irony is not lost on me.

"Blindfold?" Selena tilts her head, eyebrow raised.

I scoff. "Oh yes. I guess it was his nod to this." I gesture vaguely toward the scene in front of me with Selena and Pet in all their bondage-clad, candlelit glory. "Wesley liked to surprise me in the bedroom. He'd tie silk scarves over my eyes. But when it was my turn to blindfold him, I could never get the knots right. I tied them so loosely they basically slid off, and he teased me for being weak with rope. Funny, considering I work with metal, fire, hammers. But knots? Not my thing."

I let out a breathy chuckle. "One day, I got tired of the teasing and signed up for a knot-tying class. Came in handy on the boat—docking, raising sails— but in the bedroom? I still kept the ties loose. Just to mess with him. It was our watered-down version of kink."

The memory warms me. I can't help but smile.

"So you blindfolded each other," Selena says, her voice glowing in the candlelight like her skin.

"Yeah, I guess. But it's not the same as…" I wave toward her whip, his chains.

"Oh, but it is."

"No. It's not. We never did this. The outfits. The restraints. The control. We never…"

"But you played games. And you found them pleasurable. No?"

I shake my head. "Not *these* games."

She throws her head back and laughs—a rich, indulgent sound that echoes off the walls. It unsettles me. "Oh, I can see the difference. But like it or not, there's a similarity."

"No…"

She waves a finger in front of my face. "Don't argue. Listen."

"Okay," I murmur, surrendering, for now.

She moves in front of Pet and bends low, letting him gaze straight into her cleavage. She sways her hips, slow and deliberate, her lips parting in a smirk as she runs the lash of her whip across his chest. It's hypnotic, like she's not seducing him but... me.

Not in a *let's have a threesome* kind of way. No. It's more like she's seducing me into her world. Her rules. Her power.

Her hips continue their rhythm as she speaks, breathy and controlled. "Wives are far too submissive. They undress, lay on the bed, and wait for their husbands to finish. Sex becomes another chore on a long list. When time's made for it, it's rushed. If the wife feels pleasure, it's usually by accident."

I shift uncomfortably on the couch.

"That's why so many couples dip their toes into BDSM. They try to spice things up with silk ties, whipped cream, and ice. It's all the same. Watered down, maybe. But the drive is the same."

She drags the crop to the band of Pet's thong and teases the edge before spinning around. He watches her hips like a starving man tracking prey.

"Dominants draw out the pleasure," she continues, "build the fantasy. Make them work for it. In a way, it's everything people miss about dating without the attachment. Pet romances me, buys me things, earns every second of pleasure he gets."

She grinds back against him and he groans, syncing his hips to hers.

"Wait," she commands, turning, placing a finger to his lips. "Not yet, Pet. You haven't earned it."

"Yes, Mistress." His head bows.

The whip snaps across his chest and he winces.

"Doesn't that hurt?" I ask, unable to stop myself. I direct the question to him, and he looks to Selena for permission.

She nods.

He turns to me. "So good," he murmurs. "More." His eyes stay locked on mine as he begs.

I flinch when the lash slices just above the waistband of his thong, hard enough to raise a welt.

"Oh yes!" he moans, shuddering.

Selena reaches into one of the Louis Vuitton bags and pulls out a silk tie. It's the same kind Wesley and I used. She wraps it around Pet's eyes and knots it tightly.

"Taking away one sense heightens all the others," she says huskily. "Like with your husband. It makes everything more intense."

Her nails glide down his chest, stopping just shy of his erection. "Tease and denial," she says, "are key. He can't pleasure himself. He has to wait. If he's good, maybe I'll do it for him."

Her voice is thick with heat. "This… is seduction. And it can last for hours."

"*Hours?*" I echo, stunned.

"Yes. Sometimes six, even longer. I use chastity devices. Sensory play. I get them to the edge again and again, and when they finally release, it's so intense they can't move."

She bares her teeth, then snaps them playfully near his cheek. It's raw. Animalistic.

"So you don't always… touch them?" I ask.

"Not always. Some are married. They want the kink, not the guilt. I spank, tease, play, but they handle themselves. Or they go home to their wives and finish there. Every client wants something different."

She leans into his ear. "Blindfolding him also punishes him. He *lives* for the reaction. But now? He can't see you. He's aching to know what you think. Aren't you, Pet?"

"Yes, Mistress," he pants.

His chest heaves. The bulge in his thong stretches taut, barely contained.

Selena grins and dips her finger inside, teasing the edge. "Almost there," she whispers.

Jolene's Adonis

A deep ache stirs low in my body—slick, warm, and undeniable. I shift on the couch and cross my legs tightly. *I know this is wrong. But it's so fucking hot.* Like watching live porn, but real. No fake moaning, no bouncing breasts, no overdone theatrics.

She continues her lesson, dragging her nails along the back of his neck as he squirms. "There are so many ways to wind them up. Fingernails across sensitive spots like the back of the neck, the spine, and the jawline. Whispering what you'll do to them in detail. Their imagination does the rest. It's pure anticipation."

She squeezes his cock through the fabric. He arches his back.

"Wait!" she says sharply.

I lick my lips. My mouth's dry. I open the mini fridge beside the sofa and grab the half-finished bottle of wine. I yank the stopper and drink straight from the bottle.

"Want a drink?" I ask. "There's another bottle. I don't usually drink when I'm working, but since Wesley died… I've been doing a lot more drinking. And a lot less working."

The words escape me before I can stop them. Selena has a way of slicing straight through my defenses.

She nods and walks over, gliding like a dancer. I hand her the second bottle—already uncorked—and she drinks from it with no hesitation before returning to Pet, wine in hand.

She pours some onto his chest and laps it up, slow and hungry. Then she holds the bottle to his lips.

"Drink."

He tilts his head back and gulps, wine trailing down his chin.

"Thank you, Mistress," he murmurs.

I sip again, the wine sliding down smoother this time. I can feel my body loosening. The knot in my shoulders unwinds. I sink deeper into the couch.

"What about you?" I ask. "Your needs? What do *you* get out of this?"

Selena presses her breasts to Pet's chest and runs a finger along his lips.

"It's business, not pleasure. But still, making men burn for me? That *does* something. Sometimes, I pleasure myself while they're blindfolded. I use filthy words. I let them hear me climax. It drives them wild. But they don't touch me. Not unless I say they can."

"Please," Pet gasps, his muscles tightening against the chains.

Jolene's Adonis

His erection crests the top of his thong. His balls tighten beneath.

I stare. I can't look away.

Is she really going to get him off… with me sitting right here?

A pulse clenches deep inside me.

She has all the control. That's what I'm missing. That's what I want.

But do I want *this*?

Maybe…

21

Orlando: The key

I park in my usual spot near Jolene's store and settle in for another day of surveillance. It's routine by now. I've done this dozens of times. But everything's different today. In the last 24 hours, my investigation hit a turning point. Now the target knows who I am and she can recognize me. I'm no longer just a watcher, a ghost behind the glass. I've stepped into the story. I'm a character now. I can affect the outcome. *Shit just got real.*

I sip my coffee and glance at the black car idling across the lot. The driver wears a chauffeur's cap and looks just as curious as I am about the "closed" sign hanging on Jolene's door. He stares at it like he's waiting for the store to open so he can dash inside and grab a trinket for his rich clients.

Why is the store still closed?

Jolene had a 45-minute head start on me. She wasn't on the bus, so she must've taken something faster. She didn't take her bike. I saw her get into a car last night, so that rules it out. And she usually makes better time than this. I once clocked her at 14 minutes. And now that she's reopened the shop out of financial desperation, the first thing she always does is flip the sign to "open."

I take another sip of coffee, watching, thinking, when a gray Mercedes zips into the parking lot and stops in the handicap spot near the front door. Amy jumps out of the passenger side and slams the door like she's ready for a fight. She storms up to the door, mutters something I can't hear, then pivots and heads straight toward my direction.

I've seen that walk before, that same fire in her eyes. Years ago, when her dad was overseas and I helped keep an eye on her, I once had to pull her out of a party she crashed in heels too big and a temper too loud. She had the same strut then, like the whole world owed her an apology. Different day, same Amy.

Shit! I duck down in the front seat, heart thudding. If she sees me…

But no, she doesn't notice. I exhale when I see the determined set of her jaw, the purpose in her stride. She's on a mission. Doesn't even glance my way.

I sit up slowly, peeking over the dashboard. What the hell is she doing?

Amy rounds the building, walks straight to the dumpster, and crouches down. She lifts one of the cement blocks from the base like she's done it before. Hidden underneath is something shiny—metal. *A key!*

She doesn't even bother putting the block back in place. She walks to the front door, sticks the key in the lock, turns it, and shoves the door open with one swift motion before slipping inside.

"Well, I'll be damned," I mutter.

The key's been outside this whole time. I could've installed cameras inside the store.

22

Jolene: Slick

The bell above the door chimes and Amy's voice cuts through the empty showroom like a blade. "Where are you, you cowardly bitch?"

Shit.

I tear my eyes away from the erotic scene unfolding in front of me and bolt to my feet. "Go ahead and finish what you're doing…I'll be back in just a few minutes," I stammer to Mistress Selena and Pet before rushing out. I think I see disappointment flicker on Pet's face, but there's no time for that now. I draw a breath and step into the showroom, pulling the door shut behind me, and say a silent prayer. *Please don't go in there.*

Amy's already stomping across the floor.

"You fucking gold digger! What did you do with my daddy's money?"

"How did you get in here?" I ask, breathless, ignoring the insult.

"Daddy showed me where you hide your spare key!" she screams, flinging it across the glass showcase. The high-pitched scrape triggers a howl from the bag slung over her arm. It's Sadie. Amy pats her nose briefly, then rounds on me again. "Why are you out of breath? Have you been screwing?" Her eyes narrow. "Find another rich, older man to suck dry already?"

"No reason. Hell no. And of course not!" I fire back, trying to stay calm. "Just working on some new pieces. What brings you by?" Maybe if I ignore her hostility, she'll get bored and leave. *Yeah, right. Like that's gonna happen.*

"I came to take your car, but I didn't see it outside. The idiot attorney took mine. Said Daddy was bankrupt and that my car had to be repossessed. He's only been gone for two months, and the vultures are already circling, picking the bones clean and leaving me with nothing." She stomps a stiletto heel into the thick carpet, which muffles the sound and ruins her dramatic flourish. I've seen this routine too many times. She frowns, clearly disappointed by the lack of impact.

"And Trina is missing her spa appointment because she has to drive me all over town. What the fuck is going on?"

Hot tears sting my eyes as I meet her glare. "I'm sorry, Amy. I didn't want you to find out like this. It came as a shock to me too."

"Why would he do this? It isn't like him!" she hisses. "Did you bleed him dry? Squeeze every dollar out of him?"

I gasp as tears spill over. "No. Of course not! I promise. I didn't know. I thought we were fine. He never told me anything was wrong. I didn't find out until after he was gone. Did the attorney tell you there wasn't even a life insurance benefit? The coroner says he killed himself." My voice cracks. "I've lost everything too, everything but the boat he paid for in cash and this leased store. That's all I have left. Amy, we've never been close, but I want you to know you're not alone in this. I'm going through it too. My whole world's been stripped away."

"'My whole world's been stripped away,'" Amy mocks in a high-pitched whine. "What about me? His heir? I'm left with nothing but bills and this fussy little bitch who has to be carried everywhere.." She jabs a finger at Sadie's trembling body.

Sadie lets out a low whimper and lowers her head.

I want to grab her and run, but I know Amy's all bark. She loves that dog. When she thinks no one's watching, she dotes on her like a child. She might be rough around the edges, but she'd never really hurt Sadie.

"I'm sorry. I really am," I say softly. "I'll help however I can. Like it or not, we're still family."

Amy's expression softens as she strokes Sadie's fur and sets her designer dog bag on the counter. "So the money you gave me—where'd it come from?"

"I sold a piece of art."

"Humph." Her gaze sweeps the showroom. When her eyes land on the phallic sculptures, they go wide. "Did you sell one of those?"

I wince but nod. I want to be honest, even if I'm afraid of her reaction. "Yes. As a matter of fact, I did."

"I like them," she says, spinning on her heel. "Not saying that to be nice, especially not to you. I'm just surprised. You seem like such a prude."

If she only knew...

I exhale and take a leap. Maybe these oddball pieces can be a bridge between us. "To be honest, I didn't realize what I was making at first. I meant to sculpt eels. You know, kind of a tongue-in-cheek thing about the local catch. Turns out... it's a niche market."

Amy nods slowly. "I know some people... Listen, you need to sell your freaky art, and I need living expenses. If I bring in my rich friends and they buy something, we split it. That'll at least get me by until I figure out my next move. Not that I want to do any kind of deal with you, but I don't really have a choice. And as far as I'm concerned, you owe me."

It hurts that she found out this way, but part of me is relieved I didn't have to be the one to break the news. I'm not sure doing business with her is a good idea, but splitting a sale beats handing over every dollar I make.

"Deal." I stick out my hand to seal it.

Amy scoffs and sneers, "We're not friends. This is just business."

Wasn't that what Selena just said to me? Just business. "Got it." I nod and pull my hand back. From behind the counter, I count out $500 from the stash I tucked away. "It's not much, but maybe it'll help."

For the first time since I met her, I see something close to gratitude flicker across her face. She takes the money and, without lifting her eyes, mutters, "Thank you," then snatches her bag and storms out the door, Sadie nestled in her arm.

"Not friends!" she yells over her shoulder as she climbs into a sporty Mercedes. Gravel spits up under the tires as they tear out of the lot.

I wave halfheartedly before locking up and turning toward the eerily silent showroom.

Did they hear any of that? I'm sure they did. Ugh!

After opening the door to the workspace, I freeze. Total darkness. I instinctively take a step backward, heart pounding. "The coast is clear!" I call out into the dark. "You can come out now!"

A match strikes. Candlelight flickers, illuminating Pet. He's now completely naked. The blindfold is gone, but Mistress Selena is still fully dressed.

My shoulders slump as I let out a long, shaky breath.

How the hell did a naked man and a dominatrix become the least shocking thing in my day?

"We waited for you," Selena says, turning to face me. "Come in, please. Have a seat."

Whatever spark I felt earlier is now replaced with regret. Sure, I was turned on. The seduction was rich, intoxicating. I felt wicked just watching. I got caught up in it.

But now?

Now I'm back in the real world. A world where a naked man is chained to my workbench. And I'm the one holding the key.

"Uh… I'm not sure," I admit.

"Bah! Don't tell me you're feeling squeamish, *cara mia*. This is the best part, and Pet insists you stay for the finale."

Selena runs a hand down Pet's naked torso and cups his balls. If she heard Amy yelling at me, she's pretending everything is normal. *Is it?*

"Please," he begs again. This time, he's not talking to her. He's looking straight at me.

I'm gonna need another drink.

I sink into the couch and grab the wine bottle, tipping it up and draining it to the last drop. Pet doesn't take his eyes off me. His desire is right there, raw and exposed, following the path of my gaze as it flicks to Mistress Selena. She lathers her palms with some kind of oil, thick and glossy, and rubs her hands together, warming it. Then she spreads it over every inch of his bulging manhood.

"Have you been a good boy?" she teases.

"Yes, Mistress," he growls, but he's still looking at me.

"What does my good boy want?"

"To come."

"Oh, he does, does he?" Her slick hands stroke up and down his shaft. His chains rattle with the movement of his hips as he starts to match her rhythm.

His balls draw up, tight, and right before he loses it, she presses her fingers against him, cutting off his orgasm.

"Did I say you could come?"

"No," he says through clenched teeth. "Please."

"Since you waited…" She doesn't even finish the sentence. He explodes into a towel she somehow grabs just in time. "My, my. You were ready, weren't you?"

"Yes, Mistress," he gasps.

My head falls back against the couch. I've never seen anything like it. It's twisted. It's perverted.

And I *like* it.

I feel a deep ache pulsing between my legs. Wet. Throbbing.

I'm so turned on.

My legs feel like jelly as I push myself up off the couch. "I'll wait in the other room while you get dressed," I mumble.

Selena just nods and frees Pet's wrists.

Several minutes pass before their car pulls up to the door. Mistress Selena and Pet reappear, now dressed in what I guess is their version of small-town activewear. Crushed velvet tracksuits and designer sneakers. Still expensive. Still too polished for this dusty Texas town.

Pet doesn't say anything. Just gives me a glance before hauling their bags out to the car.

Selena steps closer and places a hand gently over mine. "So, what did you think?"

"Mmm…" My head's spinning—from the wine, from last night's hangover, from *everything*. "I've never seen anything like it."

"Wonderful!" she claps, pulling me into a quick hug.

Huh. Didn't peg her as the hugging type.

"Do you need a ride? We can talk more in the car."

"No, thank you. I have my bike."

"Are you sure?"

I nod.

"Same time, same place tomorrow?"

"Umm…"

"We'll pay the same rate for the space. There's still so much more I want to teach you."

"I just need a little time to think about it. Can I give you an answer tomorrow?"

Selena studies me for a moment, something soft and unguarded in her expression. "You don't have to do anything you don't want to do. This is about control. I'm in control with my clients, and you'll maintain full control at all times. If it's not for you, just say no."

That's what I *should* say. I should tell her to get the fuck out of my shop and never bring her sadistic client back. But that warm, slick spot between my legs says something else entirely. It whispers that I'm not hurting anyone. That I've been through hell and maybe, just maybe, I deserve a little fun.

And my head? It says this is easy money. All I have to do is let them use the room. A few days. That's it. No strings.

I glance at Selena sidelong. "It's just a lot to take in. That's all. I'll let you know tomorrow." I offer a small, practiced smile.

"Tomorrow, then." She gives me a parting wave and slips out the door.

I lock it behind her, then head into the back room to grab my bike. Everything's been reset. Put back exactly as it was. No trace of what happened. It's like the whole scene was a dream.

I shake my head, trying to erase the images that keep flashing behind my eyes. I slip my bag over my shoulder, stuffing the leftover cash and spare key into the front pocket.

The air outside hits cold and crisp.

Good. I need to cool off.

Rounding the building, I walk toward the dumpster and find the misplaced brick. I lift it, slide it back into place neatly, then hop on my bike and start pedaling toward the marina.

All I can think about is the key.

Amy has too much time on her hands. I can't risk her finding it again, or worse, discovering my dirty little secret. I'll find a new hiding spot. Maybe somewhere on the boat.

And then there's the other thing I need to figure out. How the hell do I convince Amy to get a job?

23

Orlando: Witness

After watching Amy storm out of the store, screaming "Not friends!" before she climbs into the Mercedes and peels out of the parking lot, my patience hits an all-time low. I've done more surveillances than I can count. I've followed Jolene, shadowed her, basically stalked her for almost two months, but nothing could've prepared me for *this*.

I fidget with my keyring, sliding keys on and off the metal loop, again and again, the motion grounding me.

What the hell is going on in there?

My fingers freeze mid-loop when the door opens and a man and woman step out. They're dressed casually, blending in, but I recognize them. They're the same pair I saw last night.

What are you up to, Jolene?

I need to know.

And I want to kick myself for not figuring out the key's hiding place earlier. I should've installed cameras, should've trusted my instincts. But I didn't think there was anything worth seeing. I thought she was either waiting for customers or hammering away in the back, making her art. I was wrong.

Jolene exits the store a moment later. She pauses, glances around like she's checking for shadows, and then goes toward the dumpster and replaces the brick before walking out of sight. After a few tense seconds, she returns and mounts her bike, heading toward the main road.

It's the first time I've seen her *aware*. Really aware. For the past one month, twenty-six days, five hours, and twenty-seven minutes—yes, I'm counting—she's moved through life like she's invisible. Not in a self-absorbed way, like the world revolved around her. No. More like she was trying to shrink, trying not to be seen. Like blending in kept her safe.

But this? This is new.

What changed?

I glance at my watch. Time to shift into surveillance mode—precision timing, step one. I wait for the digital numbers to tick over, starting the count. I've got nine minutes to find that damn key before I need to head to the marina for my next encounter with Jolene.

I sit tight for two more minutes. Standard procedure. Give her time to realize if she forgot something and circle back.

Nothing. No sign of her.

I slide out of the car and press the door shut with both hands, careful not to make a sound. No need to draw attention. I glance around. No witnesses. Then I casually stroll to the spot where I saw Amy pull out the key.

I kneel down and inspect the block, checking for anything that would indicate a trap or test. Nothing. Satisfied, I lift it. Nothing underneath.

Damn. She must've moved it.

I head around to the other side of the dumpster—where Jolene disappeared earlier—and start working a grid pattern, moving methodically from block to block. Closest to furthest. One by one. Still nothing.

Five minutes left.

I stand frozen, thinking.

Where would she hide it? Or did she take it with her?

The dumpster's boxed in by a wooden fence on three sides. I walk the perimeter, then duck inside, running my hands along the slats, searching for anything out of place. A nail. A hook. A wire. Anything.

Nothing.

Two minutes left.

I abandon the search and head back toward the car, my brain turning over every image, every frame of her disappearing behind that dumpster.

What did I miss?

Did she move the key because she was scared someone might find it?

Or because it would lead to something she's trying to hide?

I'll have to come back when I have more time. This job isn't over.

I climb into the driver's seat and buckle my belt. This is Texas, after all. "Click it or ticket" isn't just a slogan here. I fire up the engine and head toward the marina.

Two miles out, I pass Jolene on her bike. Back to her old self. Head down. Eyes on the pavement. Oblivious to the world around her.

At the marina, I pull into a center space in the lot, angled for a fast exit. Just in case. I kill the engine and walk with purpose and past the pool, the bathrooms, the laundromat, the restaurant, and finally down the dock, which feels like a damn obstacle course today. I nod when I have to, but I keep moving. Eyes forward. Focused.

I make it to the boat just in time.

Once on board, I rip off my shirt and throw on a tank top. It's hot, and I need to cool my nerves before she gets here.

I step onto the deck and wait. This is it. My opening.

Something shifted in Jolene. She's no longer oblivious. She sees the world now. That means she'll see *me*.

This is my specialty—the part of the job I know better than anyone. Time to seduce the suspect.

But this one? She's different.

I take a deep breath and exhale. I'm going to have to handle Jolene carefully. Differently.

She might be my target. But she's also my silver bullet.

24

Jolene: Puzzles

The ride to what I now accept as my new home is uneventful, and it gives me much-needed time to think. A lot has changed in a short amount of time. I feel like I have mental whiplash. It's as if a giant boulder rolled over what was once my life and smashed everything into rubble. The only salvageable pieces are tainted with deception. On the surface, they appear to be normal, as if something of my old life still exists, but as I get closer, inspect them, and try to fuse them back together, I find they no longer fit.

Who am I kidding?

What I thought was my life was never a real part of me. Just tattered edges of the cloak of secrecy that shrouded everything I once knew as truth. The worst part is that I want to take that tattered cloak and mend it and throw the fucking thing back over my reality and hide underneath it!

The frightened widow inside me wants to live in the make-believe world that Wesley created and pretend everything is okay. But the enraged, betrayed female who also inhabits my body wants to gather the tatters and set them on fire and dance around the flames, and then stomp on the ashes and damn them to hell, where I can only guess is the current residence of Wesley's wretched soul. It's bad enough that he lied to me, but to leave his daughter with nothing…the man really is insufferable.

I press the handbrake and slow down enough to make the sharp turn into the marina. The early afternoon sun has started its slow descent to the west, and the crisp air makes me wish I wore a jacket or at least longer pants. I ride past the parking lot and onto the sidewalk leading to the docks before dismounting and rolling my bicycle the rest of the way.

The winter months offer a chance for boaters to do maintenance without spending too much time docked or working in the heat that can become unbearable in the warmer months. During the day, the docks are lined with toolboxes and boating gear, and everyone in the marina is busy. I wave and nod to several of the boaters and maneuver my bike around tool and tackle boxes.

As I approach my boat, the fine male specimen from this morning is bent over the far railing of his small sailing craft. He's wearing a wife-beater shirt, which I would normally find repulsive, but on him, *ooohh!* With his back to me, his pants cling to and enhance his tight glutes.

Michelangelo himself couldn't have sculpted a better form.

I'm so distracted that I trip over a dock line and try to catch myself on the handlebars of the bike, which tips forward as the rear tire flies into the air.

"Oh shit!" I yell just as the bike folds over onto itself. I shove it away from me and throw my bag onto the dock, trying to balance myself. I teeter on the edge of the narrow concrete before crashing into the slimy, cool water. Panicked, I doggie paddle and grab for something, anything, to hold onto, but since the only surface within reach floats, it bounces with the waves that my plunge created, and I can't seem to get a grasp. Small fish and other creatures are attracted away from the barnacles at the bottom of the boats and come to nibble at my legs. The sensation startles me.

"Help!" I gasp in a panic. "Help!"

The sound of footsteps pounds on the dock, heading toward me. Pairs of hairy, sandaled feet come into view just as hands reach into the water to grab me. I take hold of the hand that's closest to me and entwine my fingers in his. He grunts under the strain as he pulls me out of the water. My feet land on the concrete, and I find myself face to face with Larry, Lisa's husband.

"You look…cold. Are you okay?" he asks, staring boldly at my soaked shirt.

"I am. Thank you for pulling me out," I say between clenched teeth.

A cold shiver winds its way up my spine as I look around at all the boaters staring at me. I then look down. My tank top is not only soaked, but it's completely see-through. My nipples stab into the wet fabric. Instinctively, I wrap my arms over my exposed breasts and cover myself. This is what I get for not wearing a bra!

When Wesley and I started spending more time at the marina, I noticed that none of the other women wore bras or makeup. I envied their ability to be so carefree, so I decided *when in Rome*. It felt liberating! I never realized how comfortable life could be without the confines of the straps and the wires. It's the one aspect of boat life I enjoy the most. I do, however, wear at least some makeup. I won't go totally natural.

Orlando grabs a towel from the railing on his boat and wraps it around me. "It's dusty. But it's dry," he tells me.

A series of groans erupt, and the onlookers clear out, returning to their respective chores.

"Thank you!" I call after them. I'm left standing awkwardly between Orlando and Larry. "So…at least my bike didn't go into the water along with me."

"No," Larry says, looking anxiously down the dock.

I wonder why Lisa isn't the first person on the scene, but then I remember it's her day on the court. "Just let me go put something on and I'll come back for my stuff."

"Allow me," both men respond, lunging for the handlebars. With the fluidity of a cat, Orlando grabs my bag and still manages to reach the bike first. He pulls it upright and straps my bag to the front. He grins triumphantly.

Larry rolls his lifeless eyes. "It looks like you're okay. So, I guess I'll see you later?" He frames the statement as a question.

"Sure. Thanks again." I clutch the dirty towel around me as I make my way to the boat with Orlando close behind. He helps me onto the deck and then chains my bike to the nearest post. I pull on a sweatshirt, slide my bag off the bike handlebars, and hand him the towel. For a moment, our hands touch. He feels soft, warm, sensual.

I blush and let go of the towel, stepping away from the rail. "I appreciate everything, and this morning…your hangover cure really helped. I'm not usually this pathetic and in need of assistance."

"It's been my pleasure. Are you okay? Nothing hurt?" Orlando asks.

"I'm fine. The fall just shocked me. Let me make it up to you. How about dinner, tomorrow night, on me? I happen to know a great chef at a little place that's not too far from here."

"Jolene, are you asking me out on a date?" He flashes that heart-stopping smile.

"No!" I blurt. "Not a date. I don't even know you." I laugh nervously and slap my forehead. "I've been married for so long that I don't know the rules anymore. Is dinner considered a date now? I was just thinking that I'm not at the marina during the day and I thought it would be nice to share a light dinner to express my thanks, and to welcome you to the marina."

Orlando chuckles. "It's okay. You don't have to defend yourself. I get it. It's not a date and I accept."

Defend myself? What the hell is his problem? Am I not good enough to date? He'd be lucky to date me. Does he think I'm nothing but a gold-digger, like Lisa claimed? It's not like I'm ready to date anyone. Besides, why would I want to put myself out there for some man to betray me like Wesley did?

I hide my feelings and plaster on a fake smile. "Great! Seven?"

"Seven. Until then." He nods, and I notice a slight shift in his usually jovial demeanor before he makes his way back to his boat.

Relieved that the awkward encounter is finished, I look around at the pile of opened boxes and the mess Amy made while digging through my stuff. I place my bag on the main salon table and take out the extra store key and look around at the sparse decor. Where to hide it? I decide it'll be safe underneath the white orchid. It's fake, so it doesn't require water or ice cubes or whatever one does to keep flowers alive, so there isn't a reason to move it, except for dusting, and I'm the only person who would do that. After I feel confident the key is safe from Amy, one by one, I throw everything back into the boxes and carry them into the forward stateroom and pile them on the bed and floor. The day has been too exhausting for me to unpack.

Once everything is inside, I curl up on the bed that I shared with Wesley and hug a pillow to my abdomen and close my eyes. The sun is still bright in the late afternoon, but exhaustion takes over and I fall asleep. Images of whips, chains, and Pet's lust-filled eyes haunt my dreams. It's a re-enactment of the morning, only I'm the one holding the whip. I pull my arm back and then lash out at Pet's bare leg. The whip cracks as it hits his skin. He writhes in pain.

"More!" he begs.

I raise the whip further and hurl it at his upper thigh. It cracks and he writhes.

"More!" he begs.

His erection is huge! It pulses just below his belly button and busts out of the thong.

I smile wickedly. "More?" I touch the top of his penis and laugh wildly.

"No!" he screams. "Not there! Please, not there!"

I raise the whip higher and pull back my arm, but before the crack, I'm startled awake. I open my eyes to a pitch-black room. The sheets are twisted around my legs and the pillow is between my thighs. A faint knocking sound echoes in the darkness.

"Hello? Is someone there?" I ask.

Silence.

I reach for the flashlight on Wesley's side of the bed and flip it on.

No one's here but me.

I crawl out of the bed, realizing I'm still wearing the wet clothes and sweatshirt, and walk around the cabin and confirm that I'm alone in the room.

It's nothing.

Jolene's Adonis

I peer out of the curtains over the stateroom window. The marina is dark, quiet. There's nobody in sight. I turn on the light and search the drawers for a t-shirt and panties and feel the outline of my vibrator in its sock, which is nestled on the side of the drawer. The dream leaves me feeling uneasy, yet strangely aroused. I haven't used my vibrator since before Wesley's death, so the mere thought of using it makes me feel as if I'm doing something bad.

But maybe I want to be bad.

I pull the vibrator out of its sock. Slowly, I work my way out of the damp sweatshirt and remove the smelly shirt, shorts, and panties. Nude, I lie back on the bed and flip the switch. The vibrator hums in my hand, but I'm paralyzed, confused. I didn't die with Wesley. I'm still living, breathing, and I have desires and needs. It's time to keep living. I touch the vibrator to my clitoris and an electric pulse shoots through my body. I arch my back and hear a loud thump.

Startled, I drop the vibrator onto the bed. I fumble to turn it off and hold my breath and listen.

Silence.

Maybe it's just the boat rocking against the dock.

I shove the vibrator back into the sock and its place in the drawer and head for the shower. The sound of the water drowns out all the noises and I'm able to relax. Wesley and I were at the marina for years, but we never slept on the boat at the dock. So, the noises are unfamiliar, I reason. I'll get used to them. Anyway, I'm surrounded by people on neighboring boats. *If I scream, someone will come to rescue me like they did earlier today. Won't they?*

25

Orlando: Guilt

Torment surrounds me as I kneel quietly, peering through the opened hatch over the main cabin. Guilt pulses through me as my cock presses against the soft fabric of my shorts. I'm engorged with shame, like I'm a twelve-year old boy, spying on the hot babysitter through a crack in the bathroom door with my penis firmly grasped in one hand and my head on a swivel, mortified of getting caught, but too sexually charged to stop.

I can't believe what I saw. Jolene was naked on the bed, lying on her back, a vibrator in her hand. The shock caused me to lose my footing, and I stumbled backward, and went flat on my back and froze, waiting to see if Jolene stormed out onto the deck. She never came, so I resumed my position, hoping she'd resume hers. She didn't.

Though Wesley died almost two months earlier, seducing his wife for a confession seems like a betrayal, even though I'm only doing it because of my friendship with Wesley. I want to know the truth. But can I treat Jolene as I've treated every other widow I've surveilled in the field? *I'm not sure.*

J. Jaden

When I'm near Jolene, there's a spark or some kind of connection I can't explain. I've spent years pretending to be interested in people for the sake of a case, but this isn't that. This isn't make-believe. It's different. It feels easy. Natural. I'm not pretending. I'm genuinely intrigued.

Now I understand why Wesley risked everything to be with her. If I were in his shoes, I would've done the same.

All this time spent watching her, studying her—it's made me feel like I know her. Like I understand what she needs. And that's the problem.

My desire for her is going to be my downfall.

And I can't help myself.

26

Jolene: Desperate

I roll onto my side in a deep sleep and find myself back in my workroom, but something's different. In the center of the space is a bed draped in satin blankets and pillows, with rose-colored netting cascading around it like a fantasy.

A man pushes the sheer material aside and beckons me toward him. He's completely naked, sprawled across the bed like he owns it. His body is powerful and perfectly sculpted. Dark, wavy hair frames his strong features, full lips part to reveal white teeth, and his almond-shaped eyes are hooded with thick lashes.

"Come," he says.

I step forward and glance down. I'm wearing embroidered purple satin slippers and a sheer lilac gown, with nothing underneath, that brushes my ankles. My breasts ache beneath the soft fabric, practically begging for his touch. I move closer.

"Come," he says again.

His erection is long, wide, and full, resting on a soft patch of black curls. His balls are pulled up tightly, and I can feel the heat of his desire from here.

He wants me. Oh God, he *wants* me.

I slip between the sheer panels and crawl on top of him. He takes up the entire bed. His cock throbs against my belly, and his body is hard and hot beneath mine. I shift so the head of his thick length presses right into the slick, aching crevice between my legs.

"Take me," I order.

He moves his hips, and I can feel the delicious pressure, but he isn't kissing me. He isn't sliding inside.

"Fuck me, damn it!" I growl.

Whoa. I'm a badass bitch in this dream. I like it.

But just as suddenly, the weight of his body disappears. His beautiful almond eyes fade into darkness.

"No!" I try to scream, but nothing comes out.

It's one of *those* dreams.

"No! Come back! Fuck me, please!" I beg, but he's already gone. He doesn't hear me.

He fades completely, and I jolt awake.

Jolene's Adonis

Light pours into the stateroom. The blankets and pillows are scattered across the floor. My hand is between my legs, rubbing furiously.

I groan, yanking my hand away, frustrated beyond words.

Dragging myself out of bed, I mutter, "Cold shower. Now."

As the icy water hits my skin, I sigh.

This is going to be a long damn day.

27

Orlando: Focus

I spend the night sorting and reviewing everything I've gathered so far—evidence, timelines, observations, and gut instincts. It's a sobering process. I lie on my bunk in the main stateroom of the boat, tossing a rubber ball against the wooden ceiling and catching it on the way down, over and over again. The repetition grounds me. Calms me.

It's a trick I picked up from a Thai monk while chasing a lead across Asia. Throw. Breathe. Catch. Repeat. Slow the heart rate. Focus the breath. Sink into the rhythm.

Thunk. The ball hits the slatted roof. *Slap.* It drops into my palm. Marina sounds fade behind the mantra forming in my body. *Inhale.* Water sloshes against the hull. *Thunk. Slap. Exhale.*

Inhale.

Slosh.

Thunk.

Slap.

Jolene's Adonis

Exhale.

Inhale.

Slosh.

Thunk.

Slap.

Exhale.

I stay for hours like this, slipping into a meditative trance. But the silence isn't perfect. Jolene intrudes.

Visions of her, sprawled across a bed, her hand between her legs, a vibrator buzzing.

I toss the ball harder, breathe deeper, force those images away. There's time for that later. Not now. Now, I have a job to do.

I shift my mind back to the timeline. By this point in most investigations, I'm convinced of the target's guilt, and my remaining task is to draw out a confession.

But *usually* doesn't exist in this case.

Usually died the day I learned about Wesley's death.

Now I'm navigating uncharted waters. I'm not closing in on a suspect. I'm still trying to figure out *who the hell the suspect even is.*

I took this job believing Jolene killed her husband. But now? I'm not so sure. That certainty I usually lean on? It's nowhere to be found. I keep chasing it like a mirage on the horizon, something shimmering just out of reach. Sometimes I think I catch a glimpse, a shadow of truth, but when I reach for it, it dissolves. An illusion. A trick of the mind.

For the first time in my career—and against my nature—I find myself hoping I'm wrong.

I want to clear her.

I want to find out who *really* did it.

And that realization guts me.

Instead of the thrill I usually get when zeroing in on a perp, I feel this weight. An ache in my chest, like anxiety tangled with guilt. I walked in assuming she was guilty. Hell, two times out of ten, the wife *is* the one who does it. But what about the other eight?

I toss the ball higher. *Thunk. Slap.*

I start working through the classic motives—the ones I've seen a hundred times before.

1.) Money. *Breathe. Slosh. Toss. Catch.*

> There's no big life insurance policy. Wesley's accounts were nearly empty. She wouldn't lose anything in a divorce. Doesn't add up.

2.) Jealousy. *Breathe. Slosh. Toss. Catch.*

From what I've seen, she isn't competitive or possessive. No signs of insecurity.

Wesley wasn't the jealous type either.

3.) Child custody. *Breathe. Slosh. Toss. Catch.*

They didn't have kids. No custody battle. No leverage.

4.) Abuse. *Breathe. Slosh. Toss. Catch.*

No police reports. No whispers. Nothing that suggests violence at home.

5.) Affairs. *Breathe. Slosh. Toss. Catch.*

I've found no evidence of cheating on either side. No lovers, no side flings. Just... silence.

6.) Mental health issues. *Breathe. Slosh. Toss. Catch.*

She has no documented history. Wesley passed a full psych eval when he joined the agency. Nothing unstable there.

7.) Narcissism. *Breathe. Slosh. Toss. Catch.*

Jolene doesn't show any signs. She's not grandiose, not manipulative. Wesley, maybe, had some tendencies—he could be arrogant—but he had empathy. He mentored me when I was greener than fresh paint. He had his flaws, but not enough to push someone to murder.

No motive. No clear suspect. No confession to chase.

I'm drifting in unfamiliar territory, and worst of all, I *care*.

Caring isn't part of the job.

But I do.

And that, more than anything, could cost me everything.

Wesley's death doesn't enrich her life in any way. She gained nothing. No payout. No property. No new freedom. So, as I breathe through the rhythm of my meditation, I make a decision. I need to broaden my suspect list.

If she didn't do it, then who did?

And why?

I've been laser-focused on Jolene since I arrived in South Texas before the funeral. If someone else had been following her—or if anyone in her orbit looked suspicious enough to be involved—I should've seen it by now. *Shouldn't I?*

Am I missing something?

Maybe it's time to shift my approach. Stop shadowing Jolene every damn day and look outward.

Jolene's Adonis

But the thought of not following her anymore sends a jolt through my chest. My pulse spikes. For almost two months, she's been my assignment. My focus. My fascination. I can't just walk away now. I'm embedded.

I *am* Orlando, the guy who sails from port to port, minding his own business, running an import-export hustle as he drifts down the coast. I can't just pull anchor and disappear. That would raise eyebrows. Blow my cover. Or am I just making excuses?

No. I'm not leaving. I'm not ready. I'll keep up appearances. Business as usual. But instead of watching *only* Jolene, I'll widen the lens. I'll dig into the people around her, starting with the couple I saw leaving her store.

First, though, I need rest.

I let the ball fall from my hand, landing softly beside me on the bunk. I exhale and allow my body to release. One breath at a time, I sink deeper into stillness, tuning in to the rhythm of the rocking boat and the low hum of the marina. Somewhere in the distance, a freighter calls out its departure—three long honks echoing through the night.

The stale scent of fish and damp wood fills my nose.

And finally, I drift into sleep.

28

Jolene: Salvation

"You look like hell," Jessica announces the second she strolls into my studio. "And I don't mean that in a biblical sense. I mean it in the 'I'm your best friend, we're not at church, and no one's here to judge me, so I'm just going to say it like it is' kind of way. And there really is no other way to say it. You. Look. Like. Hell."

"Well, thanks," I smirk, glancing up at the cowboy clock over the door. Wesley's not-so-subtle reminder of the life I *could* have lived. Mistress Selena and Pet won't arrive for another hour. There's plenty of time to get rid of Jessica. "You look nice," I add, and she really does. I wish I could say otherwise, but Jessica's always put together. Today it's a yellow maxi dress with faint sunflower outlines that cling perfectly to her curves. It's basically wearable art.

Me? I had to dig through boxes to find anything that didn't smell like the bottom of a gym bag. I landed on a faded t-shirt with a parrot wearing a floral lei and sunglasses, sipping a margarita under a pair of palm trees. "Parrot Head" is stamped across the front. Paired it with cut-off jean shorts and a haphazard braid down my back.

I really need to do laundry.

"Are you sleeping okay?" Jessica asks.

"I'm trying. Living on the boat takes some adjusting. And the nightmares aren't helping," I admit.

Jessica gives me one of her soft, reassuring smiles. "That's to be expected. I just want you to know my door's always open."

"You've already done so much. I owe you."

"Don't even think about that. Just take care of yourself."

I nod, and then my fingers drift toward my wedding ring. I slowly twist the diamond around, letting the weight of it settle in my palm before sliding it off. For the first time since I said, "I do," my finger is bare. There's a deep indent where the band lived, and now it feels… naked. But it's time. I'm not Wesley's wife anymore.

"Do you think your husband could sell this for me?" I ask, holding it out to her. "It's used, but it's a good cut. Almost three carats. It has to be worth something."

Jessica lifts it, squints at it like the pro she is, and then smiles. "Are you sure you want to let it go?"

"I need the money. And honestly, it didn't mean anything to him. Just a gold band and a carved rock. Clearly, he didn't feel the way I did about it."

"If you're sure, I'll show it to George." She tucks it gently into her bag.

I hesitate, then shift awkwardly on my feet. "There's something else…"

Jessica senses it immediately. Her eyes narrow. "What is it?"

Come on, just ask her. She's my best friend. She won't judge me… right?

"Now I'm worried," she says, brow furrowed. "You're scaring me."

I exhale. "What do you think about me dating? Do you think it's too soon, considering… everything?"

Coward.

Jessica laughs, clearly relieved. "Mama always said, 'The only way to get over a man…'"

"Is to get under a different man," I finish with a smirk.

She winks. "I was going to say, 'find another man to ride,' but yours works too. Any prospects?"

"Maybe. I have dinner plans tonight with a hot Hispanic guy. But he insists it's not a date. I'm not sure how to take that. It wasn't supposed to be a date. I just wanted to thank him. He came to my rescue."

"Ooooh, a hot Hispanic hero? The visuals dancing in my head right now…"

"Seriously, Jess! What do you think?"

"I think you've been lonely too damn long. It's time to figure out who *you* are and what *you* want out of life. And you're not going to find that answer by locking yourself away in here or hiding out at the marina."

I open my mouth to protest, but she raises a hand to stop me.

"I get that Wesley didn't want more kids, but you're still young enough to have a family. If that's what you want. The sooner you let someone in—someone worthy of your love—the more time you'll have to build the life you deserve. Maybe the first frog wasn't your prince. That doesn't mean you stop looking."

My smile fades. "Wesley *was* my prince. For a long time."

"Was he?" she presses. "You say you were happy, but were you really?"

"For a while," I whisper.

"You deserve more than *for a while*, Jo. You deserve *forever*. But before you can find that, you've got to figure out who you are. Who is Jolene Brown?"

I shake my head. "I wish I knew."

Jessica pulls me into a hug. Her arms are skinny, but there's strength in them—a quiet, fierce strength that makes me believe she could conquer the world if I needed her to.

I should trust her. I want to. But these days, trust feels like an outdated concept. A fantasy. Like world peace.

"Thank you," I tell her as I step back. "I needed a friend today."

"I'll always be here. That's why I stopped by. I knew you were too stubborn to call."

"I have a feeling everything's going to be okay," I say, letting a bit of hope slip into my voice.

As Jessica walks out, she passes beneath the cowboy clock. That ugly thing's been there since the day I opened the store. I barely notice it anymore. Wesley picked it. His reminder that if it weren't for him, I'd be barefoot on a ranch, married to some bull rider, never knowing what I missed.

But when Wesley showed up in my life, he was a portal to something different. I chased that. I lived it. Even if I never imagined it would lead to Mistress Selena and Pet.

Still… maybe this is just the prologue to my next story.

Bob Marley's "Everything's gonna be alright" echoes in my head as I begin prepping for tonight.

And for once, I believe it.

29

Orlando: Answers

I oversleep. The second I jolt upright, my stomach clenches with hunger and disappointment. I rush around the cramped space of my boat, grabbing clothes, pulling on jeans, barely breathing. When I finally glance out the portside bull's-eye window and see that Jolene's bike is gone, I assume she's already left for the day.

The gnawing in my gut settles, not from the protein bar I haven't eaten, but from the jolt of purpose kicking in.

Time to find that damned key.

I ease open the cabin door and pause, holding my breath, listening for footsteps on the dock or the unmistakable drawl of Lisa, the marina's resident gossip and all-around buttinsky. But it's quiet. The breeze is light, the boat's still. Last night's soothing motion—the slosh of water, the hum of distant ship traffic—is gone. In its place is stillness. Calm. The occasional screech of seagulls slices through the silence, but I barely notice. To tourists, they're a nuisance. To all those who live out here, they're just background noise, like a humming refrigerator.

I take a deep breath, fill my lungs with salt and sea, and step onto the deck. Stretching my arms upward, I slowly pivot, scanning a 180-degree view of the docks. From here, I can see nearly the whole marina.

My Knotty Jolene is moored on the first pier from the entrance and is long enough to take up two slips. My smaller boat is tucked on her port bow side. I'm her closest neighbor. From this angle, I have a perfect view of the parking lot and, more importantly, a front-row seat to my favorite show: Jolene.

Satisfied that she's gone, I step onto the dock and walk with purpose toward her boat. If anyone sees me, I don't want to look like I'm sneaking. I rehearse my cover story as I cross the few feet between us. *I didn't know she was gone. Just swinging by to visit.*

I climb aboard *My Knotty Jolene* and give the galley roof a couple of knocks. No movement. I grip the handle, open the door, and slip inside, closing it quietly behind me.

Time to move fast.

The place is chaos—boxes everywhere, clothes and random items spilling out. I recognize almost everything. I've watched her pack them, piece by piece. But a key? She wouldn't stash something that important inside a taped-up box. She'd put it somewhere accessible. Logical. If I were Jolene, where would I hide a key?

I open drawers, peek into cabinets, lift everything that might conceal something small.

There it is .Under a fake plant.

Aha.

I grab it and turn it over in my hand. Could be a boat key, but she never locks the cabin. Not a storage unit key either. Her lock's a combination, and I already cracked it. It's their wedding date—etched right into Wesley's headstone. Along with the words "loving husband and father," a pair of interlocking rings, and a date. But no second name. No matching plot. No room for her next to him.

Did she just not have the money for a double plot? Or… did she never plan to be buried beside him?

I study the key again. Purple silicone sleeve over the head, the word *store* burned into the metal beneath.

Bingo.

I pocket the key and slip out the door, crossing back to my boat, and then straight to my car. I need a copy. *Now.* Before she notices it's gone.

Jolene's Adonis

Back in my usual parking spot outside her shop, I settle in with a protein bar and a thermos of coffee. Lights are on inside, but no movement. I sink lower in my seat, eyes on the storefront.

A few minutes later, the same black sedan from yesterday pulls up to the curb.

I sit up, just enough to get a good look.

The driver steps out, walks around, and opens the back passenger door. The couple I saw yesterday emerges. The man's wearing a black thong. The woman's in a halter top and a black mini skirt.

My breath catches.

No way they're going inside. Not dressed like that.

But that's exactly what they do.

The woman leads the way to the door and tries the handle. Nothing. Locked.

Why would Jolene lock the door? She's usually open by now.

My pulse spikes as worst-case scenarios flood my brain.

Did something happen to her on the way over? Did she get jumped while unlocking the store? Is she inside, hurt? Tied up? Unable to call for help?

Should I use the key?

Damn her. She's making me care.

That's dangerous. That's the kind of entanglement that gets agents killed.

The woman knocks. After a few seconds, the door opens and she steps inside.

I let out a long, slow breath and slump forward, releasing all the tension I didn't realize I was holding.

The man follows her in. I catch a glimpse of Jolene's face—she's upright, not restrained. She pulls the door closed behind them. There's a hint of paranoia in her expression, the same haunted look I've seen on her face recently, but she's not in distress.

The sedan rolls forward and tucks into a space along the side of the building, out of easy view.

Something's going on. And it's not just bondage-clad tourists on a road trip.

I sit in my car, trying to figure out my next move. I need to know what's happening inside that shop.

I turn the ignition and pull forward into a space right at the front. Nothing strange about that. I'm new in town. It's a tourist shop. As far as anyone knows, I'm just another guy checking out the local businesses. I had no idea it was her store. What a surprise!

I get out, stretch like I've got all the time in the world, and try the door.

Locked.

What the fuck?

Now I *really* need to know what's happening in there.

I glance up and down the road. The sedan is parked at the side of the building—close enough to approach casually.

But should I?

I wait.

Right outside the door.

Heart pounding.

Options narrowing.

I walk toward the sedan at a slow, casual pace, fixing my cover story in my mind. I need a reason to approach, something natural, something that gives me a purpose for asking questions. I run through possibilities and pivot on instinct and head back to my car.

I unlock the door, pop the hood, and bend over the engine. I tug on wires, fiddle with tubing—anything to make it look convincing. I'm banking on the driver seeing me and having some kind of mechanical knowledge. Car trouble's always a solid conversation starter, especially with gearheads. Guys like that usually end up in some kind of driving role—chauffeurs, mechanics, or retired racers. And they love talking shop.

I walk from the front of the car to the left side, then the right, banging on the battery wires for good measure. Then I pull out the transmission dipstick and pretend to study it like I know what I'm doing.

Footsteps approach from behind.

I keep my head buried under the hood until I glance sideways and see an older guy in a chauffeur's uniform and cap.

"Car trouble?" he asks.

"I think so," I say, putting on my best confused-and-slightly-panicked face.

"What's it doing?" he says, leaning in to look under the hood where my focus is fixed.

"Temp gauge started climbing just as I pulled into town," I tell him. "Figured I'd better pull over before it blew. I wasn't sure if it's too hot to remove the cap or if I just need to top off the water."

"Let me take a look," he says. He moves to the radiator cap and rests his hand just above it, testing the heat. Then he gently presses his palm to it before gripping and unscrewing it. "It's warm, but not too hot. Let's see what's inside."

He peers in, nods. "Slightly low on coolant. Nothing major. Definitely not enough to overheat."

I lean in, play along. "Yeah, I see what you mean. Doesn't look terrible." I make a thoughtful noise. "Hmm…"

"Could be something else," he offers. "Salt air can corrode your radiator. This close to the water? Wreaks havoc on cars, bikes, even homes. Could be buildup. Could be anything. How long since the last flush?"

"It's a rental," I say, shrugging. "No clue about maintenance."

He chuckles. "Well, I'm no mechanic. But my old man was. Taught me everything I know."

"Oh yeah? You seem to know your way around an engine."

"I do what I can. I drive for a family when they need me. Part of the job's keeping their fleet running smooth."

Fleet, he says. That perks me up.

"Must be a sweet gig," I say, trying to sound impressed. "You get to drive anything exciting? I've always wanted to try a Maserati. Or at least a Benz."

He grins. "They've got a Benz. Never a Maserati, but there's a Corvette."

It's working. Keep him talking.

I smile and nod, not too eager. "Well, I'm Orlando." I extend my hand, watching him carefully. "Really appreciate you stopping. I'll definitely get the radiator checked out just in case. Ever drive for anyone else? I may need a reliable driver soon. Be nice to know someone who won't leave me stranded. You have a card or something?"

He shakes my hand, firm grip. "Name's Roger. I don't have a card, but I'm usually based out of the D'Angelo Hotel in San Antonio. Just ask for Roger, the family driver."

Perfect. That's all I need.

"Appreciate it, Roger," I say, grinning as I lower the hood. "Hope to run into you again."

I climb into the car, wave, and pull away from the storefront. I don't let the smile fade until I'm out of sight.

Now I know who I'm dealing with, and exactly who just walked into Jolene's shop, wearing a thong.

I have work to do.

I steer toward the docks, board the ferry to Aransas Pass, and ride across the water with my mind racing ahead. Once I hit land, I head straight for Corpus Christi.

There's a CIA field contact office in town. It's time to start digging.

30

Jolene: The whip

I open the storage box I've been meaning to take to Goodwill—the one filled with old Halloween costumes I no longer wear. It's been sitting here for months. As I dig through the pile, my fingers find something I'd forgotten about.

A sexy little outfit.

It's nearly identical to what Mistress Selena described wearing during her first foray into the fetish world. Just holding it makes me feel wicked. Naughty.

When I wore it for Wesley, he couldn't keep his hands off me.

It's perfect.

I want to be in the right headspace, open to possibility, unafraid to explore whatever Selena has in mind. Who knows? I might even enjoy it.

I squeeze into the skimpy, form-fitting costume in front of the mirror. Hazel eyes stare back at me, dulled with fatigue.

What happened to me?

I yank the band from my ponytail and let my hair spill over my shoulders. Then I brush it smooth and fluff it up. The burgundy and black lace corset hugs my waist and lifts my breasts. The booty shorts are so small that half my ass hangs out the bottom. The fishnet stockings lead the eye straight into the thigh-high lace-up boots.

Damn.

This corn-fed girl still has it.

If Wesley could see me now…

I grin at first, but it quickly fades into something darker, colder, more deliberate.

Wesley once said I could never wear this outfit for anyone but him. He threatened to spank me if I even thought about it.

Wesley spanking me… the irony continues.

A knock at the door makes me jump.

Showtime.

I throw on a bathrobe and go to the front. "Hello?" I call, holding my breath.

"It's us, *cara mia!*" Selena's voice rings out.

Relief washes through me as I open the door and let them in. Instinctively, I glance around the parking lot before locking up.

"Wait here for one minute," I tell them and rush to the back, ditching the robe on the way.

I hurry to the couch and cycle through poses, trying not to look desperate, but not too stiff either. I want Selena to see I'm open, willing. Not begging, just… ready. Sort of. I settle on an upright position, legs crossed. The outfit says enough.

"Ready!" I yell.

Selena steps into the room and freezes.

She stares, eyes wide. Her lips part slightly before curving into a slow, smoldering smile. Not a happy one. A claiming one.

She doesn't say it out loud, but her look is clear: *You're mine.*

Pet bumps into her from behind, then leans around her with a grin and nods in approval. He's wearing nothing but a leatherette thong. His erection strains over the waistband. Selena shifts as it brushes her backside.

It hits me that I didn't even notice their clothes. *Jeez!*

"My, aren't you the eager boy," she purrs in her thick Spanish accent.

She's wearing a black leatherette halter top, silver rivets outlining her breasts and revealing flashes of nipple. Her matching mini skirt barely conceals anything. Her shoes are six-inch Louboutins—clear tops, red soles, five black bows lining her feet. They make her look mostly naked from the ankle down. Her black hair is braided; her eyeliner winged like Cleopatra.

She's stunning. Otherworldly.

Next to her, I feel… underdressed. Exposed.

She moves toward the workbench like a predator—slow, deliberate, and unthreatened. My breath catches. I count her steps.

One…

What the hell was I thinking? There's still time to back out.

Two…

Pet looks absolutely ravenous. And he's not looking at her. He's looking at me.

Three…

I can do this. I can do this. No, I can't.

Four…

This is for every time Wesley made me feel invisible. Someone *wants* me. Look at Pet.

Five…

Oh no. I haven't touched another man's dick in over a decade. *Breathe!*

Six…

I could run. I could bolt.

But I don't want to get off this couch.

Selena reaches for the chains. Pet lifts his wrists without hesitation.

I watch her secure him, then she glides over to me and sits beside me on the couch. She wraps her fingers gently around mine. I realize my hands are shaking.

"We've decided to stay a few more days," she says. "No pressure, *cara mia.* You can watch. Or join. Pet is very patient."

"I thought I could…" I start, but she silences me with a finger to my lips.

"Shhhh."

Selena begins the session with a loud crack of her whip as Aaliyah's "Rock the Boat" fills the air, eerie and slow. The low, pulsing rhythm matches my heartbeat.

I sink into the cushions, watching her tease Pet with calculated precision. Her focus is completely on him, but Pet's eyes keep drifting back to me. Every time they do, Selena lashes him again, and it only makes him more eager.

It's almost funny.

Almost.

The tension eases. I begin to relax. The scene doesn't feel so foreign anymore. Selena circles him, brushing the whip along his chest, whispering in his ear. He pulls against the chains, muscles flexing as he tries to touch her.

The song ends.

The room shifts. A throbbing beat kicks in—dark and charged.

Nine Inch Nails' "Closer" plays through the speakers, raw and primal.

Selena dances, slow and teasing, letting the rhythm move through her as she circles Pet. But then she turns, locks eyes with me, and her whole energy shifts. She struts over, climbs onto the couch, and lip-syncs straight to me:

*"I want to f** you..."*

She mouths the words with wicked intent, dragging her fingers along the edge of my corset, then laughs softly.

And just like that, my fear fades into heat.

I don't feel invisible anymore.

I relax even more as Selena performs. She's a natural performer. Pet and Selena are so open, so accepting.

I can do this! I chant it like a mantra.

Selena goes to the stereo and puts on "Butterfly" by Crazy Town. Her expression shifts, turning serious as she crosses back to the couch and reaches for my hands. I pause, then submit. She pulls me to my feet and hands me the whip.

"Come," she sings along.

I nod and step toward Pet. I toss the strands of the whip lightly toward his chest. He smiles, and I giggle awkwardly.

Selena blindfolds him with a tie and cranks the volume.

"You can do this!" she shouts over the music.

I echo in my head: I can do this. If I'm going to, I need something to lash out at. With the first real crack of the whip, I see Wesley's face, sneering. I strike again. It feels good. His scars he never explained. His condescension. Gone, even for a moment.

I pull back for another strike, but now I see Wesley's cold, lifeless face. My scream cuts through the room as the whip crashes to the floor. Pet jumps.

Selena wraps an arm around me and leads me to the couch, turning the music down.

"It's too soon," I whisper. "I want this. It feels powerful. Holding that whip… I just need time."

She nods and switches the song. "Soldier" by Eminem pulses from the speakers.

Pet pulls against the chains, singing along, and almost keeping up with the rhymes.

Selena cracks the whip near him. He wiggles his hips, straining toward the sound.

"Please," he begs, tilting his chin up under the tie.

Selena sings the lyrics, looking at me.

I nod and sink back into the couch. I grab the wine bottle, take a long drink, and offer it to her as she dances over to me. She gulps it down and hands it back with a wicked smile.

Selena returns to Pet, lashes him with force, and removes his blindfold. He looks at me with sympathy and desire mingling in his gaze. "More," he whispers.

Selena frowns.

"Please, Mistress," he adds.

"That's better." She slides down his thong and strokes his arousal.

His gaze shifts to me. Selena taps his chin with the whip.

"You like to watch her?" she asks.

He nods.

She blindfolds him again, unlocks one hand, coats it in oil, then sits beside me.

"We want a show. Don't we, cara mia?"

"Yes," I say, my voice rough.

"You're going to perform for us, and you won't get to see our reactions. How's that, Pet?"

"I like it very much. Thank you, Mistress."

"We're waiting," she says, taking another swig and passing the bottle to me.

I drink. My throat is dry, but my body is not. The ache between my legs intensifies. I watch Pet touch himself, slowly at first, then with growing intensity.

He moans.

My lips part.

Selena drinks.

We share the bottle like old friends.

Pet strokes faster, then groans.

"Wait!" Selena cries, diving for her bag. She pulls out a small clear ring, coats it in oil, and slides it onto him.

"Thank you, Mistress," he gasps, stroking again.

Selena collapses beside me. "Shoop" by Salt-N-Pepa starts playing.

"What's that ring?" I ask, pointing. "Doesn't it hurt?"

"It's a cock ring. It enhances pleasure. Builds pressure. Makes it stronger."

"Oh." That's all I can manage.

Pet groans louder, faster.

"Wait!" Selena yells again, but she's too late. His orgasm splashes across the floor.

"Sorry, Mistress," he pants.

"You have cleaning to do," she says, untying him.

"I'll wait outside," I blurt, fleeing.

"Wait," Selena calls, catching up. "He made the mess. He cleans it."

In the showroom, she hands me a thick wad of cash. "This covers our stay. There's more if you participate."

"Maybe tomorrow?" I say, eyes on the bills. I've never held this much money.

"Take your time. Pet's infatuated."

"My stepdaughter's bringing friends tomorrow. After noon?"

"Perfect. We'll pick you up. We'll shop for something more suitable."

I look down at my outfit, suddenly self-conscious. "It's all I had. I thought…"

She hushes me. "I get it. Pet likes to gift the women who intrigue him. And you, cara mia, have him hooked."

I blush. "He's different. Refreshing. It's like living without shame."

"You can be free," she says, pressing my hand over the cash.

Pet strolls in wearing nothing but his thong. "Ready?"

They smirk as I gape.

"Aren't you going to change?"

They both shake their heads.

"Into what?" Selena grins. "We came like this."

What the fuck?

They slide into the waiting car. I glance outside. The streets are deserted. Thank gawd for off-season.

Just before the driver shuts the door, Selena lifts a hand. "Do you bake?"

I blink, then shake my head. What a weird question.

She waves, and the car pulls away.

I lock up fast and hurry to the back.

"Shoop" is on repeat. I count the money—$5,000 in hundreds. Enough to pay for Wesley's funeral, plus extra.

But I can't deposit this. Joint account. Debt collectors. No safe, either. Wait…the lock box in the bow. Wesley hid one. Combination's my birthday. Maybe the investigators missed it. Maybe there's more in there. I'll hide it.

I brush my hair, untie the corset, glance at the table, the chains. The memories flood me. My hips sway to the beat.

Inspired, I grab my welding gear and dig through scrap until I find four pieces. I crank the music, fire up my torch, and shape the metal. By the time I install the manacles to the blank wall facing the couch, the lyrics are etched in my brain.

And damn, I feel good.

31

Orlando: Lust

After spending a few hours at the local field office, combing through every file and media mention about the D'Angelo family, I'm confident I can identify the couple visiting Jolene's store. Their faces are splashed across gossip magazines everywhere. They're infamous for public displays of near-nudity and a long list of fetishes.

They're the same couple Jim used to talk about on stakeouts. "Jim," of course, is just his undercover name. I never knew his real one. Most of us don't share that kind of intel, not unless trust is built over time. Wesley was different. He was one of the few agents I ever really let in. The kind of guy who made you feel safe, who never judged you, and who'd never stab you in the back.

"Hey!" Jim would start casually, always with that grin. "You read about that D'Angelo dude and his mistress?"

I shook my head at the time, only half-listening, eyes locked on a passerby down the block. I watched the same door for two hours and twenty-seven minutes. Any moment now, Abdul-Bari, the Afghan student I tailed for twelve days, would exit the university, and I needed to be ready. He was our best lead in the disappearance of a college professor and journalist, last seen writing about al-Qaeda activity in the U.S.

The man vanished twenty-three days before then. His wife had a solid alibi, officially cleared. But then Abdul-Bari hit the radar. No red flags on his visa, not at first. But after a few classmates reported strange, drunken rants about jihad and martyrdom, the agency took a second look. Turned out he spent time in Kabul with relatives just before arriving on U.S. soil. Kabul is an al-Qaeda breeding ground.

On paper, he was a mechanical engineering major. But he just happened to take the missing professor's journalism class. He also seemed to be constantly in proximity to the professor, both on and off campus. *Coincidence?* I don't think so.

As an immigrant myself, I know how easy it is to get caught in the gears of the United States justice system. I double- and triple-check my facts, especially with cases like this. But everything pointed to him. My gut said he was guilty, and my gut rarely lies.

Sooner or later, perps return to the scene, just to check. To see if the soil shifted, if the earth has whispered their secrets to someone. That's when they slip.

Jim kept talking, ignoring my lack of interest. "Dude's rich, like *D'Angelo Hotels* rich. Private planes. Family owns exclusive clubs. He went to some elitist school for kids of celebrities and old money. He could have anyone, but he's only ever seen with this dominatrix chick. Don't get me wrong, she's fine as hell, but she's *paid* to whip dudes and play their games."

That actually got my attention. I glanced at Jim, raising a brow, then returned to watching the door.

"Dude's got balls," he went on. "His dad's probably ready to strangle him. My pops thinks he's hot shit for making five figures, and he'd still tan my hide if I embarrassed the family name like that."

Good ol' Jim. Turned out he wasn't just talking to kill time. He was paying attention.

It took four more days of his ramblings before we got our break. We were driving down Old Sawmill Road, tailing our suspect, when Jim suddenly shouted, "Got the bastard!"

"Huh?" I blinked, frowning at him.

"Brake check. Quick, but definite. About 800 feet back." He dug the map out of the glove box and circled our location. "Marking it. We'll come back after we follow this asshole home. Just in case." He gave me a cocky wink, flushed with adrenaline.

Jolene's Adonis

I didn't take my eyes off the gravel road or the car we followed. Steady at forty miles per hour. I figured Jim was seeing things.

But he wasn't.

We trailed the guy home. It was the same routine: parked, garage door closed, lights off except for the kitchen. After that, we doubled back to the spot Jim marked. A few minutes of tromping through brush with flashlights, and boom! There it was. That sickly-sweet, unmistakable stench of decay. A shallow grave.

Before the sun rose, we hit Abdul-Bari's place with search and arrest warrants. We found enough to tie him to more than one murder. Jim's eagle eye paid off. His gossip tangents about D'Angelo? Somehow, they gave me more context than the damn files.

Still, D'Angelo isn't a killer. He's into sex. Kinky, maybe extreme, but not criminal. So why is he mixed up with Jolene?

He already has a dominatrix. Jolene doesn't act like a woman wrapped up in that world. No suspicious meetings. No secret rendezvous. But she *has* changed lately.

It doesn't add up.

WTF.

I leave the office, running over potential conversation starters on my way to the marina. Maybe dinner will give me the opening I need.

Once I get there, I climb aboard Jolene's boat, scan the area to make sure no one's watching, then quietly try the door. It's unlocked.

I duck inside and install the hidden cameras. One in the main salon, one in each stateroom.

I miss watching her. All those hours studying her, even while she slept. It became comforting. Like having her there beside me.

Back on my rented boat, I strip down and step into the shower. The warm water eases the tension in my muscles, the citrus-scented soap coating my skin like armor.

My mind drifts.

Will she show up tonight in black, holding a whip? Or will it be white lace and garters?

I close my eyes and try to picture it.

God help me. I hope I'm wrong.

But I'm going to find out.

I close my eyes and picture her—Jolene— unclipping a stocking from her garter belt and slowly rolling it down her long, sculpted leg. Her hair falls forward, veiling her breasts like silk.

Jolene's Adonis

My cock throbs. I grip it in my right hand, bracing myself against the narrow shower wall with my left. She keeps undressing in my mind, stripping away each barrier between us. I stroke slowly at first, imagining the sensual glide of those stockings down her skin. Then she straightens, her breasts bouncing slightly with the movement, her body clad in nothing but a garter belt and thong.

She looks straight at me—teasing, inviting.

My strokes speed up.

"Jolene," I murmur, then louder, "Oh… Jolene."

The pressure builds. I grit my teeth as it overtakes me, my release splattering across the shower floor. My body collapses forward, forehead resting against the curved fiberglass enclosure, breath coming in shallow gasps.

She's in my head.

Too much. Too deep.

After a few moments, I rinse off what's left of the shame and step out, grabbing the towel. I dry off fast, like if I move quick enough, I can scrub the guilt away too. I pull on my lucky blue shirt—the one that never fails when I need to charm a lonely widow— and splash on cologne. Brush through my hair.

In the mirror above the tiny sink, I stare at my reflection, leaning in, both hands gripping the edge of the counter.

This mission was never supposed to go this far. I tell myself I'm doing this for Wesley. I *am*.

But I can't stop thinking about Jolene—those legs, that hair, that supple body. She's carved herself into me.

Since learning who her mystery guest is, I haven't been able to stop picturing her holding a whip, delivering pain, but not to me. That part makes me twitch with something darker. Want. Jealousy. Rage.

It turns me on.

And it pisses me off.

The line between lust and vengeance is too thin. It's starting to blur, and I need to get control. I can't let her live in my head like this, twisting my thoughts, warping my judgment.

I have to keep things professional. Business as usual.

I check my watch, exhale sharply, and hop down onto the dock. The sun is lower now, throwing warm light across the marina as I stroll toward the small restaurant nestled between the parking lot and the pool.

Inside, I get why people rave about this place. It feels like a bistro in some tucked-away coastal town. Tables dressed in crisp white linen. Carved chairs with ship anchors. Flickering candles set in metal holders shaped like sea creatures cast shadows across the walls—octopus arms, fish tails, and jellyfish drifting like ghosts.

A waiter walks over, wearing navy cargo shorts and a marina-logo polo.

"A menu, sir," he says, handing me a laminated card and flipping over the wine and water glasses. "Wine list's on the back. Would you like to hear the specials?"

"I'm actually waiting for someone. She should be here any minute. Can we wait?"

"Of course. Just flag me down when you're ready."

I nod, then glance at my watch again. I'm on time—always am.

She hasn't come back to the marina yet, far as I know. But I was… *preoccupied* in the shower.

I drum my fingers on the table and mutter under my breath, "She better not be off whipping that damned fool."

32

Jolene: Diamonds and Desire

A sharp ring slices through the music, jolting me upright. My phone! I scramble for my bag and shut off the music, but I'm already too late. When I flip it open, four missed calls glare back at me. All from the marina's restaurant.

Shit!

Orlando.

I quickly dial the number. Chef John picks up, his tone laced with annoyance.

"Jolene, where are you? I was starting to worry. You never miss a reservation or ignore your phone."

"I'm so sorry," I say, trying not to sound as flustered as I feel.

"You're forgiven," he says with a chuckle. "I'm just glad you're okay. But your gentleman is still here, and he doesn't look pleased."

I glance around the studio, taking in the mess of tools and freshly set displays. A satisfied smile tugs at my lips. "The store got busy and I completely lost track of time. Would you mind apologizing to him for me? And go ahead and charge his meal to my boat slip account."

"No problem. I'll take care of it."

"Thank you. Please tell him I'm on my way."

"I'll try to keep the kitchen open a little longer."

"No need. Just let him know I'm coming."

I hang up, toss the phone back in my bag, and rush to the bathroom. Peeling off the costume takes some effort. I've basically sweat through it. Once I'm free, I speed-dial the local cab company.

"Jolene's Treasures," I tell the dispatcher. "And I'm in a hurry."

Clothes go on fast. I flick off the lights in the backroom and step into the showroom, now dark with the sun fully set. The cowboy clock reads 8:30. *Damn.* I lock up and pace on the curb, foot tapping impatiently. Luckily, the cab pulls up in under five minutes. One perk of living in a small town, no traffic.

I spot Orlando waiting at the marina entrance as I jump out of the cab and shove some cash into the driver's hand.

"I'm so sorry!" I plead to Orlando, breathless. "I lost track of the time."

He eyes me, suspicious. "Chef said the store got busy."

"It did."

"Strange. Everyone in town's been complaining how slow things are in the winter, yet your store's packed?"

"It's *usually* slow. But I've got two clients visiting from out of town. I'm working on something special for them."

"Really?" He lifts an eyebrow. "Like what?"

Here we go again. Explaining what I do to a man who probably assumes I make friendship bracelets and sell them at craft fairs. I swallow and slow my words, just a touch patronizing. "I'm a blacksmith. I make jewelry, custom pieces out of brass, platinum, gold, silver—basically anything that can be melted and shaped when heated."

That grin of his spreads slowly. "A woman who knows her way around a toolbox. I'm impressed," he teases with a low chuckle.

But when he catches my expression, the humor in his eyes softens.

"Seriously," he adds, voice more sincere. "You're full of surprises, but this one shouldn't be surprising. Women are a hell of a lot more capable than most men give them credit for. Luckily, I'm not most men. I'd love to see your work sometime."

"I'm booked solid the next few days, but once I finish my current piece, I'd be happy to give you a tour." *I wonder how he'd react to the cocks.*

"Well, busy lady, you missed a great meal. Kitchen's closed."

My stomach rumbles loudly. Perfect timing. "I'm starving."

He lifts a foil box and grins. "Hungry for Chef John's vegan crab cakes?"

I nod eagerly. Chef John must've told him I don't eat meat.

"Too bad. These are *my* leftovers."

I swing my bag toward him in mock outrage. "You monster!"

He laughs, eyes sparkling. "Relax. Chef took care of you. And apparently, *you* bought *my* dinner. Just so you know, that doesn't guarantee I'm sleeping with you."

"Oh? It takes more than dinner, huh?" I lift an eyebrow and lean in just slightly. "I've got a chilled bottle of sangria on my boat. It would pair perfectly with those leftovers... if you're interested."

"After you stood me up?" he shoots back, amused.

"I thought we agreed this wasn't a date," I say, playing innocent.

He just laughs.

We head down the dock together, passing Lisa and Larry's boat. Heated voices float from the cabin, mid-argument, but stop the second they hear us. We stifle our laughter. Orlando's barely moved in, and he already knows Lisa wears the pants in that relationship.

Once we reach *My Knotty Jolene*, he climbs aboard first and offers me his hand.

"You cleaned," he notes, eyeing the now-clear deck.

"Not completely unpacked, but at least the boxes are inside in case it rains." I step into the cabin and toss my purse onto the bench. I grab a fork, the sangria from the fridge, a corkscrew, and two plastic cups.

"Aren't you afraid of being robbed?" Orlando calls from outside.

"What do you mean?" I ask, arms full as I join him without bothering to shut the cabin door behind me.

He's sitting on the padded bench near the helm. "I mean," he says slowly, taking the bottle and corkscrew from me, "your door wasn't locked."

"Oh, *that*." I smirk. "Aren't you observant. What did you say you do again?"

Before he can answer, I open the box and inhale the delicious scent. Inside are two golden-brown veggie cakes with a colorful etouffée on the side with kale, tomato, and a hint of lemon.

I spear a bite and pop it into my mouth. The flavors explode—spicy, rich, and tangy. I close my eyes, throw my head back, and moan.

"Chef John is the best," I gasp. "My mouth is having an orgasm right now."

Did I just say that?

I open one eye and glance at Orlando.

Yep. That grin is back.

Orlando pulls the cork from the bottle and pours sangria into one of the plastic cups, setting it in front of me. His expression doesn't change.

Maybe I didn't actually say it…

"Then we can skip the foreplay," he says.

Oh fuck.

Too much sex on the brain. I just talked about an orgasm to a complete stranger.

I smile awkwardly and shove another bite into my mouth. I'm too hungry to let a slip of the tongue ruin my appetite. "What were we talking about? Oh, right. What do you do, Orlando?"

"I deal in imports. Exports. Whatever pays."

"Hmmm… that's what my husband, Wesley, did. Traded everything from cattle to car parts, whatever brought the biggest profit." I glance up at him, wondering if their paths ever crossed.

"What a coincidence." He brushes it off casually. "So, your door. Why was it unlocked?"

"I'm not sure where the key is, and Wesley never locked it. There's always someone around at the marina, so it never felt necessary. When we're out sailing, it's just us and the water. Locks don't mean much out there." I narrow my eyes at him. "Should I be worried?"

"No. No, I get it," he says quickly, studying me like I'm some exotic bird. "You like to eat."

"Is that a question or a statement?" I ask, licking the last grain of rice from the fork. I take a sip of the sangria and lean back, satisfied. For the first time in days, my stomach quits growling. I hadn't realized how many meals I've skipped since Wesley died. I really need to start taking better care of myself.

"Just stating a fact," Orlando replies, his tone tinged with apology.

"Would you rather I pick at a salad and starve while you dig into a plate of bloody steak?"

He laughs, an honest, deep laugh. "So you *did* spy on my last date."

"Isn't that every guy's 'last date'? The woman orders a salad, whines about being fat, then goes home and cries into a tub of ice cream wondering why the man didn't like her. I want to grab her shoulders and scream, *you weren't being real!* If you can't be yourself, what's left to be attracted to?"

"Do you always say what's on your mind?"

"Unfortunately." I sip again.

"I find it refreshing." He finishes his wine and pours more for us both.

"My late husband found it annoying."

"I'm not him."

His voice dips when he says it, like there's something beneath the surface. Sadness? Regret? No way. Why would there be?

But he's right. He's nothing like Wesley.

I take a long look at him. Canvas shorts with cargo pockets. Faded blue V-neck. A small tuft of dark curls peeks out of the collar, hinting at the unshaved chiseled chest beneath. His legs are tan and muscular, his sandals exposing large, strong feet.

The word that comes to mind—MACHO. Capital M.

Gawd, I want him. I want his big hands tangled in my hair, yanking it until my head tilts back. I want that mouth on mine, on my neck, my breasts.

My lips part as I imagine his tongue circling my nipple.

I shift in my seat and shake my head, trying to chase away the graphic images flooding my brain.

I need a man. Just one night. Just one delicious, reckless night.

"You look tired," he says, standing and downing the rest of his wine. "I should go."

No, don't go. Take me to bed. Drag me there by my hair and…

I clear my throat and stand too, thankful I'm not a man with an obvious bulge giving away my thoughts. "That's probably a good idea. Thank you for bringing my dinner, and for the non-date."

Offering a sly smile, I step forward, pulling him into a hug. His biceps flex under my hands, and my nipples brush against him, sending a jolt straight to my core.

I tilt my head, aiming for his chest, but his lips land squarely on mine. He wraps his arms around me and kisses me. Really kisses me. Deep. Intense. My lips tingle under the pressure, but I freeze, eyes wide open.

He pulls back, flustered. "I'm sorry. The wine… the hug…"

"I shouldn't have hugged you. My fault," I say quickly.

But damn I want more.

"You just lost your husband. I crossed a line. It won't happen again."

"It was nice," I admit. "It's been a long time since someone kissed me like that."

His gaze darkens. "Your husband didn't kiss you?"

"Not lately. He had other… interests. I haven't felt like a priority in years. So please, don't apologize. You have no idea how good it feels to be touched, to be seen, to be wanted."

"Can I ask you something?" I say before he can respond.

"I have a feeling you're going to anyway."

I grin. "True. Are you married?"

"No."

"Ever been married?"

"No."

"Kids?"

"Just a goddaughter."

How sweet.

"Girlfriend?"

"No."

"Boyfriend?"

He laughs. "No. What's with the interrogation? I said one question."

"You're single. I'm single…"

"And?"

"Why are you so opposed to going on a date with me?"

He exhales. "Believe me, I want to. I just don't want to be *that guy*—the one who swoops in on the lonely widow and takes advantage."

Lonely widow. Ugh. That's what I've become? How utterly pathetic.

He pulls me into his arms. My cheek presses against the base of his throat. I inhale the scent of citrus body wash and expensive cologne. Masculine. Clean. Comforting.

His heart beats fast. His breath ruffles the top of my hair.

"You're a very desirable woman, Jolene. Your husband was a lucky man," he whispers.

I tilt my head back to meet his eyes, and then his lips crash into mine.

This time, I kiss him back.

His tongue explores mine. His hand slides to the back of my head, fingers fisting in my hair, tugging just enough to make me gasp.

He presses against me, hard—his erection firm against my stomach.

Oh yes. Right here. Right now.

His other hand slides up my side, cupping one breast. He moans when he realizes I'm not wearing a bra.

I thrust my chest forward, aching for his touch.

I feel like Pet on a leash—eager, exposed, and aching to beg.

And then… he stops.

His hand drops. His grip on my hair loosens.

"We can't," he says, panting.

"Why not? I want to… so badly."

"Me too," he says, stepping back. "But it's too soon. You just lost your husband. I can't be that guy."

He shakes his head and adjusts his shorts. His arousal is still obvious, thick and tempting.

My nipples ache, desperate for his touch again.

He steps off the boat and onto the dock, putting space—and fiberglass—between us.

"Thanks for the wine. And for dinner." His voice is strained. "It's been… nice."

"It's been *very* nice." I don't even try to hide the longing in my voice. "I'll see you tomorrow?"

"Tomorrow," he nods, then turns toward his boat.

I carry the nearly empty bottle and my cup inside, locking the door behind me.

Another man to ride, huh?

I sigh.

If only.

I scoop up my purse from the bench and collapse against the cabin door. Holding it tight to my chest, thinking of the money inside, I try to slow my breathing. I shift my focus away from the rush of adrenaline, away from my wildly inappropriate attraction to Orlando and toward Wesley's lock box.

Orlando is so damn sexy. Too sexy. Distracting in the most dangerous way. Around him, I feel like I'm on autopilot, as if my body overrides my brain.

Honestly, it's like my vagina flops outside my body and starts running the show—like a man with a dick leading him into danger with no thought of consequences. Screw safety. Screw common sense. Just… screw.

Ugh. He's a stranger. I don't know him. I have to be more careful. Next time, I swear I will be.

I make my way to the forward cabin and slip off my sparkly purple boat shoes. I keep a couple of pairs on deck so I can switch into something more boat-friendly when I board. A girl's gotta have her glam, even in boat-safe footwear.

I crawl across the bunk to the wooden panel where the shelving forms a V. I slide my forefinger into the little hole at the corner and lift. The panel creaks open, revealing the small compartment beneath.

Chains fill it halfway, leaving a gap at the top. The wood looks solid, but Wesley showed me months ago how to press on a certain spot to make the panel in the back slide open just a little. I find the spot and press. It resists for a second, then squeaks softly as it shifts along the swollen rail.

I wince at the sound. It stops. I reach inside, half-expecting to touch a hairy spider or a nest of something awful. *Ick.*

My fingers brush something rough and metal—the handle of the lock box. Got it. I grip it tightly and tug. Something inside jingles. Coins? It's heavier than I expect. I brace on my knees and pull harder.

With a grunt and a little sway, it finally breaks free.

I drag it out of the compartment and plop it on the bed, positioning myself cross-legged in front of it. It's much larger than I remember and it's heavy…

My hands shake as I press the code into the keypad. The familiar click makes me exhale, and the lid pops open just enough to tease what's inside.

I lift it the rest of the way and gasp. *Cash!* Thick stacks of hundred-dollar bills, each bundle wrapped in a paper ring marked $10,000. And gold. So much gold. Rings, earrings, and necklaces. Some studded with diamonds, others glittering with deep green emeralds that sparkle even in the dim cabin light.

Whoa!

I lift a few pieces, letting them dangle from my fingertips. Then I notice a thick manila envelope tucked beneath the treasure, my name scrawled across the front in Wesley's handwriting.

Jolene's Adonis

I rip it open.

Inside, I find a handful of official-looking documents in Spanish with gold-embossed seals. I'm not sure what they are, but they feel important. Carefully, I lay them out on the bed, my mind racing. How am I supposed to interpret these?

Then I find a folded letter addressed to *me*. And another smaller note tucked behind it, this one addressed to Amy.

My throat tightens. I set Amy's note aside carefully. I'll give it to her later.

My letter is dated four months ago.

Tears fill my eyes as I unfold the page. Wesley's familiar handwriting stares back at me.

It says:

> My dearest Jolene: As you may have guessed by now, there are a few things about my life I have never shared with you.
>
> For your safety, I regret that even in my death, I must remain secretive. Just know that from the moment I saw you on your father's ranch, you took my breath away. You have consumed every one of my thoughts since then.

Things have changed between us, but I want you to know that I have never stopped loving you. I want you to go on, find happiness, find someone who can give himself to you fully, as I never could. This is my final wish for you.

You may be shocked at the contents of this box. Use the money to continue your life in the way you choose. I don't want you to end up back on the farm. I've put away enough to last for at least one year. That should give you time to get back on your feet. And you have a home, purchased with cash, in Mexico. The information is here. Go there. It's yours.

I've also set aside a small trust for Amy. It won't get her too far. No amount of money I give to her will suffice. She's reckless and she hasn't learned the value of a dollar. Now she'll be forced. Now she'll grow up. Don't let her bully you. This is for you and you alone. Keep it a secret. The trust is hidden away. My attorney doesn't know about it. In this envelope, you'll find a letter that gives Amy everything she needs to access it. Give it to her, but don't tell her where you found it.

Unfortunately, the jewels aren't for you. They're not mine to give. I'm just keeping them safe. They are valuable and there are people who would kill to have them. Since you're reading this letter, they have killed for them. Please be careful. The only diamond that is mine to give is in your ring. I traded for it, so keep it, or sell it. It's yours to do with as you wish. Just don't take it to George.

The jewels once belonged to the Columbian cartel. Get them to my contact from Mexico. Amy has his information. Ask her where to find Uncle Franco. Tell him to search for the raven. He knows what that means. He can be trusted.

I know you. You're wondering why I'm instructing you to go to a stranger and to not take your ring to George. You have no reason to trust me now, but I'm begging you to follow my directions. Everything isn't as it seems.

My love, be safe and know that you carry my heart with you always.

Yours, Wesley

I fold Wesley's letter and press it against my chest, tears falling freely, soaking into the paper. He really did leave a note for me. And he provided for me.

Maybe that bastard had a heart after all.

Did someone kill him for the jewels?

My mind races with questions I can't answer.

I unfold the letter again and read it once more, scanning for hidden meaning, any sign of logic in his madness, but nothing makes sense.

I return the letter to the lockbox and stare at the jewelry. The stones are enormous, expertly cut, probably priceless. If they're as dangerous to keep as he implied, I want them gone.

And yet... why can't I just take my ring to George? He's a jeweler. He's married to my best friend. I've always trusted him, more than I trust Wesley. Right?

So why the secrecy? Why the warning?

Why was Wesley worried about my safety four months ago, yet still chose to kill himself? If he was afraid for me, why leave me behind to deal with this?

Didn't he want me to take care of Amy? Nothing he wrote adds up.

I'm even more confused now than I was the day he jumped into the water with that damn rope around him.

I decide to put everything away for now. I need time to figure out who to trust, what to do, how to even get to Mexico to find this supposed contact.

Wesley always warned me it was too dangerous for a woman to sail alone. "Too many pirates," he'd say with that crooked smirk of his, half-joking, half-serious. Back then, I rolled my eyes and shrugged it off. But now, the warning feels heavier, like a shadow cast over everything he left behind. Because as I stare down at the box brimming with cash and glittering jewels, I can't help but wonder: was Wesley one of them? A pirate in disguise? Who else hides a chest full of treasure on a boat?

I pull the cash from my purse and add all but a hundred dollars to Wesley's stack. Then I lock the box and slide it back into its hiding place, tucking it away like a secret I'm not ready to carry. One that feels heavier every time I touch it.

I have no idea how much he left me, or where it came from, but for the first time since his death, I don't feel the crushing panic of how I'll pay the next bill.

I can breathe.

Do I send Selena and Pet away now that I no longer need them?

No.

Wesley said to live my life in the way I choose.

And I choose them.

Instead of a restful sleep, I toss and turn, trapped in a storm of dreams featuring jewels, pirates, Wesley, Orlando, and Pet…

In the dream, I'm dressed like a wench in a lace-up corset, ruffled skirt, and knee-high boots. My hair is curled and pinned on one side, cascading in soft ringlets over my bare breasts. I'm dripping in emeralds and diamonds with a necklace around my throat, and rings on every finger.

Orlando lies across a satin-draped brass bed, surrounded by velvet pillows and a thick down comforter. He wears tight black pants, tall boots, and a white button-up shirt open at the chest. His dark wavy hair is tousled, his face rugged and unshaven. He looks dangerous. Irresistible.

"You're still wearing your boots," I murmur, crawling toward him like a cat on the prowl.

"So are you," he replies with a smirk.

I climb on top of him and drag my nails down his chest. He sits up, untying my corset, and the strings loosen in his fingers. My breasts spill out.

I grab strings and tie his wrists together. "You're my prisoner now. You'll do as I say, or suffer the consequences."

He raises an eyebrow. "I like the sound of that."

His hands reach for me, but I push them back to the pillow above his head. "Did I say you could touch me?"

He shakes his head.

"Good." I loop the tie around the brass headboard and begin stripping him. First the boots. Then the pants. He's wearing nothing underneath.

"Going commando?" I ask, pleased.

"Yes," he breathes.

"My kind of pirate." I tear his shirt open. Buttons scatter across the floor, clinking as the roll away. I straddle him again, still mostly clothed except for my exposed breasts resting atop the corset. I pull the pins from my hair and let it fall, tickling the coarse hair on his chest as I rock my hips back and forth.

I trail one finger through the hair on his head… down his chest… to his pubic hair. I twirl it slowly around my finger, careful not to touch his fully erect cock.

He groans and lifts his hips, desperate for contact.

"Do you want something?" I tease.

"You," he pants, licking his lips.

I kiss him, tracing his lips with my tongue. He tastes like saltwater. His stubble scrapes my cheek just right.

Then I hear it—another voice.

"You can't have her," Pet says from the foot of the bed. "She's mine."

He moves beside Orlando, completely nude. His cock is just as thick and hard.

They both look at me, waiting.

I crawl to Pet and climb on top of him. His lips crash into mine, his hand grasping my breast, his mouth tasting of wine. He reaches behind me and pulls my hair hard. I groan into his mouth as wet heat floods between my legs.

Then I turn my gaze back to Orlando—still bound, still watching.

His erection softens. His expression shifts.

Hurt.

Betrayed.

"I thought you were mine," he whispers.

His eyes change. They darken.

Wesley's eyes.

I gasp, jolting away from Pet. But he grabs my waist, slides my panties aside, and thrusts up into me.

"She's mine," he pants. "She's mine."

My body quakes. He fills me completely.

I throw my head back, letting go.

Orlando.

Wesley.

Gone.

Only Pet remains.

His fingers tease my nipples. His cock hits just the right spot. My voice rises.

"Oh!"

I'm close! So close.

Pet fills me. Steady. Certain. Driving into me with fierce purpose.

I let it all go—the confusion, the fear, the grief, and the guilt.

"Yes!" I scream, coming undone in a burst of white-hot pleasure.

For that moment, I am free. My body is spent. Fulfilled. Numb.

Yes.

33

Orlando: Clarity

I position my head against the pillow beside the small monitor, eyes fixed on the screen. Jolene shifts in her sleep, her face flushed, lips parted. She moans softly, and her hips jerk as her thighs press into the twisted mass of blankets between her legs.

This is new.

I've seen her cry in her sleep. I've seen her toss and turn, haunted and exhausted. But this? This is desire. It's raw and uninhibited. Her dream must be vivid. Intense. Her body moves like it's reaching for something or someone.

I swallow hard, trying to refocus. I'm not here for *this*. Not tonight.

But damn if it isn't hypnotic.

The monitor glows softly, and I can't tear my eyes away.

She whispers something. It's unintelligible, but it sounds like a name. Could be mine. Could be Wesley's. Could be someone else entirely.

I clench my jaw and drag my attention away.

I don't go back to the monitor.

Not tonight.

I saw enough in the way she twisted in the sheets, moaned through whatever fantasy her mind created, legs wrapped around tangled blankets. It stirred something in me I try to keep locked away. She's not mine to want.

But more than that, she's sitting on a landmine, and I need to figure out how close I am to the blast radius.

Instead of sleeping, I sit with the moonlight slicing across the cabin and replay everything I've seen since I arrived at the marina. Wesley's disappearance. Jolene's confusion. Her grief. Her resilience. Her dreams. That box.

I don't trust easily, but I trust my instincts. And my instincts are telling me something isn't right. Wesley didn't just die. He *planned* something.

I wait until the first bird cries out, then lift the binoculars to my eyes and keep watch through the forward porthole.

At 7:32 a.m., she exits the cabin.

Hair done, makeup flawless, strappy sandals, and a flowing dress, the kind of beauty that looks a little tired around the edges. She left her bike at the store last night, having arrived by cab, which means she must've dressed up for her big clients. Hmm… I fight the urge to dig into what she's up to, but I have bigger plans this morning.

She doesn't look toward me.

Good.

She disappears up the dock.

I give it two full minutes. Then I move.

I climb up, jump off my boat, cross the dock casually, and step onto *My Knotty Jolene.* No one watches. No one questions. I know how to look like I belong.

I slip inside the forward cabin the moment Jolene disappears up the dock. The marina is quiet, still wrapped in morning haze. No one sees me. No one ever does.

Inside, it smells like linen and lavender. Her scent lingers in the sheets. I block that part out.

I head straight to the forward cabin with the V-shelf. The hidden compartment has to be here somewhere. I run my hand along the wood until I find the panel, press it, and slide the box free. It's heavy, solid. I set it on the bed and punch in her birthday.

Click.

I know my partner, and now I understand his obsession with her.

The lid opens with that quiet, ominous breath of air.

Aside from the jewelry I spotted on the camera last night, there are stacks of hundreds—bundles of cash so crisp they probably haven't even seen sunlight. I don't need to count to know we're well past fifty grand—maybe closer to a hundred. Enough to run. Enough to disappear.

But it's the documents I want.

I lift the envelope and slide out the papers.

Most people would see nothing but government seals and panic.

But I read them like a second language.

Because they *are* my first language.

The first document is a property transfer in Baja California, which is beachfront land in Mexico, registered under an alias. But stapled to the back is a notarized Transfer on Death Deed, dated just weeks before Wesley died. It names Jolene as the beneficiary—her full legal name, printed in crisp, deliberate type. No explanation, no letter, just a clean, quiet handoff. Typical Wesley. Always two steps ahead, always hiding the truth in plain sight. Now I have to wonder... how much of this was meant to protect her, and how much of it was meant to bury something deeper?

The second shows proof of a dormant offshore account in Belize, holding half a million dollars. Clean. Hidden. Untraceable. Also in Joleen's name.

But it's the third document that hits like a kick to the chest. A formal report—intercepted and likely smuggled out by Wesley. Stamped with the insignia of *El Sindicato del Norte*—the northern syndicate.

The same cartel I infiltrated before everything fell apart.

It references a "missing asset," tagged as *cargo confiscado por el traidor americano. Confiscated cargo by the American traitor.*

Wesley.

I knew he was in deep.

But I didn't know how deep.

Then I see it: *Las joyas de sangre fueron robadas del envío pactado con los colombianos. The blood jewels were stolen from the shipment arranged with the Colombians.*

My stomach clenches.

He didn't just steal wealth.

He stole the language of corruption.

The jewels weren't just a luxury stash. They were blood-soaked currency, exchanged behind closed doors for everything from weapons to silence.

And sometimes… people.

Each gem carries hidden laser markings. Tracking codes. Identifiers.

Each one tied to a transaction, a bribe, a payoff, or a smuggled shipment.

This is a laundering pipeline disguised as elegance.

Precious stones masking filthy power. Funding everything the syndicate needed to keep its grip on entire regions: corrupt officials, protected routes, brutal enforcement.

And Wesley stole them.

No wonder he tried to bury it. He knew the stakes. He knew the monsters he poked.

I remember the night we raided a stash house in Monterrey. We were expecting crates of rifles. What we found were diamonds. All tagged. All cataloged.

Wesley held one up to the light and murmured, "The jewels are the language, but the raven is the voice."

I didn't get it.

He clarified, "The ledger. The raven holds the story. Without it, the jewels are just glitter."

He already knew. The gems were code. But the ledger—the raven—was the key.

And now he's gone.

I flip to the final page. A grainy black-and-white photo of Wesley. His face circled in red ink.

Below it: *Muerte a él y a quien herede su deuda. Death to him and to whomever inherits his debt.*

I sink onto the edge of the bed, my pulse roaring in my ears.

Wesley didn't take the jewels for profit. He took them to dismantle something unholy. To expose it. To stop it. To protect innocent lives.

He gave everything for this.

And Jolene—God help her—is sitting on a box of blood currency.

And she has no idea.

I slide the papers back into the envelope, careful to place the note addressed to her on top.

Then I see it, tucked into the bottom, folded three times.

A separate sheet in Wesley's familiar scratch.

No salutation. No signature.

But halfway down, the words stop me cold: *Franco, encuentra al cuervo. Franco, find the raven.*

Instructions. Meant for me.

I stare at the note, letting the weight of it settle like a stone in my chest.

Then I slip it into my pocket, close the lockbox, return it to its hiding place, and smooth the covers with the flat of my hand.

Jolene thinks she's grieving a husband.

She doesn't know she's in possession of cartel blood property. She doesn't know she's already on their list.

And she sure as hell doesn't know that the man he told her to find… is already watching her sleep.

I leave the cabin quietly, stepping out into the rising sun.

One step ahead of the storm.

For now.

34

Jolene: Adventure

Where are you?

I text Amy again and stare at my phone. It's almost noon. She should've been here hours ago.

No response.

I open and close the flip phone repeatedly, checking the signal, checking the power, but still nothing comes through. Maybe I should've ignored her cryptic message:

"mommie d. be there at 9 tomorrow. bringing friends. TRY to look ok -_-"

It took me a while to decode that mess. I rarely text and when I do, it's full sentences and proper punctuation. Still, some parts were obvious. "Mommie D." That's Amy's name for me. She thinks it's hilarious to call me *Mommie Dearest*, pretending I'm Joan Crawford with a vendetta against wire hangers. I remind her often that I'm only three years older, and she's the one who rants, not me.

But she's Wesley's daughter, and I've tried to keep the peace. I wanted to be the stable one, to prove to Wesley that the two women in his life could get along.

Yeah. Like that was ever going to happen.

I smooth my halter dress and glance at my reflection in the window. It's BCBG, silk chiffon blended with polyester, and wrinkle resistant. Perfect for someone living on a boat. The bright Caribbean paisley print and handkerchief hem scream "look at me," but in a tasteful way. The strappy six-inch heels complete the look.

Try to look okay? Please. I look better than okay. I haven't looked this good since before Wesley died, unless I'm lying to myself again, like yesterday.

Pet and Selena probably think I have no style. Maybe that's why they wanted to take me shopping. They've only seen me in casual clothes and that corset, the one I thought was sexy, until I caught a glimpse of myself from their perspective.

Still, Pet practically drools whenever I'm around. I wonder how he'll react to this dress.

And then there's Orlando. He called me *desirable*. That word clings to my skin like heat. It's been years since I've wanted anyone besides Wesley. Now I want two men who are complete opposites.

One rugged and brooding, the other sharp and refined…when he's not in a dungeon. I want both. *Hell,* I even got up early this morning to do my makeup. The cinched waist, the low back of the halter, it all makes me feel alive again. *Sexy.*

But beneath it all… I'm carrying something far more dangerous.

That lockbox.

The cash.

The jewels.

They weren't just Wesley's stash, they were a secret. A signal. A reason to run. No one hides that kind of money unless they're planning for a worst-case scenario. And Wesley didn't get the chance. He was killed for it.

That thought clings to me like a shadow, threading beneath the paisley and perfume. I'm trying to look like I belong in this world again, but part of me knows… I'm not dressing up for fun. I'm dressing up for war.

This morning as I stepped off the dock and into the waiting taxi, I glanced around. No Orlando. Lisa glared from her boat. Her husband, Larry, and a few other men whistled in my direction. It felt…nice. But I'm not trying to impress them.

I wanted *him* to see me. The one who kissed me, held me, pulled my hair. I wanted to stir something inside *him.*

But he wasn't there.

Isn't that just my luck? I look like a zombie, and he's hanging around. I dress like a goddess, and he's vanished. Classic.

Well…Pet will see me.

The thought heats my core. My nipples tighten, and I cross my legs. The memory of last night's dream creeps in… Pet's mouth, his hands, his…

Gawd. I need to get laid.

But no. Like Selena said, Pet's a client. Off-limits.

Still…

Just as the ugly cowboy clock in the store strikes noon, the bell above the door jingles. Amy bursts in, shoving three well-dressed strangers in ahead of her like she's storming a runway.

"You're hurting me!" one of them whines—a brunette in an aqua pseudo-suede mini and silk blouse, clutching a Birkin bag like it's a newborn. Her face twists as she looks around. "What *is* this place?"

A guy with a bleached-blond mohawk and perfectly tailored plaid shorts raises one sculpted eyebrow. His voice is calm, deep, and full of dry sarcasm. "Very *postmodern garage sale.* Are we here to buy art or audition for *Trading Spaces?*"

He's clearly the smart one in the group—observant, confident, and dressed like he came straight from brunch at the Omni.

Amy waves them toward my display of sculptures. "Just buy something, bitches." She drops Sadie's designer bag on the counter in front of me, giving me a warning glare. *Don't screw this up.*

Sadie's tiny eyes peek out, and I gently pet her silky fur. Poor thing. She doesn't deserve the chaos of her environment.

Behind the others, a tall figure lingers—tangled auburn hair, oversized sunglasses, and a maxi dress flowing around them like they've just stepped off a runway in Milan. Their voice is low, masculine. I hesitate. I'm not sure which pronouns they use. He? She? They?

I remind myself: Just ask if it matters. Don't assume. Don't label. Don't screw this up either.

Still, I brace myself for a round of insults. Anyone Amy brings usually comes armed.

"Look!" Amy thrusts a sculpture at their faces. "What does *this* remind you of?"

The stylish one with the mohawk—Brad, I think his name is—laughs softly. "It's art, Ames. But yes, it's definitely…suggestive."

"Don't tell me you don't know," Amy says. "You've… let's just say you're well acquainted with the anatomy."

"Oh, I'm not ashamed," Brad replies coolly. "Knowledge is power."

The prissy brunette makes a face. "Gross."

"Grow up," Brad says with a wink. "It's sculpture. Some of us can appreciate the finer things."

They look at me. I try not to flinch. My art. My sweat. My hands burned shaping that piece. Do they see that? Or is this all just a joke to them?

Amy beats me to the punch. "Seventeen hundred. Each one's unique. Handmade right here by the talented artist behind the counter."

They gape at her.

"Support local art," Brad says, pulling out his wallet. "I'll take the biggest one. This is the only thing you've dragged me to that doesn't suck."

He lays a black AmEx on the glass with a decisive slap. "You take AmEx, I assume?"

I clear my throat, fighting off the tight lump. "Yes. Absolutely."

Two more black cards follow his. Slap. Slap.

I want to sell to Brad. He actually *sees* the art. He appreciates the detail, the craft.

But the others? Being forced into it like it's some kind of inside joke?

I want to cry. I want to scream. I want to snatch my work off the counter and shout, *You don't get to mock it and own it, too!*

But I don't.

I smile.

Because bills don't pay themselves. And a sale… is still a sale.

Even when it leaves the taste of humiliation in my mouth.

Mohawk chooses the biggest sculpture without hesitation and places it on the counter like he's laying down a poker hand. "This one's got presence," he says with a wink.

The friend in the flowing dress shrugs, nonchalant and elegant. "You pick for me," they say with a smile. "I trust your eye. I'm not picky when it comes to beauty."

That actually means something. Brad might be showing off, but this one—the quiet one—gets it. Still, the moment doesn't last.

"Just wrap them quickly," the prissy one snaps, clearly over it.

J. Jaden

My heart lurches. My fake smile fades. I glance at Amy, who raises her eyebrows and gives me a coaxing nod, like I should be grateful for the scraps.

Sadie peeks out from her bag and stares at me. Somehow, the little dog seems to understand what it feels like to be unappreciated.

With a sigh that feels like surrender, I process the cards and start wrapping each sculpture carefully in bubble wrap, then brown paper, and slide them into logo-stamped bags. My hands go on autopilot. My heart doesn't.

Just as I'm sealing the final bag, the bell over the door chimes, and a collective gasp sucks the air right out of the room.

My head jerks up, expecting a robbery or a paparazzi ambush. But it's neither. It's Selena and Pet.

And they look...normal. Elegant, even. Both wear matching navy pinstriped suits, tailored to perfection. Pet's shirt is unbuttoned at the top, his dark hair slicked back. Selena's wearing a white silk camisole beneath her blazer, her hair twisted into a soft bun.

"It's him!" Brad hisses to Amy. "The one we told you about last night."

"Him?" Amy drags her gaze across Pet's frame and lands hard on Selena. Her expression shifts from interest to instant dislike.

Why the fuss?

"Selena," I say, trying to cover my nerves. "You're early. It's only 12:30."

"Oh, cara mia, we just couldn't wait." She strokes Pet's arm with practiced ease.

Amy edges up beside me, sizing Selena up like a competitor. Her friends surround Pet like he's some kind of celebrity meet-and-greet.

"Aren't you going to introduce us?" Amy asks, her smile tight and teeth-gritted.

"This is my stepdaughter, Amy. Amy, this is Selena and…"

I stop. I can't call him Pet. Not now.

"I know who he is," Amy cuts in. "Obviously."

"You do?"

She waves me off and turns to him. "We were just talking about you last night, weren't we, girls?"

They all nod like bobbleheads on speed.

My mouth goes dry. If Amy knows who he is, that means other people do too. That means people are watching—watching him, watching me.

"Haven't you heard?" Brad asks me, incredulous.

"I... I..."

"I met Jolene a few days ago," Pet says smoothly, saving me. "I bought one of her sculptures. I've contracted her for something special."

"Oh?" Amy glares at me. "And you didn't tell me?"

Pet's grin is calm and composed, full of subtle mischief. "I've sworn her to secrecy. I can't have everyone copying my taste. That would be so... ordinary."

Selena chuckles softly and releases his arm, stepping toward me. She squeezes my hand, just a gentle press. Like she knows this scene all too well.

"You bought the phallic piece, didn't you?" Amy teases, elbowing Pet.

He shrugs and shares a private smile with Selena. "Maybe."

The chaos resumes. Amy and her entourage scramble to grab whatever's left. Amy even yanks one from the prissy one. "Mine," she says, triumphantly.

"We'll take these," Brad tells me, cool as ever.

Three black AmEx cards slap the counter.

Jolene's Adonis

Amy hands me her sculpture separately and leans in. "This one's on the house," she whispers.

I nod and start bagging everything, faster now, while they fawn over Pet and jostle to be seen. Selena watches it all with the calm of a woman who either doesn't care or has already won. Maybe both.

I stop trying to figure them out. Their world is a different planet.

But one thing settles in my gut: Amy is smiling. Genuinely. For the first time since Wesley died.

And my art? For once, I know it won't end up in a trash bin.

That should be enough.

But as I glance back at Pet, I know it's not. Not really.

Who *is* he?

My only concern right now is Pet… and who he really is. I know he has money and he's definitely eccentric, but people *know* him? How the hell does Amy know he bought the phallic piece? Does she know that kind of art suits Pet's very obviously public lifestyle?

Maybe he's a porn star. Amy would know if that were the case. Or maybe he's some sort of Hugh Hefner knockoff, parading beautiful women around town and flaunting that chain in public just to stir up attention for his adult-themed empire.

If that's true, then people have *definitely* noticed him coming into my store, dressed like a damn sex fiend. This is a small town. People talk. Gawd, what are they saying about *me*? Maybe that's why no one else has come in since I met that strange couple.

I slide the final piece into a logo bag just as the bell over the door chimes. Of course! It's Jessica. Perfect. All my worlds are colliding in one surreal scene. At this point, the only one missing is Orlando. May as well toss him into the mix and call it a circus.

Jessica struts in wearing a black Gucci knee-length dress with a hand-painted fern motif down both sides, paired with black studded Gucci wedges. Her red hair is woven into a tight fishtail braid that rests neatly over her left shoulder. Diamonds drip from her ears and throat like she walked straight off a fashion spread.

Amy's face drops as Jessica glides across the floor, flashing smiles at everyone mid-sentence who now stands slack-jawed, staring at the red-haired beauty. Compared to Jessica's $3,000 ensemble, Amy's $200 raspberry Diane von Furstenberg sundress and Giani Bernini sandals might as well be from K-Mart. I never got deep with Amy, but I know *exactly* what she's thinking right now.

Pet nods along as Brad, the guy with the mohawk, launches into a spirited rant about the struggles of life in South Texas. "Like, there isn't even a Michael Kors or Kate Spade," he says, exasperated. "I have to drive three hours to San Antonio just to get a decent manicure." He holds up his hand dramatically, showing off his nails to Pet.

Pet forces a polite smile, but his eyes are locked on Jessica's hips.

And just like that, a sharp pang of jealousy hits me.

Jessica gives Amy a haughty little sneer, then beams at Pet and Selena, drinking in the attention like champagne. When she reaches me, she grabs both my hands in hers and kisses my cheeks like some European socialite. "Looks like you've got a full house today. That's great!"

"Yeah. I guess. What are you doing here?" I ask, more blunt than I intend.

"Is that any way to greet your *best friend?*" she replies, exaggerating the best friend part while staring daggers at Amy. "I just stopped by to give you some news on your ring. George wants to talk to you about it. Are you free for dinner tonight?"

George. My heart stutters. Wesley's words echo in the back of my mind—*everything isn't as it seems.* Maybe I shouldn't have handed over my ring for George to sell. But Jessica is still my best friend. And

Wesley, I'm still confused by him. If nothing else, he's still a liar. The bastard who left me in this mess and mystery. I just need time to figure it all out... to figure out who the hell I can trust.

"Tonight..." I glance at Selena, who shakes her head slightly. "Tonight's not good. How about tomorrow?"

"Tomorrow's perfect. Come by around seven and I'll order in," Jessica says, nodding in Selena's direction like she already disapproves.

"Sounds like a plan. You know you could've just called. You didn't have to come by here. I'm doing fine."

"I can *see* that." She holds me at arm's length, scanning my outfit. "Tomorrow then." Another set of double cheek kisses, then she turns and strides out, tossing Amy a strained smile on her way.

I mentally clock the difference in how Jessica reacts to Pet compared to Amy and her crew. She doesn't seem to recognize him. Okay... so maybe I'm not the only one who's been living under a rock.

I hand over the bags and pull Amy aside.

"Since they paid with credit cards, the charges have to clear through the bank. The funds will be available next week. I went by this morning and removed your dad from the account, so I don't expect any issues. But you'll need to wait a few days."

"I'm not an idiot," Amy grits out.

What I don't say—what I can't say—is that there's a lockbox back on the boat filled with enough cash to buy this entire strip of shops. Thick stacks of hundreds, bundled and clean. A stash that screams escape plan. And maybe that's exactly what it was. But Amy still thinks I'm broke, and for now, it's better that way. I don't know if the money's traceable. I don't know who's watching. And if Wesley was killed for what he knew… that money could be bait, or worse, a target on my back. So, I keep playing the role.

"Okay then. Just making sure we're clear. Oh…" I reach behind the counter and pull out the envelope I'd tucked away earlier. "I found this. It's for you. I haven't read it."

I hand her the letter, and for a moment, Amy just stares at it. Her posture stiffens, her tough-girl exterior cracking. She wasn't expecting this, not today. Not another message from her father after all the chaos. Her eyes flicker as they scan his handwriting on the front, and I catch the subtle tremble in her fingers as she takes it from me.

For a brief second, she looks like a child again—hurt, confused, and maybe even hopeful.

Please let it be something helpful, I think. Something about the trust fund. Some clue she can use. Something to keep her from falling off the deep end.

"Thank you," she says quietly, her voice softer now, the edge dulled.

But the moment passes, and she straightens again, lifting her chin toward Pet. "What are you doing for Matt?"

Matt, huh? Nice. He has a name now.

"Just some blacksmith work. Nothing you can help with."

Her demeanor returns to the same old Amy. "I can't believe you've been holding out on me. I want in. I don't care what it is. I'll roll in the dirt and hammer until my hands bleed. I want to be involved. But only when *he's* here. Just so we're clear," she says.

Sometimes I swear Amy's stuck in permanent teenage rebellion, trapped in a woman's body. What the hell am I supposed to do with her? One minute she's sentimental, kind, and caring. The next she's....well...*Amy*.

"You can't. I wish you could, but like he said, he's sworn me to secrecy."

"Well, the cat's out of the bag now, and I *will* be involved. So you'd better tell me when he's coming back. I *want* to be here." She jerks her head toward Selena. "And who's that skank with him?"

"Selena? She's not a skank. She's his companion, that's all."

"She *looks* like a skank," Amy snaps, sizing her up again. "And I don't want your trashy friend screwing things up. I want Matt *all* to myself. Got it?"

I stare at her, floored. She has no right to demand anything, but the weird part? She'd probably be *perfect* for Pet. She wouldn't bat an eye at whipping him. But if she found out what I'm doing? She'd turn on me in a heartbeat. I'd be the skank.

"Absolutely not. Matt's my client. You're not in charge. And Selena isn't going anywhere. She's become a good friend."

"Pft." Amy folds her arms. "I won't back down."

"Why do you even want to be around him so badly?"

Her voice softens. "Not that I owe you an explanation, but the girls keep up with the gossip mags. He's been on the cover of a few. They said he was spotted in town. Our plan was to go find him after we finished here, and boom! There he was. Right here. In *your* store. He's exactly the man I need in my life right now. I'm telling you, Jolene—it's fate. I don't want to beg, but I will. That's how much this means to me."

"We'll see," I mumble. My head is spinning. He was *spotted?* Where?

"I'm ditching these losers." She waves toward her friends still orbiting Pet. "Call me *every* time he comes in."

I shrug. "I'll think about it."

"If you don't, I'll be here every day from open to close. I've never wanted anything like I want him. I'll do whatever it takes."

I glance over at Pet. He's entertaining the girls, but I can see it—the boredom behind the smile.

Amy snatches Sadie's bag. "Let's go, bitches," she barks. "I'll see you again," she says to Pet, then throws Selena a daggered smirk. "That's a promise."

They leave arguing about who Pet liked the most. Funny, ten minutes ago, they called this place a dump. Now they can't seem to leave.

Hmm…

I theatrically wipe my brow and lock the door behind them. "I'm grateful for the business, but *that* was close! Thanks, Pet, for helping me dodge that bullet. Or should I say Matt?" I grin at him.

The boredom disappears from his eyes. Amusement replaces it. "You're welcome, my lady. Call me Pet. I guess there are a few things we haven't told you yet. We were just surprised you didn't recognize me. This place felt safe. But I guess you had to find out sometime."

"Who are you?" I finally ask, unable to keep it in anymore.

"The car's ready," Selena says, nodding toward the black sedan pulling up outside.

"You two can talk on the way."

I grab my purse, shut off the lights, and lock up. As we walk out, Pet leans in close.

"You look beautiful. I've never had a MILF before," he whispers. "Always wanted one. I can be a very naughty boy who needs to be spanked by his mommy."

His hand glides down my bare back… to my ass. He cups it. Warmth shoots through me.

Of course, *today* I decide to wear a thong and no bra.

I slide into the back seat. Pet climbs in beside me. Selena takes the other side. The car pulls away. Pet rests one hand on my knee and one on Selena's.

It feels… natural.

Just days ago, I would've recoiled, called it inappropriate. But now? It's oddly… normal.

Ain't that a kick in the head! Am I turning into one of those sister-wives? Some cultish woman who shares a man with the girl next to her because they bonded over trauma and trust issues?

That's not me. Right?

Or am I just a lonely widow living out some throuple fantasy with a hot stranger and his mysterious, sultry companion?

The car veers off the main highway, bypassing the causeway to Corpus Christi and pulling into the ferry line headed for Aransas Pass. As far as I know, there aren't any shops worth visiting on the other side of the bay.

But maybe they know something I don't.

35

Orlando: Seasick

I inch my way up the ferry line, keeping one car between me and the black sedan while holding a safe distance from the car in front of me. The line is longer than usual, stretching over a quarter mile down the island. This is going to take a while.

With the driver's window cracked, the salty breeze barely whispers inside. I lower it halfway, desperate for relief. The cool air tousles my hair, cutting through the thick, sweltering stickiness of pre-spring. It helps, but just barely.

The cars crawl forward, then stop again as the ferry ahead finishes loading and begins its undocking procedures. A tight knot forms in my chest. I think the black sedan might make it on. If they do and I don't, they'll have a ten-minute lead. I watch, pulse quickening.

But they don't make the cut.

I exhale slowly, relieved. I'll be on the same ferry and close enough to keep eyes on them. Still, there's that anxious buzz in the back of my mind. What if I'm forced to park right next to them? I hate leaving things to chance.

I breathe deeply and try to settle my nerves. Time to make a plan, just in case.

Reaching for the gearshift, I move to put the car in park and cut the engine before it overheats, then I hear it—a high-pitched buzz that triggers a reaction before I can think. My face stings. My left arm jerks up and slaps. Got the bastard.

I pull my hand away and stare at the crushed mosquito. Its tiny body smeared in red. I look at my palm, then check the rearview. A smear of blood dots my cheek.

Whose blood is it? Mine? A stray dog's? Someone else's?

I lean to the right, searching for anything—a tissue, a towel, even a damn napkin. As I shift, my foot slips onto the accelerator and the car jolts forward.

"Fuck! I didn't put it in park!"

I shoot upright and slam the brake. Tires screech. I stop just shy of rear-ending the car ahead—the one right behind Jolene's sedan.

I nearly blow the whole thing.

Sweat clings to my back, soaking through my shirt. My heart pounds in sync with the car stereo thumping behind me. *Thump. Thump. Thump.*

Jolene's Adonis

I slam the car into park and kill the engine, then sink low in my seat, hiding. Missy Elliott's "Hot Boyz" blasts through someone's subwoofers behind me. The bass rattles through my chest, distracting me from the screw-up.

Still hunched down, I scrape the mosquito remains onto the floorboard, then yank up my shirt to wipe the blood from my cheek. Not exactly sterile, but this isn't the time to get squeamish. Living at the marina, I know mosquito season's just getting started.

A few songs later, the ferry returns. One by one, engines come alive, including mine. The attendant motions me forward, and I drive onto the far starboard side at the bow. The black sedan parks across from me on the far port side, directly to my left.

Close. But not too close.

I stay in the car. I don't want Jolene—or her companions—to spot me. Instead, I sit still and let the ghosts drift in.

How many ferry rides like this have I taken? Heading toward uncertain destinations, chasing people or running from memories?

Too many to count.

There's something about being trapped on a moving vessel inside a steel box that makes my stomach twist. It stirs up things I'd rather keep buried. But here they come anyway.

This is going to be a long ride.

36

Jolene: Liftoff

The driver idles the car onto the ferry and parks us near the outer railing. The moment the engine cuts, I open the door and step onto the deck, needing fresh air and a moment to breathe. The wind carries the scent of salt and diesel, and I lean over the edge, watching the water churn beneath us.

A pod of dolphins appears, dancing along the wake and leaping high on either side of the ferry. From inside the car, Pet and Selena clap and grin like kids at a theme park. Their joy is contagious, but I'm grateful they stayed in the car. I'm not ready for someone to recognize Pet, and definitely not ready for anyone to link me to him. Not until I figure out who he really is.

When the ferry captain blows the horn, signaling our approach to Aransas Pass, I return to the backseat on the driver's side. The driver waits his turn and then rolls us off the ferry and down a narrow, mostly deserted two-lane highway. Bait shops, weathered docks, and industrial buildings blur past the window.

Pet still hasn't said a word. I keep waiting for him to explain… something. I assumed he'd address the whole identity thing by now, but nope. Silent. Amy didn't recognize him either—not until her friends clued her in—so maybe he's not as famous as I thought. Or maybe he is, and I've just been too checked out to know.

Either way, I can't take the guessing anymore.

"Pet," I say, turning toward him, "I asked you something earlier. Who are you? I need to know what I'm walking into. If someone recognizes you at the store, I'd like to be prepared. Are you… a porn star?"

He throws his head back and laughs, loud and unbothered. "No."

Selena grins at me, clearly loving the suspense.

Before I can follow up, the car jerks to a stop right in the middle of an open field. A black helicopter waits ahead, its propellers spinning in a blur, whipping dust into mini cyclones around it.

A man in a navy collared jacket approaches the car, thick headphones clamped over his ears. He pulls one aside and leans in to speak to the driver.

"The chopper's ready, sir," the driver says, opening the door for us like we're royalty.

I freeze. "Where are we going? I thought we were shopping in Corpus Christi. That's like twenty minutes from here. This is… unnecessary." My voice rises a few octaves as nerves crash over me.

Pet reaches for my hand, calm as ever. "We're heading to San Antonio. Selena's favorite boutiques are there. Only the best for my girls."

His girls.

I take his hand, shielding my eyes against the swirl of grit kicked up by the rotors. The man who just helped me sell a kinky metal sculpture is not the same man I see now. The leash-wearing submissive I met a few days ago is gone. This Pet is in control, commanding, leading the way. And Selena? She's taking a backseat, letting him take charge for once.

Is this what she meant by *switch?*

My dress flaps violently around my legs, wrapping tightly as I duck instinctively beneath the spinning blades and climb into the chopper. The bench seat is unfortunately leather and not animal-friendly, but it's luxurious. There's room for at least ten, with cup holders built into a sleek ottoman in the center. This is a level of opulence I've only seen in magazines.

The only downside? The deafening roar.

Pet picks up a headset and hands it to Selena, then gestures for me to grab one. I fumble for a pair to my right and slip them on, adjusting the mic awkwardly in front of my mouth.

"Have you ever flown in a helicopter?" Pet's voice comes through my headset, clear and smooth.

I shake my head.

"You can talk," Selena says, pointing at the mic. "We can hear you."

"Oh… can you hear me?" I ask, feeling ridiculous.

They both give me a thumbs up.

"I've flown commercial. A couple of private flights. But never in a helicopter."

"You're in for a treat," Pet says as the chopper lifts.

It's not like a plane. There's no runway, no build-up. It's like a giant hand yanks us straight up into the sky. I grip the seat, trying to find my balance. "Whoa!"

We soar higher. Fishermen in tiny boats along the channel shrink below us. Then come the pastel homes dotting the coast, little inlets sprinkled with shrimp boats and fishing vessels. We pass the long intracoastal bridge, where an oil barge creeps beneath, headed toward the Gulf. A few of the crew look up and wave.

I wave back with both hands, laughing at myself.

For a moment, I feel like a rock star, gliding over everything I've come to love about living on North Padre Island.

The chopper dips low toward downtown Corpus Christi, and I spot the replica Columbus ships—the Niña, Pinta, and Santa Maria—moored in the bay. Their tall masts rise high above the surrounding boats like sentinels of another era. We glide past the USS *Lexington*, where tourists on the deck pause to wave as we fly just a few hundred feet overhead. A group of girls outside the Texas State Aquarium jumps and shrieks, waving wildly and blowing kisses.

That giddy rock star feeling fades fast as I glance at Pet, the *real* reason they're reacting that way. It's not the helicopter. It's *him*.

Curiosity curls hot inside me, spreading like wildfire. I lean back against the seat, thoughts swirling.

Pet reaches over and laces his fingers through mine. His grip is steady, comforting. "I'll tell you everything you want to know," he says, his voice low in my headset. "For now, just enjoy the ride."

I manage a small smile and turn back to the window.

When I met Wesley, he introduced me to a life so different from the farm I grew up on with hot summers, rough hands, and dirt under my fingernails. I thought I saw it all once I was with him. *Boy, was I wrong.*

This? This is a whole new world. Pet's world.

I've visited these tourist spots a dozen times, but from up here, everything feels different. Magical. Untouchable. The view from this height is surreal. The boats are no bigger than ants, and the roads look like ribbons threading through the coastal sprawl.

Butterflies stir inside me as I gaze down at the South Padre Island Drive, *SPID*, as the locals call it. The tiny cars inching along look like toys, each one carrying someone with somewhere to be.

And me? I'm going somewhere too. For the first time since Wesley died, I have no idea where that *somewhere* is.

But maybe that's okay.

I glance at Pet and give his hand a gentle squeeze. For now, I'll take his advice.

I'll enjoy the ride.

37

Orlando: Discovery

I sit at the helm of my sailboat, pretending to relax while watching the neighboring boats. One by one, people start to leave. They're heading into town, to dinner, wherever. I wait them out, counting heads, waiting for the last goodbye wave. When I'm sure no one's paying attention, I make my move.

I survived the ferry ride without another incident. Just sat back and watched Jolene lean against the railing, smiling at the water like the ocean whispered her name. There was something about the way she stood—unguarded, peaceful—that kept the ghosts away. I wanted to believe she was safe. Maybe even happy.

And yeah, I'm still trying to understand what the hell she's doing with D'Angelo and his vinyl-clad companion. But nothing about their body language said "hostage." They moved like three people wrapped up in something consensual… even if I don't understand it.

But watching that helicopter lift off with her inside? That set something off in me.

Jealousy. Frustration. Possession.

She's *mine*. Isn't she?

I hate how that sounds even in my own head. She's not mine. She's not a prize or a damsel or a damsel-prize. She's a damn hurricane in heels with a blowtorch in one hand and a broken heart in the other, and she doesn't need saving. But me?

I need her.

I shake off the heat crawling under my skin and board *My Knotty Jolene*. I don't even hesitate this time. Her scent hits me like a memory and I let it linger. It's not Wesley's space anymore. It's hers. And it's mine, at least for now.

I step into the cabin, pull the storage panel open, and retrieve the lockbox from its hiding place. No need for guesswork. I know the code—it's etched on my soul. I crack it open and stare at the contents again, this time with the clarity to really *see*.

There's enough wealth in here to disappear ten times over—jewels, gold coins, precious stones, some loose, some in antique settings. A couple of them still have tags in Spanish. Museum-worthy. Blood-won.

I pull out one ring and hold it to the light. It's old. Filigreed. Ruby center, but not quite red. It's too deep, like the color of drying blood. I remember Wesley showing it off once, joking that it belonged to a dead cartel boss's mistress and still carried a curse.

I thought he was bluffing. Bragging.

Now I'm not so sure.

I open the envelope again—the one Wesley addressed to Jolene. My eyes scan the page, reading between the lines.

For your safety, I regret that even in my death, I must remain secretive.

Find Uncle Franco.

I exhale slowly and lean back, heart pounding.

He didn't just leave her a warning. He left her a path.

He told her to find me.

He wanted her to trust me.

To follow the trail he buried in shadows, hoping it would lead her to what...

And now Jolene's carrying the weight of this without even knowing what she's stepped into. She's sitting in a goddamn helicopter with two people I don't fully trust, and she's holding a box that could get her killed.

I shut the box and place everything back exactly the way I found it. If anyone else gets their hands on this, she's dead. If they know she has it—or *had* it—she's already in danger.

I'm halfway to the door when I hear it—a thump on the deck. A suitcase. The telltale yap of a spoiled poodle.

I crack the door open just as Amy steps on board.

"Uncle Franco!" she gasps, eyes wide as she nearly trips over her own suitcase lunging toward me.

"Bella," I breathe, using the name I've called her since she was knee-high to a grasshopper, and reaching out to steady her before she trips over her own feet.

She pulls me into a one-armed hug, the dog crushed against her side. "When did you get here? I've been leaving messages. I thought you were in Panama or who knows where."

"I got here the day of the funeral," I say gently. "I couldn't make contact. I've been working undercover. I need to find your dad's killer, and I couldn't risk blowing my cover."

She swallows hard and nods. "I get it. That's all I want too. Justice." Then her eyes narrow. "Do you have what you need to nail her?"

Before I can answer, I see movement up the dock. I gently guide her inside.

"I can't be seen on this boat," I whisper. "Not yet. I know you're suspicious of Jolene. I was too. But you have to trust me now. She didn't do it."

Amy's brows furrow. "Then who…?"

"I can't tell you yet. But I'm close. If you see me out there, you don't know me. My name is Orlando, and we've never met. The case depends on it. Can I count on you? After we've met publicly, I can join you here. Not until then. Got it?"

"Of course," she says, her voice barely audible. "Your mission is mine. I just… I miss him."

I lift her chin until her tear-filled eyes meet mine. "I do too. I'm across the dock on my boat. If you need anything, I'm there. You're not alone."

She pulls me in for another hug, tighter this time.

And I hold her with one eye on the window, the other on the fire building in my chest.

I'm going to finish this.

For Wesley.

For Amy.

And for Jolene, before it's too late.

38

Jolene: The D'Angelo Hotel

The helicopter lands with a soft bounce on the rooftop of a luxury hotel overlooking the San Antonio River Walk. As the rotors slow, I glance out the window and blink at the line of staff. There must be twenty of them, lined up in single file, like they're expecting Prince Harry and his entourage to make an appearance.

The moment we touch down, a man in a tailored suit opens the door. His nametag reads "Bob." He extends a hand to Selena and helps her out like she's a visiting dignitary. Then he turns to Pet.

"Welcome back, Mr. D'Angelo."

"Thank you, Bob," Pet replies smoothly.

He turns and offers me his hand. I take it and step out onto the rooftop, grateful for something solid beneath my feet, even if we're still stories above the street. But the second I let go of the helicopter's edge, the ground shifts. The concrete beneath my heels tilts like a boat in open water. My legs wobble, and before I can catch myself, I stumble into Pet's arms.

"I've gotcha!" he says, holding me steady. "It happens to everyone."

"I fell off my stilettos the first time I flew," Selena adds with a wink. "You'll get used to it."

I cling to Pet for another second before I find my footing again. Bob is already waiting near a sleek grey door, the luggage beside him. "Do you need assistance, Miss?"

"I'm fine now. Thank you," I say, releasing Pet's arm. The wooziness fades, the ground stills beneath me.

Bob turns his attention back to Pet. "Did you have a pleasant flight, sir?"

"Perfect. Clear skies, and two beautiful ladies to keep me company." Pet gestures toward me. "This is Jolene. Please show her around and make sure she has everything she needs."

"Yes, sir," Bob replies with a polite nod. He's short and stout, with patchy hair and a limp on his left side, but his smile is warm and genuine.

We follow him inside. The staff bows as we pass, murmuring "Welcome" and "Enjoy your stay." I've never been bowed to in my life. It's... unsettling. This isn't a check-in. It's a procession.

We enter a wide, carpeted hallway. A young man holds the door open to a private suite and bows silently before excusing himself. Bob leads us inside and deposits Pet's luggage in the corner, then motions for me to follow him on a quick tour.

Selena and Pet immediately claim the sofa like they've done this a thousand times. Which, judging by their comfort level, they probably have.

The suite is massive. More like a penthouse apartment than a hotel room. A fireplace with a slate mantel takes center stage, surrounded by cream-and-beige furniture, a full bar tucked into the corner. Photos line the mantel, and one stops me cold.

The president. Arm around Pet. Smiling.

My jaw drops.

I glance at Pet. He's laughing at something Selena just whispered in his ear. Not even looking in my direction.

Why would a hotel room have *personal photos* of a guest?

Bob opens the doors to three adjoining rooms, each one unique in color but identical in layout: king-sized bed, nightstands, bathroom with a jacuzzi tub, granite tile. One lavender with floral wallpaper. One navy with anchors and rope details. One pale aqua, minimalistic and serene. Each bed has throw pillows embroidered with the letter D.

The fourth door stays closed.

Oddly, there are no TVs. In any of the rooms. Who designs a hotel room without a TV?

Back in the main area, Bob pours champagne for us and excuses himself to stand outside the suite in case we need anything. Strangely, he doesn't linger for a tip.

I take the glass, trying to hide the swirl of confusion inside me.

Why are we in a room like this for *shopping?*

Pet stands and gestures toward the cushion beside him. "Have a seat."

I arch a brow and drop into the seat with a smirk. "You got some s'plaining to do, Ricky," I say in my best Lucille Ball voice.

He laughs, amused by the impression, no matter how awful it is. "Fair enough."

Selena perches nearby, already sipping her drink like this is all perfectly normal.

Pet's voice softens. "I'm sort of well known."

"Yeah," I say, heartbeat picking up, "I got that part."

"This is my hotel," he says, gesturing around us. "One of several. I own a chain, along with a few malls, a country club, other real estate stuff."

I blink. "This... *this* is yours?"

He nods. Selena confirms with a small, satisfied smile.

"That explains the pictures. The fireplace. The staff." My eyes drift back to the photo of him with the president. "That's why the room has personal photos?"

"I forgot they were there, honestly," he says. "Why didn't you ask about them earlier?"

"I was trying to respect your privacy," I say honestly.

His expression softens as he exchanges a look with Selena. "I appreciate that. Most people don't."

I lower my gaze, a strange sense of compassion settling over me. People like him probably never get a moment of peace. Everyone watching. Everyone wanting something. No wonder he plays into it. Better to give them a show than let them dig.

"This is home," he adds. "Selena lives nearby in one of my buildings. That's how we met. It was pure coincidence."

I nod, looking around the room again with new eyes.

Eccentric. That's the word. Rich men who do weird things aren't weird. They're eccentric.

And Pet? He's *very* rich. Loaded. That explains the "D" pillows. The staff. The tips I never saw. The generous payments. The ease with which he bought my sculpture like it was a pack of gum.

But he leans closer, voice lower. "I'm not a real estate genius or anything. My grandfather started with one tiny motel in Dallas. Dad turned it into a hotel empire. I'm just the next guy expected to leave a mark and double the wealth."

"It's like Monopoly," I murmur.

"Exactly." He smiles. "Buy, build, expand."

"So... Port Aransas?"

"I have a high-rise condo on the beach. One of my units was foreclosed. I was there on business. I hired Selena to keep me company while I sorted it out. Then we stumbled across you."

"You mean, *me* collapsed in grief at the edge of a gallery?"

"You were hurting. We saw that. And yes, we were... intense. But we couldn't exactly *pretend* to be normal, not once you saw me on a leash."

"No. No, you couldn't," I say, the corners of my mouth twitching.

"I thought you were a celebrity," I admit. "A porn star, maybe. Everyone seems to know who you are."

"I'm in all the tabloids," he says with a shrug. "I was named 'most eligible bachelor' a couple weeks ago. Apparently, that makes people a bit starstruck."

Selena grins. "He gets photographed a lot. Makes our scenes even hotter."

Pet throws her a look. "Ignore her."

"Oh, come on," she teases. "The public *loves* him on a leash."

"I'm not looking for a wife," he says. "Not yet. I want someone who doesn't worship me. Who challenges me. Who treats me like a person, not a prize. That's why I find *you* so intriguing."

"What about Selena?" I ask, unsure where this is headed.

"She's taken," he says.

"You are?" I blink at her.

"Yes, I am," Selena says. "Besides, can you really see me married with a baby on my hip? That life's not for me, and my partner understands."

"He's okay with… all of this?" I gesture toward Pet, trying not to sound judgmental, but needing to understand.

"Yes, of course. Like I told you, I've been in the fetish world for years. I couldn't be with someone who didn't accept that. We have an open relationship. It's my job. He gets it." She grins. "Hell, I left him tied up when we left town. I'm sure someone's at my place right now, servicing him, which reminds me… I need to get home before he's too tired to fuck."

I try not to picture that. I fail.

Pet chuckles. "Don't worry. I'm not proposing. I just want to enjoy you, as long as you're willing."

I lick my lips. "I thought we were coming here to *shop*."

"We are! Bob's setting up lunch. After we eat, the nautical room is yours to freshen up. We've arranged for private showings from Selena's favorite boutiques. You can shop right here."

"You should know that I'm vegan if lunch is involved…and that sounds expensive."

"Don't worry about it. We'll take care of everything. You just became even more interesting. And don't worry about the cost. It's on me. Trust me, I can afford it."

"Clearly you can afford it." I raise my glass. "Thank you."

"You're welcome."

"One question though. If you're not famous, why did people wave at us from the street?"

"Oh, that," he laughs. "My last name's on the bottom of the chopper. When I fly over, people know it's me. My dad's idea, not mine."

Then, in a flawless Italian accent, he switches into full *Godfather* mode. "Mattie, when are you going to settle down with a *nice* girl and give me grandchildren?"

I burst out laughing.

"Okay," I say, catching my breath, "that was actually a pretty good Marlon Brando."

"He sounds just like him. I swear!" Pet chuckles, shifting the mood. "Every time I talk to him, it's the same thing. Talk about guilt! My dad lays it on thick. You've gotten to know me well enough by now to realize I'd suffocate with a nice girl. I'd be bored to death. I need excitement and someone to tie me up and whip me, yet not treat me like a freak. That's my father's word, by the way. I want a woman confident enough to leash me and walk me in public. Someone bold enough to expose herself just to please me, and still loyal to the core."

"I see." I'm starting to put the puzzle together now. The eccentric rich boy who's been controlled his entire life. Never had to ask for anything. Then comes Selena. She flips the script on him. He gives up control, and it hooks him. It makes sense. She's into bondage, and clearly some other things I hadn't anticipated. She kinks for a living, and he pays her well. It still feels weird to think of him as Matt. He'll always be Pet to me, except when I have to introduce him. Yikes, I hope I don't have to do that again. *Awkward!*

Selena kisses Pet on the cheek, gives me a quick hug, and leaves us alone in the oversized suite. I can't believe she just leaves her partner tied up or lets others tend to his needs. *Freaky.*

After a few minutes, there's a knock at the door. Bob walks in with a massive silver tray loaded with sandwiches, fruit, and salad fixings. He places it on the bar, then walks to the left side of the window and pulls the drapes even wider, revealing a small door I hadn't noticed. He steps through it and onto what looks like a balcony, one with a glass floor. He arranges a round table and two chairs off to the right side.

I can't help but stare. Pet moves behind the bar and pulls out plates, silverware, and cloth napkins like he's done this a hundred times. He plates a couple of sandwiches, fruit, and salad for each of us, then carries everything to the balcony, setting a perfect little table for two.

"Shall we?" Pet asks, offering his hand.

Bob follows us with two glasses of freshly poured champagne.

I inch toward the balcony like it might bite. I avoid looking at the glass railing, or worse, the transparent floor. From inside the suite, the balcony is basically invisible unless you know exactly where to look.

"Should I take off my shoes?" I ask, hesitant. Stilettos and glass don't mix. What if they crack it?

"No, it's thicker than it looks," Pet assures me, wrapping his arm around my shoulders. "Perfectly safe. Just like a wood floor. Trust me."

Right. Trust the man with the leash kink.

I step cautiously onto the glass, all my weight balanced on my toes. I lock my eyes on the table like it's the finish line of an Olympic event. I don't dare relax a heel. Every step feels like crossing a tightrope fifty feet in the air. My calves scream, but I make it. Pet pulls out my chair, and I sit slowly, watching only him.

The railing's taller than the table, at least five feet, so the wind isn't as bad as I expect. Still, one gust almost grabs my napkin and flutters my skirt around my knees.

"Don't you just love this view?" Pet asks, looking out over the city.

"I wouldn't know."

"Why don't you look around? It's thrilling."

"I can't. Not if you want me to eat. Why are we out here?"

"Because sometimes I like to be in control. I could tell from the helicopter you're afraid of heights. Which gives me the upper hand."

"You're torturing me?"

I give him an exaggerated grimace but don't take my eyes off him. I'm convinced he installed this balcony just to mess with women like me. *He's a sadist. Confirmed.*

"Not torture. Fun. Just ease into it. Don't look straight down. The swimming pool is over there," he says, pointing right, "and the cabana is underneath us. I sit out here sometimes just to imagine what the people below think. It looks like I'm floating. There are no other balconies in the building. Can you imagine what people think when they see us? It's an engineering marvel."

"We look like we're floating?" I ask, then immediately regret glancing down. To stabilize, I stomp my heel on the glass, then wince, bracing for death.

But nothing happens.

"See? You're okay. Now just move your eyes slowly until that building comes into view, right there." He points to a high-rise a few blocks away.

I follow his finger. The building is made of glass and metal, balconies lined with iron rails.

"That's Selena's place," he says. "Her apartment's one floor down from the top. No blinds, no drapes. She's an exhibitionist. At night, lights on, you can see everything. That's how I discovered her profession. Spent a few white-knuckled nights watching her spank her boyfriend before I got the nerve to ask her out. She turned me down, but offered a private session. That was my intro to the fetish world."

I'm not panicking anymore. I use the same technique I learned while clinging to the top of the mast. Focus on something steady, look straight ahead, and *don't* look down. Ground myself in what's in front of me. In this case, it's not a sail or a skyline. It's Pet. And somehow, that works.

The conversation helps. It distracts me in the best way, pulling me out of my spiraling thoughts. And strangely, it's comforting—this glimpse into who he really is beneath the theatrics. Learning what drives him, how he thinks, how he became *this* version of himself. I never would've pictured him as the head of a major corporation. Not with the way he submits so willingly, so openly. But now I get it.

It's not weakness. It's balance.

He spends his days being the boss, the heir, the empire-builder. Everyone bows to him, hangs on his every word, tells him he's brilliant whether he is or not. Of course he craves the opposite behind closed doors. Of course he wants someone else to take control, to challenge him, to strip him of all that weight, even if just for a while.

And maybe that's what he sees in me. Not someone to coddle him or chase after his money. But someone who doesn't need to be impressed. Someone who sees both versions and doesn't flinch.

For the first time since Wesley died, I feel my curiosity outpacing my grief.

I want to know more.

About him.

About me.

About who I'm becoming in all this.

Just hours ago, I imagined Selena dragging him through boutiques by a chain while I trailed behind, mortified. I pictured paparazzi snapping photos and headlines shouting *throuple scandal.* But that's not what this is.

I sit back and pick up a dainty cucumber and hummus sandwich. Pet's almost done with his. The toppings melt in my mouth, rich with paprika and onion. The fruit is fresh—strawberries, blueberries, and sliced melon. The salad is crisp, with vinaigrette on the side. I didn't think I could eat while sitting on see-through flooring, but somehow, I clear the plate.

I finish my champagne and slide the chair back. "Thank you for lunch. It was delicious. I'm going to freshen up."

"You're welcome." Pet rises and offers his arm again.

I tiptoe faster this time, emboldened by champagne. "Maybe after another glass, I'll find the courage to look down," I joke.

"You've already made it further than Selena. She still won't step out here."

"Really?"

He nods and makes a mock-boy scout gesture over his chest. "Cross my heart."

I laugh. "I wouldn't have guessed she's scared of anything."

"She puts on a good front."

We reach the door of the nautical room. "Bob's stocked everything you need," Pet says.

I glance across the suite, pointing at the door that stayed shut during the tour. "What's in there?"

"My dungeon," he replies with a glint in his eye. "I'll show you, if you're brave enough."

The champagne and adrenaline rush to my head. I smile, running a finger down his arm. "I might take you up on that."

"Oh! Don't tease me."

"I'm not." I smile. And I mean it. The idea of us? Not entirely absurd. Not long-term. I couldn't leash-walk anyone or flash strangers for fun. But behind closed doors…

I step into the room and blow him a kiss before closing the door.

I'm enjoying the escape. But suddenly, disappointment hits. A pang of regret. What happens when the fantasy ends, and I'm thrown back into reality? When I wake up in the tiny stateroom on the boat, uncertain again? I wish it were Orlando on the other side of the door. Orlando makes my palms tingle, my pulse spike. He's reality. Pet is fantasy.

I've been dropped into a dream, a place where I can be whoever I want, do whatever I desire, with no consequences. What woman wouldn't want this, even for a day?

I just want to forget. For once, I want to stop worrying about tomorrow.

And today—today is mine.

39

Jolene: Matchmaker

Pet wasn't exaggerating. The room I'm offered is stocked like a backstage fashion tent during Fashion Week. The vanity holds enough toiletries to supply an army of models, including Chanel's full skincare line and cosmetics in every skin tone from ivory to mocha. In the corner is a vegan-friendly setup. Pet didn't just prepare, he prepared for *anyone*.

The closet is just as over-the-top: designer dresses for every occasion, red-bottomed heels in sizes six through ten, and shelves lined with lace bras, panties, and thongs so delicate they look like they'd dissolve in water. There's even a drawer filled with naughty outfits like fishnets, feather boas, and leatherette accents. All brand new. Someone clearly thought through every detail of what a fashionista… or a lover… might need.

I pause, staring at the overwhelming abundance.

How many women is he expecting to pass through this room? Jeez.

I step up to the mirror and touch up my makeup, trying to collect my thoughts. The heat I felt for Pet when I walked in here is quickly replaced with a cold dose of reality. I glance around one more time before heading back out, but something stops me. The earlier pang of doubt turns into a crashing wave of emotion that nearly knocks the breath from my lungs.

I freeze.

I can't do this.

I can't play with this man's feelings, or mine. Pet doesn't hide what he wants. He's been clear. He's looking for someone open, someone sexually uninhibited, someone who fits effortlessly into his world. Even if I let myself fall into the moment and give in to the desire, it won't last. It *can't.*

I still love Wesley, no matter what a lying asshole he turned out to be, and I'm definitely not ready for anything serious. But if I were... it wouldn't be with Pet. It would be with someone like Orlando. *Someone who makes my heart race just by being in the room.*

If I give myself to Pet, it wouldn't just be temporary. It would be dishonest. I'd be pretending to be someone I'm not, and I've already lived too many lies. I couldn't do what Selena does—sleep with someone and walk away like it meant nothing. When I let someone in, I want them to *stay.* I want someone to hold me at night, to grow old with me on a porch in rocking chairs while we wait for the grandkids to visit.

That's who I am. That's what I want.

Wesley never wanted more children. But now that I'm free from him… maybe it *is* possible. Maybe I really could start over. Reinvent my life. And in that vision, that's so clear and bright and painfully honest, Pet doesn't fit. Any man who has a curated wardrobe of lingerie in a dozen sizes and shades isn't looking for *forever*. He's looking for rotation.

A sob rises in my throat, and I choke it back. I stare at the stranger in the mirror, trying to find the woman I want to be in her reflection.

This lifestyle works for him. I get that now. I even understand why his father's desperate for him to settle down. And it makes sense why Selena always looks flawless. She has *all of this* at her disposal.

But me?

Nope.

"I can't do this," I whisper. The words harden my spine. Resolve settles in.

There's someone else more suited for him. Someone I know.

A plan starts forming, fast and bright.

"I'm a genius," I murmur to my reflection.

I dig through my bag and grab my phone. Three texts from Amy. One from Lisa.

Lisa? That's... weird. She hasn't contacted me directly since before Wesley died, and even then, she only ever reached out to him, not me.

Her message is short. *Ring me.*

Ugh. I *hate* those kinds of texts. "Ring me." "Call me." Like I'm just supposed to drop everything and come running without context?

"Tell me what you want, and maybe I will," I mutter under my breath.

Amy's messages are more predictable. She's already been to the shop *twice*, looking for me. Wants to know where I am. Who I'm with. Of course. I should've known. The way she looked at Pet? She's obsessed. And relentless. That girl doesn't stop until she gets what she wants.

Even if I wanted something with Pet, I couldn't have it. Not with Amy gunning for him. But maybe... maybe they *could* work. Pet's odd, but he's decent. And Amy? Amy needs someone to match her intensity. And Wesley said that no amount of money he gave Amy could satisfy her. Pet has resources that would keep Amy satisfied for a lifetime, if that's what they want...

I tap out a reply.

Amy, I'm in San Antonio on a shopping trip with Pet.

Pause.

No. That'll trigger a frenzy.

…with Matt. He's showing me some pieces he's interested in for the special project I'm doing.

That's better.

I think I can set something up so the two of you can spend time alone. After getting to know him, I think you might be well-suited. BUT, you can't be clingy or starstruck. He hates that. I'll text you more later. Be patient. Mommy D

Satisfied, I fire off a quick reply to Lisa too.

I'm in San Antonio with a client. Did you need something urgent?

Short and sweet. Let's see what she has to say.

I silence the phone and tuck it back in my bag. No doubt Amy will blow up my inbox. That girl treats men like shiny toys. And she always gets the toy.

I glance at myself in the mirror one last time and decide to leave my bag on the bed. Then I step out into the suite.

Pet's already up, waiting. He's changed into beige linen pants and a steel-blue polo shirt, barefoot and casual, but somehow still polished. He looks like a preppy surfer who wandered into a GQ shoot.

And damn it, he looks good.

I walk toward him, twirling once in the flowing dress I found in the closet, vintage Gucci color block print, of course. I paired it with a pair of lavender red-bottom heels that match one of the print's colors perfectly.

Pet smiles when he sees me. "I wasn't sure of your size, so I had Bob stock the closet. I'm glad you found something you like. It suits you."

"Thank you. I can't help but be excited about the selection. I may work with metal and grime, but when it comes to fashion, I'm weak."

"I figured that about you," he says with a grin.

I do another little spin, giggling like a girl in a new dress.

"I'm so excited to see the fashions! Do you think they'll have more vintage pieces? Or is this all just… lingerie?"

He doesn't answer. Instead, he slips into the hallway. A moment later, he returns with a grin. "Vintage it is."

I clap my hands and laugh, genuinely delighted. For a second, I forget everything—Amy, the plan, even Orlando.

But it doesn't last.

"Pet," I say, slowing my steps. "I've thought about what you said… about who you are and what you want. And you're right. It's not for me. I thought maybe I could try. I'm attracted to you. You have so many good qualities. But I'm not what you're looking for."

I take his hands in mine.

"I'm sorry if I misled you. I understand if you want to cancel everything. I can't be the exhibitionist you need."

His eyes hold mine. There's a flicker of disappointment, but also something else. Maybe… relief?

"Jolene, when you dropped the whip, I knew," he says softly. "You were trying too hard. And it's okay. This life, it's not for everyone. But I still want you to enjoy today. No lingerie, I promise. Just a few nice things that will be my gift to you. You stepped out of your comfort zone for me. Let me do this for you."

"And the shop?"

"I want to lease the back room for my own use. I'll be in Port Aransas for a few more weeks. You're welcome to join me anytime. I'm attracted to you. You make things interesting. But if you want to walk away, no strings, no guilt, just say the word. Keep the money. It was never about that."

I breathe out, shoulders relaxing. "Thank you! I really wanted to be honest with you. I haven't felt much of anything in so long. You have brought me happiness again. Plus, I didn't want to give up the shopping part. Is that terrible?"

He laughs. "Not at all. It's *refreshing*."

There it is again. That word. The same one Orlando used. What is it with men and this theme of being *refreshed* by me?

A knock interrupts my thoughts.

"Are you ready, sir?" Bob's voice floats in from the hallway, polite and professional.

"Yes," Pet says, gesturing for me to sit back. "Bring them in."

And just like that, a private runway show begins.

Models stream in, one by one, each one a vision of confidence and poise. They don't just walk. They float. Every turn, every pose is practiced, precise. The fabrics whisper secrets as they move, silk and satin sliding over skin like water.

The first model wears a vintage Versace slip dress—liquid silver, bias-cut, the kind of gown that hugs the body like it was poured on. Another spins in a Roberto Cavalli halter dress, wild with leopard print and accented by a scarf tied at the hip. I suck in a breath. That one was everywhere in the magazines. Then comes a Tom Ford Gucci piece—

deep navy and burnt sienna color block, low back, plunging neckline, slit to the thigh. *Iconic.*

A few wear flowing pieces I can't quite place at first, but then I recognize the distinct drape. It's Halston, revived for the modern runway. Chiffon layers flutter like wings. One woman enters in a Donna Karan open-back jersey gown that somehow looks as effortless as a T-shirt, but slinks like sin. And there's one with a pale gold Fendi coatdress, cinched at the waist, with oversized buttons that catch the light like polished brass.

The men come next, scattered between the women like punctuation marks—sharp, deliberate, unforgettable. One wears a white Prada suit with a lavender shirt open just enough to suggest mischief. Another dons a slim-cut Dior Homme jacket with satin piping, paired with tailored trousers that hit just above a vintage loafer. There's even one in a deconstructed Jean Paul Gaultier ensemble. It has a sheer undershirt, pinstripe vest, and a chain necklace that reminds me of the ones I make in my shop.

I grin at Pet. "Seriously?"

"What?" he protests. "I couldn't let you have *all* the fun. I enjoy shopping just as much as you do."

I find myself smiling. There's something so gratifying about recognizing the artistry behind each piece. I may spend my days with fire and steel, but this fashion is also creation. Each outfit is a story stitched in thread. And somehow, Pet knew. He understood the magic of surrounding someone like me with designer pieces that span generations. He didn't just stock a closet. He curated an experience.

It shouldn't surprise me, but it does.

Pet isn't just eccentric and rich, he's thoughtful. Intentional. Every detail of this show is a testament to that. He knew I'd appreciate this on more than a superficial level. That I'd study the tailoring, admire the drape, recognize the craftsmanship the way some admire sculpture or glasswork.

Maybe that's what's messing with my head. It's easy to dismiss him as a fetishist or a spoiled collector of women, but this display… this is something else. It's generous. It's art.

And for a moment, I let myself forget the past. I just sit back and let the show wash over me like molten gold.

And for now, at least, I let myself enjoy it.

The fashion show ends and Pet decides to buy everything, including the men's clothing too. Every last piece.

"I want the shoes, the accessories, all of it," he tells the shop owners, who nearly faint with glee.

With a wave of his hand, he dismisses them after arranging delivery: the men's items to his hotel, the women's clothes and accessories to my marina address. They shower him with thank-yous and even call him a saint, which makes me hide a smile. If only they knew…

The female business owners shoot me looks—half jealousy, half suspicion—as if I'm the competition they're dying to run out of town. Amy will be perfect for them. She'd annihilate those women with a single glance.

Once the room clears out and it's just me and Pet, I put my plan into motion.

"First, I want to thank you from the bottom of my heart," I say. "I know you can afford all this and it's probably just a drop in a very deep well for you, but it's still incredibly generous. You have no idea how much I appreciate it."

"No thanks needed," he says, brushing it off like it's no more effort than buying a loaf of bread. Never mind that he just dropped seventy grand in one afternoon.

"Second…" I take a breath, ready to shift the conversation. "It's my turn to do a favor for you…"

"About that," he cuts in. "I have a proposition. I'm a man with needs, as you already know. I'd pay you handsomely if you'd consider spending the night with me. We don't even have to use the dungeon. I have a very nice bed. And I haven't had normal sex in a while. I'm still interested in you. But I'd never push you into something you're uncomfortable with."

My face burns.

Oh no. He did *not* just say that.

I should've seen it coming, but I didn't. Not really. I thought we were on the same page. Is he that obsessed with sex that he can't keep it out of the conversation for five minutes? Then again… what have I thought about since the moment he strolled into my shop on a leash?

Sex. Just not with *him*.

Someone else keeps invading my thoughts. Someone with a firm mouth and intense eyes. I drift back to Orlando's kiss.

"I see I've surprised you," Pet says, misreading my silence. "How does fifty thousand dollars sound?"

I snap.

"You've got to be kidding me! I'm not for sale!" I jump to my feet, pacing furiously. "You may have leased a space in my shop, but my vagina is not for rent. There is no price high enough!"

My words hit like fire.

Wesley always warned me my mouth would get me into trouble. He was right. Again. I walk right into vulnerable territory with my usual impulsiveness.

Selena said she never had sex for money. She swore she wasn't a prostitute. So, what the hell does Pet think *I* am? Some lonely widow he can toss a bone and save with his fat checkbook?

Oh my fucking gawd.

Pet steps in front of me, blocking my pace. "Please. Calm down. I didn't mean to offend you." He runs his hand through his hair, clearly flustered. "Please, sit down with me."

I shoot darts at him with my eyes but sit anyway.

He places his hands over mine. They're trembling. "I have a confession," he says, voice low.

I watch him carefully, still fuming, but I force my breath to slow. No man should ever tell a woman to *calm down*. Nothing spikes fury faster. But I don't do it for him. I do it for me.

"I've never been good at this. With women, I mean." He sighs. "I'm used to buying everything I want. Sometimes I forget how to speak like a decent human. What I meant to say is that you need money, and I need someone to hold. I'm not just into being whipped and degraded. I'm still a man. I need comfort… connection. Just for one night."

He looks up at me. His eyes aren't lustful, they're apologetic. Hopeful. He tries to laugh, almost embarrassed. I can feel the edge of my anger start to soften. Sympathy slips in.

"Do you know how hard it is to have everything?" he continues. "You forget how to function in normal society. Dating. Women. Relationships. I haven't paid for intercourse, ever. Not even with Selena. So, if that counts, I guess I'm still a virgin in that sense."

He chuckles sadly. "I would never be with someone I didn't respect. I'm not looking for a whore. I like you because you're real. You don't tell me what I want to hear. You're genuine."

He pauses, pleading. "Please… say something."

I study him. If he hadn't interrupted me, I would've offered him exactly what he's asking for, but framed differently. Now, I hesitate. Can I trust him? What if he's lying? What if he *does* pay women regularly?

Amy doesn't deserve to be used. No matter how cruel she acts, I love her. It's a fucked up kind of love, but I do. She's all I have left of Wesley. I open my mouth, ready to cut him down, but then… I don't.

I want to see who he *really* is behind this most-eligible-playboy crap. The man behind the curtain. I want to know the wizard.

"I accept your apology," I say carefully. "But let me be clear… just because you bought me clothes doesn't mean you get to unzip your pants and cash in. You're mistaken if you think that."

"I don't think that," he says quickly. "I'm sorry if I gave that impression."

"You're forgiven," I reply, though my tone is still stiff. "Even if you hadn't made such a tragic misstep, I couldn't go through with anything."

"Oh?"

"Sex is a big deal to me. I haven't been with anyone since Wesley, and before him, only a couple of others. I don't have a long list of experiences, not because I couldn't, but because I choose not to. I want connection, not compensation. Even if I needed the money, even if I were open to something casual, I still wouldn't do it. I don't sell myself. I never will."

He exhales and drags his fingers through his hair again. "Though I'm disappointed… I respect your decision." He offers a small smile.

"You do?"

"Of course."

Maybe he's not the villain I thought.

"Before you opened your big mouth," I say, "I was going to offer a solution. But now I'm not so sure. How do I know you're even sincere about wanting a relationship? What if all that stuff in the dressing room is just for your consorts?"

"Consorts?" He flinches. "Okay, I deserve that. But I'm not a perv. I'll prove it to you."

He stands, energized. "Bob!"

The door cracks open. "Yes, sir?"

"Come in here a minute."

"Yes, sir." Bob hobbles in cautiously, looking like he expects a landmine to go off.

Pet clasps his hands behind his back like a trial lawyer. "Bob, tell the lady how many days a year I spend here on average."

Bob looks between us, confused. "Sir, it'd be easier to say how many days you're *away*, if that's alright."

"Fine. How many days am I away?"

"If you count holidays and your birthday at the family ranch? Maybe twenty days, tops. This trip's been your longest stretch away in years."

"And how long have you worked here?"

"I worked for your father before you. Twenty-two years this August."

"What did you do before that?"

"I was in special ops, sir. Military."

Pet stops, surprised. "Special ops? I didn't know that. Thank you for your service."

"Thank you, sir."

Pet nods and continues pacing. "And what's your primary job at the hotel?"

Bob glances at me again, looking like he's under cross-examination. "I'm your butler, sir."

"Why did you leave the military to become a butler?" I ask, folding my arms across my chest, not out of suspicion, just curiosity.

Bob's face flushes. His eyes drift toward the floor, like the weight of the memory is too much to look me in the eye.

"I was in Beirut with the peacekeeping force in '83," he says quietly. "Got caught in one of the bombings. Got lucky. I came home alive."

My breath catches.

He says it so plainly. No drama. No edge. But it lands like a brick in my gut. Beirut. I remember my parents talking about the news coverage of burning buildings, broken glass, and bodies. And here he is, standing in front of me, the human echo of that headline.

I don't say a word, but my arms fall slowly to my sides. I feel stupid for asking now, stupid for thinking this conversation was just casual.

Pet freezes mid-pace. His expression drops the usual eccentric charm, replaced with something deeper, something I hadn't seen before. Reverence, maybe. Or guilt. He lifts a finger like he's about to deliver a final verdict, but his tone softens instead.

"So…" he says, gently, "you're trained to be observant, even with the injury. How is it, by the way?"

His voice is different now. It's not performative. It's careful. Respectful. Like Bob's pain cracked open something in both of us.

Bob lifts his chin but doesn't smile. "It's fine, sir. No complaints."

I look between them, the billionaire and the butler, one who's never had to fight for anything, and one who fought just to stay alive. And yet, somehow, they've both built cages for themselves.

And for the first time, I realize I'm not the only one in the room carrying invisible scars.

The silence thickens, heavy with the weight of things unspoken. For a moment, no one moves.

Then Bob clears his throat, cutting through the tension. "Sir, were there any other questions?"

Pet shifts, his voice more grounded now. "As my butler, you're either just outside this door or in this room nearly every day, right? Watching the comings and goings?"

"Yes, sir. I live just down the hall. I'm always around."

"And you see how many women I bring into this room."

Bob shifts on his feet but nods. "Yes, sir."

"Would you please tell Jolene the exact number of women who've come in and out of this room over the past year?"

Bob hesitates.

"Come on, Bob. Be honest," Pet encourages.

Bob thinks for a moment, then answers carefully. "Including Miss Jolene and Miss Selena, and not counting the models earlier today, there've been two, sir."

"Thank you, Bob. Very helpful," Pet says, nodding. "You're dismissed."

"Wait, Bob," I say gently, stepping forward. I don't snap. I can't, not after what he just shared. "Can I ask you something else?"

He stops just short of the door and turns back to face me. "Yes, Miss?"

"You said you were special ops. How do I know you're telling the truth now? That you're not just… protecting him?"

He blinks, caught off guard, but I keep my tone calm. Not accusing, just real.

"I'm not trying to be difficult," I add. "I just need to understand the full picture before I make any assumptions."

He straightens his posture and meets my eyes. "You're right to question it. I've worked here for twenty-two years. I've got a roof over my head, a paycheck, security… I'd do anything to keep Mr. D'Angelo safe. But I wouldn't lie. Not even for that."

He hesitates, glancing at Pet. "And to be honest, I'm not sure telling you the truth is helping him. I don't know what kind of relationship you two have or what you're hoping to hear, but yeah, I'm probably sticking my neck out here. Not that there's been anything to report… not recently."

My chest tightens with guilt. I hadn't thought about what I was asking him to risk.

"You're safe, Bob," Pet says, stepping in. "I asked the questions. No harm done, old man."

Bob nods and quietly exits.

"You didn't have to do that," I say to Pet, my voice soft now.

"I wanted you to hear the truth from someone other than me. I'm not pretending to be someone I'm not."

I fold my arms, studying him. "So... if Bob's telling the truth, and I'm still not entirely sure he is, then it's been at least a year since you brought anyone to your room. Does that mean you haven't had sex in that long either?"

He sighs, almost embarrassed. "Unfortunately, it's been longer. I was seeing a woman I met in New York. We ended things nearly two years ago. No drama. Just... faded. I realize now why. When I said I had white-knuckled nights watching Selena, it was true. She helped me tap into parts of myself I hadn't explored. She opened a door. I stepped through it. Now I know what I need."

I actually admire that he didn't blame his ex. So many men can't wait to drag their past lovers through the dirt. But not him.

I clear my throat. "Like I said earlier, I was going to make a suggestion. Would you be open to a blind date?"

He narrows his eyes. "With who?"

"I can't tell you. Not yet. I need to prepare her, and you."

"Hmm..."

"She's beautiful, tempestuous, stubborn, a little full of herself, and not exactly known for her tact. But she's exactly what you need."

"Did you just call my mystery date *mean*?"

"Well, she's spoiled. But she's got a good heart underneath it all. You just have to dig."

He pauses, then shrugs. "Why not? I trust your judgment. When?"

I hesitate. "What about Selena? Would this... affect her business?"

"No," he says quickly. "She's hoping I find someone. She likes me, sure, but she's got plenty of clients. Some regulars, some married. She's not hurting for business. She'd be happy for me."

"Good." I rub my hands together, feeling the buzz of excitement. "I need to head back to the marina and get her ready. It's five now. If you send me in the chopper, I can have her back by nine. I think you should have your first date here, in the suite. Let her see you as you are, dungeon and all. If she can handle that, you'll know you've got a shot."

"I've never brought anyone in here," he admits. "Just dinner dates that go nowhere. Are you sure it's not too much for a first meeting?"

"Trust me," I say with a smirk. "You shocked *me* into your world. She'll need the same treatment if you want to break through."

He nods. "Alright. I'll get dinner ready. What do you need?"

"Two things," I say firmly. "One, I need a room of my own for tonight, separate from yours, in case she doesn't stay with you."

"Done."

"Two, does the hotel allow dogs?"

"Dogs?" His face falls. "Wait… you don't mean the Dita Von Teese look-alike from your store?" He recoils. "Please tell me that's not who you mean. She's hot. That's not the issue. She was just…."

"Perfect."

"She's terrifying."

"She's *exactly* what you need."

He exhales like a man accepting his fate. "If you say so… Bob!"

The door creaks open. "Yes, sir?"

"Get the chopper ready. Miss Jolene is heading to Port Aransas and returning tonight with a guest."

Bob's eyebrows shoot up. Relief floods his face. He nods quickly. "Yes, sir."

"Bob, don't go far," Pet adds before the door closes. "You and I have some work to do."

"Yes, sir." Bob shuts the door behind him.

I race through the suite toward the nautical room like it's Christmas morning and I'm about to roll out a shiny new bike. I dial Amy.

She picks up on the first ring, her voice a mix of impatience and curiosity. "Hello!"

"Amy…"

"You didn't answer my texts. What the hell did you mean by…?"

"Shut up. Do you want to go on a date with him or not?"

There's a pause. Then she exhales, defeated. "Yes."

I grin. *Knew it.*

"Great! I'll be at the ferry landing at 6:15. Try to look okay."

She snorts. "Excuse me?"

"Wear something black, short, and tight. Oh, and do you own a whip?"

"A whip?" she echoes. "Yes. Why?"

I bounce on my toes. "Bring it! I'll explain everything in the helicopter."

"Helicopter?" she repeats, her voice perking up.

"Yes. Your life's about to change, if you'll just listen to me. *For once.*"

40

Orlando: The Godfather

She didn't tell me she was leaving.

Didn't leave a note.

Of course she didn't. That would've made things *simple*.

I glance back toward the boat. Her boat.

Or so she thinks.

And now—enter stage left—the wildcard.

Amy.

She saunters across the deck in shorts that should come with a warning label and a smirk sharp enough to slice through steel. She drags a duffel bag like she's moving in, not visiting, and tosses it onto the bench without asking.

Fuck.

My little Bella.

She's grown. She's fierce. But she's still *mine*. And she's up to something. I can feel it in my bones.

"Nice day for a helicopter ride," she calls, eyes gleaming, voice light.

I bury the urge to demand answers. Keep my posture relaxed. "Didn't notice," I reply, watching the tide.

She rolls her eyes. "Wow. You're just a party in cargo pants, huh?"

I grimace. "Depends on the party."

She plants one hand on her hip and stares me down. Her attitude is thick, but her defenses are slipping. She's giddy. Nervous. Almost... hopeful. That's what scares me.

Then she drops it like a grenade.

"I've got a date. Tonight. With *him*."

I lift an eyebrow. "*Him?*"

I know exactly who. And it's taking everything in me not to handcuff her to the mast.

"Don't play dumb. You know. *The* guy. Helicopter. Money. Eyes like he invented sin. Matt. I have less than two hours to get date-ready, and I'm a mess."

The coast is clear, so I hop aboard *My Knotty Jolene* and sit on the bench. She joins me with a dramatic sigh, all tough-girl swagger fading just enough for the kid to peek through.

I see her. Not the woman-in-the-making with the sharp tongue and stilettos, but the girl in ripped tights who used to sit on the kitchen counter and demand chocolate milk while I taught her how to tie fishing knots.

"You have no idea," she says, stretching her legs in front of her. "My friends said he's weird. Like... dungeon weird."

I keep my expression still. "Weird can be fun."

"Weird can be *murder*," she snaps, half-joking. "But he's hot. And rich. And into me. So... yeah. I'm doing it."

She's not saying it out loud, but I hear the undercurrent. She wants out. A new life. A shot. Someone to *see* her.

And I get it. Because I've spent years seeing her when no one else did.

"You've got time," I say calmly. "What do you need?"

She squints at me. "What are you, the concierge?"

"No," I answer. "Just a guy who knows how to prepare for war."

That gets me a real smile. The kind I haven't seen in years. And suddenly, I'm not sitting beside a young woman chasing a rich man. I'm next to the little girl I helped raise.

She kicks at the air. "Well, General, I need help with my hair, something to wear that doesn't scream *daddy issues,* and maybe someone to tell me I'm not totally screwing this up."

I glance at her. "I can help with that."

She blinks. "Seriously?"

"I'm sorry your dad isn't here to help. But I am." I pause. "And as much as I want to throw Matt into the Gulf of Mexico and tell you to hide forever, I know you. You're tough. And I'm starting to think maybe Jolene's tougher than I gave her credit for. If she's with you... I'll sleep easier."

Amy leans against the railing, suddenly quiet. "You remember my first date?"

I smirk. "The one with the boy who showed up in a beater with a bumper sticker that said *I brake for boobs?*"

She laughs, actually *laughs,* and nods. "You made him get out and take it off."

"I offered him a screwdriver or a black eye."

"You ironed my dress that night," she says softly. "Taught me how to use lip gloss without looking like I'd been licking fried chicken."

"You were nervous. It was adorable."

"I was scared," she admits. "I didn't think I was pretty. Not until that night."

I look at her. Really look. She's stunning. Unapologetic. But the girl inside her still craves reassurance.

"You've always been beautiful, Bella. Even when you had braces and thought glitter eyeliner was high fashion."

She laughs again, a little misty-eyed now. "You always made me feel safe."

"You *are* safe. Always."

She wipes her cheek like it itches, but we both know what that was.

Then, of course, she ruins the moment. "It's so nice to have a gay godfather."

I grunt. "Not gay."

"Shame," she mutters, grinning.

"Focus," I say, standing. "Do you have anything that doesn't involve leopard print, mesh, or sequins?"

"Maybe," she says cautiously.

"Let's start there."

We head below deck, and I lead her to where Jolene keeps some spare clothes, because I know where everything is on Jolene's boat.

Amy doesn't question how I know. She just shakes her head as she rifles through the options, discarding half with a scoff. "This makes me look like I'm going to church."

"Better than looking like you're going to jail."

She holds up a sleek black dress. Structured. Classy. Hugs all the right places. My pick. I give a short nod.

She studies it. "You think this'll work?"

I look her dead in the eye. "You'll knock him dead."

And then, in a quieter voice: "But if he touches you wrong, makes you feel small, or hurts you in any way, you tell me. I'll handle it."

She nods, her lips pressed together, emotion rising again.

"Tonight," I say, "you're going to play the part. But don't forget who you are."

She breathes in deeply, steadies herself. "Thanks, Uncle Franco."

I nod.

Jolene's Adonis

Tonight, I'll be the godfather. The ghost in the shadows. The man no one sees coming.

But if shit goes sideways…

I'll burn it all down for her.

Not on my watch.

41

Jolene: Forgiveness

Before the helicopter lifts off and heads back toward Aransas Pass, I dial Lisa's number and hold my breath, hoping she won't answer.

No such luck.

"The Hicks residence," Lisa answers in a thick British accent. "Lady of the yacht speaking."

I stifle a giggle. Wesley always swore that the Hyacinth character from *Keeping Up Appearances* was based on Lisa. He may have been right.

"Lise?"

"Yes?"

"It's Jolene. You said you needed to speak to me?"

"Ring me" from Lisa is never a good sign. But I'm feeling better than I have in months, so I decide to throw caution to the wind.

"Oh yes, Jolene. I spotted her in the car park, you see."

She says it like we're in the middle of a conversation that started hours ago, like I'm just supposed to *know* who she's talking about.

"Spotted *whom*?" I ask.

"Amy, of course. She was pulling a rather lovely set of designer luggage behind her. It looked like she was moving in."

My stomach drops. "Moving in? To where?"

The last word escapes as a whisper, dread crawling up my spine like a slow fog. The peaceful sky above suddenly feels heavier, darker.

Lisa hums like she's sipping tea. "With you, of course. Isn't it *lovely* how the two of you have gotten on, even after Wesley died?"

"Yes. Lovely." I smirk at the appearance of a cloud in an otherwise clear sky.

"Did you know?"

I don't answer. I hang up. Not rudely, well, maybe a little, but I can't take one more word out of Lisa's chipper, self-important mouth. My brain splinters into a million frantic thoughts.

Maybe Lisa's wrong. Maybe Amy packed an overnight bag for San Antonio. Maybe it's nothing. But *just in case...* this trip with Pet couldn't have come at a better time.

Please, let this work.

After the short flight, the black sedan waits in the field as the helicopter touches down. Pet's stocky chauffeur greets me with a tip of his hat before opening the back door. I slide inside and glance out the window as the car winds its way to the ferry landing.

Amy is there. She's ten minutes early, for once. That alone should've tipped me off that something's up. She looks impatient, of course, but at least she followed directions. She's dressed in my favorite LBD, *little black dress*. I let it slide.

"Hop in," I tell her, and then give the driver our first stop. "Marina, please."

"I *just* left there," Amy whines.

Sadie snoozes in her designer doggie bag, undisturbed. The poor thing's used to being hauled around like luggage.

"Yeah, I know," I say. "Lisa told me. What's going on?"

Amy mutters under her breath, "She's gotta big mouth."

"Amy!" I chastise, but only mildly. I don't disagree.

Amy shrugs. "It just made sense for me to stay with you. It's Daddy's boat. Why should *you* have to pay rent on my apartment when I can just live with you?"

I blink. "You're a grown woman. You're only three years younger than I am. Why is *your* rent my responsibility? And more importantly, why would you even want to live with me? You *hate* me."

"I don't hate you."

Her fingers stroke Sadie's silky ears, and just like that, her edges soften. She looks… young. Her hair is braided over one shoulder in a fishtail, and her makeup is soft, except for the crimson lipstick, classic Amy.

"Since when?" I ask, half-laughing but feeling something shift.

"I never hated *you*," she says. "I hated that Daddy married someone young enough to be my sister. I didn't understand why he'd do that. Or why you'd want to be with him." She glances sideways at me. "You're not ugly."

Well. I think that's a compliment?

"I *loved* him," I say gently. "Isn't that reason enough?"

She shrugs, still avoiding my eyes. "I thought you wanted him for his money. I didn't know…"

"Didn't know what?" I press. "That he *didn't* have any money?"

"No. Not just that." Her voice quiets. "I didn't know you *loved* him."

She shifts in her seat, clearly uncomfortable. It's the most honest she's been in… maybe ever.

"Look, I don't want to talk about this now," she says quickly. "I want to talk about Matt. Can we agree to a truce, for now? We can unpack the emotional baggage later."

I nod. "Sure. But we *will* talk. Especially if we're going to be living together."

The car pulls into the marina parking lot. I step out before the driver even reaches for the handle.

Amy rolls down the window, her head popping out. "We don't have *time!*" she complains, drama in every syllable.

"I'll just be a minute!" I call back as I head down the dock.

Orlando looks up as I approach. A belt sander rests on the railing, but judging by the untouched wood, he hasn't used it.

"Hey, you," he says with a smile that catches me off guard. His eyes flick to the dress hugging my body like a second skin. The breeze catches the hem, teasing the edge of modesty.

"Hi. I was hoping to catch you." I smile, breathless from the sun and the rush of everything. "I only have a minute. I'm leaving for San Antonio and I won't be back until tomorrow."

"Oh." His voice dips slightly, disappointment flashing in his eyes.

"I was hoping you could keep an eye on my boat while I'm gone. I haven't had a chance to make a key for the door yet, and after our conversation last night, I'm a little on edge."

"No problem." He nods. "I did notice a woman on it earlier. Looked like she had luggage, like she was planning to stay."

I wince. "Yeah. That's Amy, Wesley's daughter. She's going with me to San Antonio."

He doesn't call me out. Doesn't ask the obvious follow-up. He just nods, respectful.

"When I get back," I continue, "I want to talk to you. I'm thinking of taking some time off. I need to sail somewhere. Maybe Belize. Maybe Mexico. I'm still figuring it out and I don't want to go alone."

His brow tightens. "Why so far?"

"I'm trying to find someone. A friend of Wesley's. It's a long story. I'll tell you everything when I get back. I just wanted to give you a heads-up… and maybe see if you'd consider going with me. Or helping me find someone who can."

He holds my gaze for a long moment. I feel the air between us shift, like the tide pulling at the shore, just before a wave crashes.

"I'll keep that in mind," he says quietly.

And the way he says it?

It already feels like yes.

"Where are you staying in San Antonio? In case I need to reach you for something… boat-related."

I pull a crumpled receipt from my purse and scribble my cell number on the back. I'm barely done when he jumps onto the dock and pulls me into him so fast I gasp.

And then he kisses me.

Hard. Deep. Like he's finally decided to stop pretending we're just friends, or neighbors, or anything other than what we really are: two people who've been circling each other like fire and kindling.

I melt.

My legs give out and I fall into him, pressed against the heat of his body. He moans into my mouth, and I feel it all the way down. It's like something long overdue just broke free.

When we finally come up for air, I press the paper into his palm and curl his fingers around it.

"Call me for anything… *boat-related*," I tease, still breathless.

"I wish you could stay," he whispers against my lips. "I'd like to see you tonight."

"I can't. But oh how I want to." I don't know what changed in him, but I don't care. He wants me, and I want more than Pet's carefully packaged seduction. I want this. Real. Raw. Messy. *Desired.*

And so does he. His erection presses into my thigh as he grazes my lips again, tasting, teasing.

"Tomorrow?" I ask, my voice catching with need. I feel heat coil low in my belly.

"I'm not sure I can wait that long," he murmurs. "You've been on my mind all day. I wanted to make it up to you… for last night."

"Oh?"

"We're two consenting adults," he says. "And there's no denying the attraction. I'd like to explore it, if you're sure it's not too soon."

"It's not. I want…"

But his mouth claims mine before I finish.

His hand pushes into the bodice of my dress, warm skin brushing over my breast. His thumb circles my nipple, and I shudder, heat flooding through me. My knees nearly buckle again. I want to climb onto his boat and strip him bare. I want to show him just how ready I am.

"There you are!"

Amy's voice slices through the moment like a bucket of ice water.

Orlando immediately pulls his hand away and steps back. He groans and adjusts himself, then positions himself behind me like a schoolboy caught in the act.

"A… Amy!" I stammer, trying to pull myself together as my pulse pounds in every corner of my body. "This is Orlando."

I gesture awkwardly behind me, bracing for her usual barrage. Some snide comment or venomous insult.

But instead, Amy surprises me. She extends a perfectly manicured hand.

"Nice to meet you… Orlando?" she says, with only a faint glimmer of that trademark sass.

I blink. *What the hell is happening?*

"I was just telling Orlando I'll be back tomorrow," I explain, still trying to catch my breath. "He's going to keep an eye on the boat for us."

"How nice." Amy winks at Orlando—mildly, not in her usual predatory way—and starts tapping her foot like a human metronome. "Can we get going? Matt's waiting."

My jaw nearly drops. I was prepared for a meltdown. A tantrum. At the very least, a passive-aggressive jab.

But nothing. No name-calling. No slut-shaming. No performance. Not even a flirt-fest aimed at Orlando.

Well... maybe the wink, but that barely counts with Amy. For her, that's restraint.

I glance toward the boat. I don't need anything from it. Pet thought of everything. He probably stocked the hotel room with enough clothing, cosmetics, and whatever else he thinks I need to keep me comfortable for the next month.

Still, I hesitate.

I turn back toward Orlando, and shyly wave goodbye. I want to tell him I wish he was coming with me. That I don't want to leave this moment. That I feel more alive from one kiss than I have in years.

Instead, I follow Amy up the dock toward the waiting car.

Just before I slide inside, I glance back.

He's still there, watching me. He lifts a hand in a slow, deliberate wave. That smile of his, the one that makes me ache, curls at the corners of his mouth.

Please help me.

I want that man.

42

Orlando: The Raven

I watch from the shadow of the dock post as Jolene and Amy climb into the back seat of the sedan and pull out of the marina lot. I track the red taillights until they vanish down the highway toward Aransas Pass.

She waved goodbye. Smiling. Trusting.

And she asked me to sail with her. To no doubt help her find Uncle Franco.

If she only knew.

I'm not used to guilt. But the way she looked at me… like I was the only one she could trust… it eats at me. I'm not lying to protect myself. I'm lying to protect her. To keep her breathing. Sailing. Laughing.

Until I know who killed Wesley, and why, the truth has to wait.

The marina slips behind me as I walk the shoulder of the highway. It's two miles to the nearest bar. That's long enough to think, and short enough to reach before the sky goes completely black. I don't plan on being in driving condition when I leave, so the walk will do me some good.

The wind off the Gulf of Mexico tastes like salt and engine oil. The kind of thick air that settles before everything explodes. I pass a weathered bait shop with boarded-up windows, then a sagging fence lined with *NO TRESPASSING* signs that gave up years ago.

Jolene's voice echoes in my head.

She wants me to sail with her.

She looked so damn hopeful. So open.

I pick up my pace. Guilt sits heavy in my chest, but guilt doesn't change the mission. I'm not who she thinks I am. I'm the man Wesley told her to find. The shadow at the edge of her story. The one who was never supposed to matter… until now.

And when she finds out who I really am—what I've done, what I've hidden—it could break her.

When I finally spot the glowing red neon of *La Hacienda*, I slow down. It's a dive bar tucked behind a run-down Mexican cafe; the kind of place that doesn't check IDs. Just pours the beer and keeps the salsa coming.

I slide into a corner booth, still damp from the walk. I order a Shiner and something fried, anything to absorb the ache that's settled deep in my ribs like a permanent bruise.

Then I hear it.

The soft ding of the bell above the door.

Jessica.

Jolene's best friend.

Wesley's old contact.

Colombian intelligence, if she's still where I last saw her.

I don't expect to see her here. Not tonight. But there she is, standing in the doorway, lit by fluorescent indifference and looking like a woman who's lost more than she's saying. She walks to the bar and orders a glass of iced tea. Sits alone. Stirs it with a straw like she's trying to summon the truth from the bottom.

She hasn't spotted me yet.

Not until I let her.

Eventually, we lock eyes.

Recognition.

Surprise.

Then that calculating gleam I remember from Bogotá. A flicker of pain quickly masked.

I nod, just once, and tilt my chin toward the booth.

Jessica doesn't hesitate.

She slides into the seat across from me, her movements fluid, but worn like a blade sharpened one too many times. Her gaze doesn't waver.

"I figured you were watching," she says quietly. "Didn't think you'd show your face."

"Didn't plan to," I admit, taking a slow sip of my beer. "But things are shifting. Fast."

She glances out the window, then back. "You've been here the whole time?"

"Almost two months," I say. "Watching Jolene. Watching you."

She doesn't flinch, but she quits stirring.

"And?"

"Didn't think I'd see you again outside of Bogotá," I add with a smirk.

She lets out a bitter little laugh. "You always had a talent for popping up where trouble brews."

"And you always had a talent for creating it."

Jessica raises an eyebrow, but she doesn't argue. "You working this, too?"

"Let's just say I've been watching a certain blonde a lot closer than I expected."

Her face darkens. "You remember George? My partner. My *cover.* Jolene gave her wedding ring to me to have George sell it."

I exhale and fight the urge to slam my fist into the table.

The one person Wesley warned her about.

Jessica continues, her voice low. "He's been off ever since I showed him the ring. He didn't say much, but I saw it, the shift. His hands trembled. His voice went cold. Measured. He asked where she got it, but he already knew."

I lean forward and lower my voice. "He knows exactly what that ring is."

I pull a worn folder from my bag and slide it across the table. "Normally I wouldn't share this, but I've been digging. George is double-dipping. Fake names, shell companies, offshore accounts. One of them used to belong to a cartel front in Montería."

Jessica's eyes widen as she flips through the pages. "So, he *is* tied to them."

"He's been laundering blood jewels and cartel cash through a string of real estate 'investments' across South Texas. And Wesley knew. In a note to Jolene, he warned her. Told her not to trust George."

Jessica falls silent. Her fingers whiten around her glass.

"There's more," she says after a beat. "I wasn't sent here by the U.S. government. Colombian intelligence brought me in after the Medellín deal collapsed. They traced a rogue asset operating along the Gulf Coast. Someone moving jewels under the radar. I thought it might've been Wesley, but now…" She trails off. Shakes her head. "I think Wesley stole something sacred. Something that was never meant to leave Colombia."

I nod slowly. "And George killed him for it."

"Or gave the order." Her voice hardens. "Either way, he's dangerous. He's circling something. I don't know what."

Find the raven. The words echo again, low and urgent. Maybe this is it… the opening. The beginning of the unraveling.

"I do," I say. "And I have an idea."

Jessica leans in, wary but interested. "Let's hear it."

"We feed him a story," I say. "You tell him Jolene's headed to Mexico. Alone. With the jewels. Make him believe she's selling them to a third party… someone cartel-connected."

Jessica smirks. "Let him sweat."

"Exactly. We wire you. Plant cameras. Let him panic. If he follows her, we've got him. If he contacts someone to intercept her, we trace it. Either way, he'll make a move."

"And when he does…"

"We have him," I finish.

She leans back, absorbing the plan. "It's dirty."

"It's clean enough to hold up in court."

She hesitates. "And Jolene? You're using her as bait."

"She's already bait," I say softly. "She just doesn't know it. She's carrying ghosts, Jessica. She's in deeper than she realizes. And until we know exactly who's coming for her, it's better she believes she's chasing a dream than running from a killer."

Jessica studies me for a long moment. Then, softer: "I'm sorry about your loss. Wesley was a good man. A damn good agent."

I nod once. "He was my brother. Blood or not, he was mine. I'm going to finish what he started. I owe him that."

Jessica holds out her hand, steady and sure.

"We've never worked a case together," she says, her voice low, steady. "But I trust you. Always have."

I take her hand. Her grip is firm, but I feel the tension beneath it—the weight of grief, of questions, of everything unspoken between us.

She studies me for a moment longer, eyes narrowing just slightly. "You wouldn't happen to be a *hot Hispanic hero* who recently surfaced in Jolene's life, would you?"

I huff a quiet laugh. "Guilty, partner."

Jessica lets out a breath, half exasperated, half amused. "Damn it. I should've put it together."

"She called me hot?" I try not to smile, but it slips through anyway. It's a rare warmth in a night full of shadows.

Jessica rolls her eyes. "Don't let it go to your head."

We share a beat of silence, something unspoken pulsing between us. A reckoning. An understanding.

"This one got to you, huh? You really care about her? Or is it business as usual?" she asks softly, almost like she's testing the words on her tongue.

"I do. I am. There's something about her…" I admit. "But I also owe her the truth. Just… not yet. Not until I know she'll survive it."

Jessica's expression shifts—respect, sympathy, and something a little like sorrow. "Then let's make sure she does. And if you hurt her…"

"Got it!" I nod, gripping her hand one last time before releasing it.

George thinks he's still running the game.

But the truth?

He just became the bait.

And this time, we're the ones holding the line.

43

Jolene: Confession

On the return flight to San Antonio, Amy fires questions at me with unchecked excitement. She's practically bouncing in her seat, demanding answers like a prosecutor in Louboutins.

"What's he like? How did you meet him? What does he want in a woman? Did you sleep with him? Why didn't you introduce me sooner?"

I decide to go with honesty. It's easier than dodging. I tell her *everything*. Well, almost. She wants the dirty details, and I give them to her. Every last naughty strap and command. Except the part where he offered to sleep with me. Some things are just too awkward to say out loud. If this date turns into something real for her, I don't want any secrets between us. Just one. That one.

"But you've never touched him, and he's never touched you, right? Not even a kiss?" she asks through her headset; eyes locked on mine like she's hunting for cracks.

"No." I drop my gaze. "I tried to be a dominatrix. It wasn't something I was looking for.

They came into my store and made me an offer. I needed money." I pause, then point at her. "*You* needed money. I'm not blaming you. I made the choice. He's good-looking, sure, but I only hit him with the whip a couple of times, and beyond that, there's been zero sexual contact. I tried. I failed. Miserably."

Amy's lips twist. "No surprise there… I can work with that." She nods, then lifts her chin like she's already sealing the deal. "I knew she was the hired help."

"Who? Selena?"

She nods again.

"How could you possibly know that?" I brace myself. Here comes the stereotyping.

"She wasn't jealous. Any woman dating a man like that would cling to him like plastic wrap. Block other women from even looking his way."

"You mean clingy?" I smirk.

"No! Not clingy. Smart. I'd make sure *all* of his attention stayed on me." She leans back, crosses her legs, and kicks a foot in the air like she's rehearsing for a power move.

Then she lunges forward, startling Sadie in her dog carrier. "Wait a minute! You said he's attracted to *you*? First of all, *gross*! I didn't think you were his type!"

"I'm not." I shrug. "He told me today he knows I'm not the one for him. That's why I planned this date. So you could meet him."

"*Good!*" She fans herself like she's about to faint. "That's a relief. I mean, I don't mind him being attracted to you. He's a man. He can't help it when you flaunt in his face what *my* daddy paid for. You're not the crypt keeper or anything, but let's be real, you do look as old as Elvira."

I let it slide. That's Amy. She has to get her jab in. "Thanks."

She softens a bit. "You know what I mean. You're not awful to look at, and he's a man with no attachments. As long as he hasn't touched you, I'm cool with it. Once I get him alone, he'll forget you ever existed. *That's* a promise." She swipes her finger through the air with all the flair of Lil Kim claiming her throne on the red carpet.

I laugh. Not because I'm mocking her, but because… in her own twisted way, she's charming. She always has this take-no-prisoners energy that somehow makes her the Alpha in every room she enters.

"I'm setting you up with him. But you *cannot* act like you did at my store this afternoon," I warn her. "You have to treat him like you would any other man. No worshipping. No fawning. He doesn't want to be idolized, and he doesn't want to be smothered.

He gets that all the time. Honestly, he was attracted to me because I didn't know who the hell he was when he walked in. I treated him like a customer. He liked that. He likes being told what to do. He likes dominance."

Amy raises her eyebrows, intrigued.

"You practically have a PhD in domination," I continue. "You've spent your entire life bossing people around and getting your way. That's why I thought you were perfect for him."

I adjust my headset and lower my voice. "You could make each other happy. But only if you treat him like someone you *love*, not like how you treat *me*. Be kind to him. Be honest. He needs someone he can trust. Take control in the bedroom, sure, but don't try to run his whole life."

Amy tilts her head, serious now. "Of course. I'm not as callous as you think. I've just had… a hard time with things. Daddy was gone all the time. Then he brought you home and stopped spending time with me. And now he's just… gone."

She turns away, looking out the window at the scattered lights of San Antonio below.

"Amy…" I reach out to touch her hand.

She jerks away. "I don't want your pity."

"I wasn't…"

"I know." She turns back to me, her eyes misty and full of conflict. "If it weren't for Matt and this whole date thing, I probably wouldn't be saying any of this. Especially not after that disgusting little scene at the marina. Who even *was* that guy?"

Of course. "He's someone I met recently," I say, already preparing for judgment.

"How recently? You looked *way* too cozy to be 'recent.'"

Guilt tries to creep in. I push it back. I'm not married. Wesley lied to me. He abandoned his daughter. He abandoned *me*. I won't let Amy make me feel guilty for wanting companionship.

"He got to the marina a few days ago. I met him then. I know it seems fast, but there's something about him. I can't explain it. I'm lonely, okay? Your father… he hurt me. But I still miss him. I miss having someone in my life."

Amy watches me closely. I place my hand on hers, gently. This time, she doesn't pull away. "I'm sorry you had to see that. I'm sure it must be confusing."

She sighs, slipping her hand free. "I'm not a kid. I get it. It just… hurt. I kind of expected you to wear black and weep by the ocean for the next few years."

"You did?"

She nods. "I did."

I narrow my eyes. "Alright. What's the catch? When's the other shoe dropping? You're *never* this reasonable without a price."

She grins. "Maybe it's the new me."

I give her a look.

"Okay, fine. Look, I meant what I said before. I want to work on things. You're still my stepmonster, and we need to look out for each other. Besides, you're not so bad."

I raise an eyebrow. "I'm not?"

"You could've told me to screw off and kept Matt for yourself," she says with a shrug. "But you didn't. You're handing him over. No drama. No games. That's pretty cool. And the trust? Turns out I'm gonna be okay because of it. You could've kept that from me too, but you didn't. So… I'm willing to give you a chance."

I let myself smile for real. "I'm glad you're finally coming around."

"Hey," Amy warns, narrowing her eyes. "I didn't say we're gonna be friends, so don't get all misty-eyed. I just said I'm seeing you differently." She pauses. "Besides, I need to talk to you about something."

"Sure. What is it?" I try to keep the excitement out of my voice. We're having a civil conversation—a real one—and for once, she's not clawing at me. I wish Wesley could see this.

"You said Matt didn't have sex with you or that other woman, right?" she asks, tugging at her seatbelt. "So what did you do? I want to be prepared. I want to know what he likes."

"Amy…" I sigh, adjusting my headset. "I already told you what happened. He was tied up, sometimes naked. Selena jerked him off or he did it himself. That's it. I know it's a lot to take in, but I'm not setting you up to be his dominatrix. He's looking for more than that. He wants a real connection. He's kinky, sure, but I think he was only with Selena because he was lonely."

"Oh." Her eyes drift to the window, staring out at the dark sky and the blinking lights of San Antonio as we descend.

"Is that a problem?" I study her expression. "I know it sounds strange."

She doesn't answer right away. She reaches down and pets Sadie, who gives her fingers a grateful lick.

"Well?" I push gently.

"It's just that… I want to go on a date with him," she admits. "I want to be the only woman to see him naked after tonight. But…" Her voice drops to a whisper. "I've never… I haven't…"

"You haven't had sex?" I squeak, not hiding my surprise.

Amy shakes her head, eyes still on Sadie.

"What the fuck, Amy? The bars, the parties, the attitude. You're how old? How?" I blink at her, stunned.

"I haven't met anyone worthy of me," she says simply. "You've seen my friends. They're all girls or guys who identify as girls. And honestly, I've been saving myself."

"Saving yourself?" I scoff. "You don't even go to church."

She doesn't take the bait. Instead, she looks out the window again, eyes glassy with reflection. And then it clicks. The puzzle pieces I've been trying to fit together for years suddenly lock into place.

"You never introduced a guy to your dad who wasn't gay. And you never talked about a serious boyfriend. Not once. I mean, sure, I wondered if you might be gay, but it didn't matter. Not to your dad, not to me. So, we never brought it up. But this…"

"Now you're getting it." She sighs and folds her arms.

"I didn't know," I say, softly. "I swear, I didn't know."

"Well, now you do," she snaps. "I'm only telling you because I want to know if he's going to expect sex from me. I'm not comfortable with… selling my virginity. But I wouldn't mind tearing into his flesh with this." She pulls the whip out of her bag like it's a trophy.

I blink again. "But you own that! Why do you even have a whip if you're a virgin?"

"I've spanked a few guys," she says nonchalantly. "I'm into it. I've done things. I just haven't had intercourse."

My mouth drops open.

"Don't judge me," she bites. "At least I didn't get paid for it like you did. I just had some fun."

"You've *never* had intercourse?" I echo again, still trying to catch up.

"Hell no. They were all spoiled little boys living on trust funds. None of them could ever be the man I want."

I lean back, absorbing that. "Are you sure you're ready for someone like Matt? If you've never… I mean, his particular appetite might be overwhelming."

"I didn't say I'm going to marry him," she says with a roll of her eyes. "It's a first date. I'm not stupid. I just want to get to know him."

"Okay." I nod. "That's fair. But leave the whip with me, maybe?"

She clutches it. "No. I'm keeping it."

"All right, but listen. I'm telling you again because this could be your one chance. Don't fuck it up. Don't act like you did in my store this afternoon. Be cool. Treat him like you'd treat any other guy you're into. Don't fangirl. Don't fawn. Don't give him your résumé. Just… be real."

She scoffs. "I heard you the first time and I got it…I am real."

"You know what I mean. When Jessica ignored him, he couldn't take his eyes off her. He likes confidence. Not desperation. So, find that balance."

"I can do that." She nods.

"You sure?"

"Give me some credit, will you?" she huffs. "Just introduce us and disappear. I can take it from there. And again, I'm keeping the whip."

"Are you going to tell him?"

"Tell him what?" She flashes a wicked little smile and removes her headset as the helicopter touches down on the hotel's rooftop.

She pulls out a compact, checks her makeup, and adds a fresh coat of red to her lips like she's gearing up for a war she knows she'll win.

Bob greets us with his usual stoic expression and escorts us off the chopper. Amy's legs wobble slightly, but she squares her shoulders and keeps walking like she owns the rooftop. She really is perfect for someone like Pet. I hop out, wobbling some at first, but I quickly gain my balance. The adjustment does get easier every time.

A hotel staffer picks up Sadie's bag, holding it away from his body like it might explode, and grabs Amy's overnight bag too. He trails behind us as we head toward Matt's suite.

Bob opens the door and steps aside. Matt stands as we enter, looking like sin in a tailored suit and Gucci oxfords. He rises from the sofa with a smile that could melt steel.

Amy extends her hand, expecting a kiss, just like she does with every man she meets.

Matt doesn't disappoint. He lifts her fingers to his lips and kisses them softly before offering me a respectful nod.

Amy owns the moment. In that little black dress with the whip handle peeking from her bag, she's a vision of self-assurance wrapped in mystery. Matt's gaze lands on the whip, then flicks back to her mouth.

His smile deepens.

Game on.

"Matt." I snap my fingers to get his attention. "This is my stepdaughter, Amy. Amy, this is Matt."

"You can leave," she says, not even looking at me.

I glance to Matt, who gives the smallest nod, his eyes still locked on her. Guess I'm dismissed.

"Okay," I say, trying not to sound offended. "I'll just… leave you two to it."

Neither of them responds. Out the window, I catch a glimpse of the balcony table, set for two, a single candle flickering in the breeze. They've got it covered.

"Please take Sadie," Amy says, still without looking at me.

"No problem." I walk toward the door and take the small dog carrier from the man still holding it like it's radioactive. "Just you and me now, kid," I whisper to Sadie, patting her on the head. She licks my hand, grateful.

"Close the door," Amy calls.

Bob ushers me into the hallway and gently shuts it behind me. The man who held Sadie's bag moves into position like he's guarding state secrets.

"This way to your room, Miss Jolene," Bob says in that calm, old-school butler voice. "We've prepared everything you need, as well as a few provisions for the dog."

Sadie wags her tail and lets out a cheerful bark.

"Thanks, Bob. I'm not sure when she was last walked, so if someone could take her out now, I'd appreciate it."

"Of course. I'll send someone right away."

We step into the elevator, and I feel that old familiar guilt stirring in my gut. "Bob," I say, just before the doors close.

"Yes, miss?"

"About earlier…I want to apologize. I didn't mean…"

He lightly touches my shoulder. "No need, miss. It's already forgotten."

There's something about him. Something about his eyes, the way he carries himself, that tells me I can trust him. For Amy's sake, I hope I'm right. But if history's any indication, my instincts about people are… flawed.

Jolene's Adonis

Amy's a grown woman. She can take care of herself.

I repeat the mantra as we glide down to the floor just below Pet's penthouse.

When the elevator doors open, the hallway surprises me. It's not what I expect in a hotel. Sleek, quiet, only two doors on this entire floor. One to the north. One to the south. The third leads to a stairwell.

Bob opens the north door, revealing a suite so luxurious it could be mistaken for a high-end mid-century modern apartment. The raised kitchen overlooks a sunken living room with low-profile furnishings and clean lines. Floor-to-ceiling windows stretch across the far wall, offering an expansive view of the city. Two bedrooms branch off the main living space. It's simple, functional, but undeniably elegant in its design. It's even nicer than Pet's place. The only thing missing is a balcony. A second penthouse, maybe?

"Mr. D'Angelo has the only balcony in the building," Bob says, anticipating my question. "It adds to the illusion of floating mid-air."

"Very cool," I say with a little smile.

Bob gestures toward a door off the kitchen. "Primary suite's through there. I took the liberty of bringing some clothing down from Mr. D'Angelo's rooms in your size, as well as toiletries and cosmetics. If you need anything else, I'm just a call away."

"Thank you, Bob." I reach into my bag for a tip, but he lifts his hand.

"No need, miss. I'm Mr. D'Angelo's private butler. I work on salary alone."

I blush and step toward him for a half-hug. He lightly pats my shoulder and backs away with a little smile.

"If that will be all… someone will be up for the dog shortly." He disappears, leaving me alone with Sadie.

I pull her out of the carrier. She spins in delighted circles, barking, tail wagging. I check her bag. It's empty. No toys. No food.

"Amy," I mutter, shaking my head.

In the kitchen, I find two labeled bowls and a can of dog food. Better than nothing. I fill the water bowl, sink into the ultra-soft sofa, and then pick up the phone.

"Front desk," a cheery voice says.

"Yes, um... I was wondering if you have any dog food or toys."

"We have a Happy Tails package in the gift shop. It includes food, toys, a brush, toothbrush, peanut butter-flavored toothpaste, a rawhide-free easy to digest bone, gourmet treats, and anything else you may need during your stay. Would you like one sent up?"

"Yes, please. But how much is it?"

"It's complimentary, Miss Jolene. Mr. D'Angelo has an open tab on your behalf in the shop, restaurant, bar, and spa. No limit."

Of course he does. "Thank you."

Sadie snuggles onto my leg while I flip through the room service menu. Eventually, I settle on a black bean burger and fries, and a glass of wine. A knock at the door makes Sadie explode with excitement.

"Who is it, Sadie?" I ask, smiling as she jumps in place while I open the door.

A young man stands outside, holding a massive gift basket.

"Happy Tails for you, miss."

He steps inside, drops the basket on the coffee table, and kneels to pet Sadie.

"Are you the little one who needs a walk?" he asks, scooping her up as she slathers him with kisses.

"There's a fenced area in back just for our furry guests," he says on his way out. "She'll have it all to herself tonight."

Room service arrives just as the dog walker returns. I tip them both and sit down for my mini feast. Sadie munches on her kibble while I finish my burger and wine, then carry her to the primary bedroom.

The silk nightgown and panties in the drawer surprise me, but I slip them on after a quick rinse. I'm too tired to blow-dry my hair, so I leave it damp and collapse onto the bed. Sadie curls into a ball beside me.

A knock on the hotel room door jolts me. I groan, wrapping a robe around me and peering through the peephole.

It's Amy.

I open the door and she bursts in, looking agitated.

"I have to talk to you," she says, breathless.

"What's wrong?"

She throws herself dramatically onto the sofa. "Remember what I told you earlier?"

"About?"

"You know…" She gestures vaguely to her pelvis. "How I've never…"

"Had sex," I say flatly.

"Yeah, that." She sighs. "I like him. I want to spend the night. He asked me. But I'm not ready for... you know."

"Did you tell him?"

"Of course not! He'd think I'm lame."

"Then make him wait. He wants you to take control. Call him. Say you're staying here and you'll see him tomorrow."

"I don't want the night to end. I think he's my soul mate."

"You *just* met him."

"I know. I just *know*." Her eyes sparkle and it hits me. I've never seen her look like this.

I reach for her hand. She lets me. Progress.

"It's a big step. You're old enough to make your own choices."

"I'm ready. I just don't want to seem easy."

"You won't. Guys like him respect boundaries."

"You think so?"

"I know so. Take it slow. Make him earn it."

Amy smiles, then pulls her hand back. "Okay. I'll tell him I'm staying here."

"Good girl. He'll respect you more for it."

I stand up. "This suite has two bedrooms. Take the one over there. I'm going to bed."

"Thanks," she whispers.

I curl up next to Sadie, too restless to sleep. I miss the boat, the marina, the lapping water, the far-off chimes of the buoys.

At some point, I hear the door open and close again. Sadie doesn't stir. Neither do I.

Finally, sleep comes.

44

Orlando: The Morning After

It's just past 3 a.m. when I start the long walk back to the marina. The walk there was easy, but in this fog of whiskey and unresolved grief, each step I take now feels like a reckoning. I'm weaving past shuttered bait shops and darkened beach motels with flickering neon signs, the kind that buzz until they give up. My boots crunch over gravel and beer caps, and the coastal wind slaps my face like a warning I'm too stubborn to heed.

Jessica bought the first two rounds. We spent the better part of the night cloaked in dim bar light, our voices low, sharing old intelligence and new suspicions. We hatched our plan—bait, pressure, confession. And I knocked back drink after drink, hoping the burn would drown the guilt I can't name out loud.

It hits harder now that Jolene's gone. The first night I've spent without her in view. No monitor. No dockside glance. No excuse to hover. I hate that I miss her. I hate that it doesn't feel like surveillance anymore. It feels like absence. And that absence cuts.

Hell.

I kept telling myself it was surveillance. Safety. Protection. But it stopped being about the mission weeks ago. Maybe the first night I saw her curled up on the couch, muttering Wesley's name in her sleep.

I didn't mean to feel this way. I judged Wesley hard for getting involved. Thought he let his guard down. Thought he was selfish for dragging her into something she never should've touched. But now I get it. She has this pull. She gets under your skin without trying.

I kick a rock down the road and watch it skitter into a drainage ditch. My mouth tastes like whiskey and regret.

Wesley. He'd hate this. Or maybe he'd laugh. The bastard always did enjoy irony.

He used to say, "You never see the bullet that kills you. You just see the girl holding the damn gun." He didn't mean Jolene. Not then. But he could've.

I flash back to the night in Bogotá when he first told me about the blood jewels. We were holed up in a crumbling safehouse with a bottle of rum and no heat. He laid out the whole twisted network: how people were being auctioned off under the guise of tourism, how certain cartel families used the jewels not just as currency, but as trophies. As proof they owned everything, even innocence.

Jolene's Adonis

He said, "You take the jewels, you take their proof. Strip them of their trophies, and they bleed shame instead of pride."

It was confusing to me at the time. I thought he was playing cowboy. Tilting at windmills. But he was right. The jewels aren't just valuable. They're proof, physical proof of unspeakable crimes. Each one connected to something. A date. A transaction. A monster. Wesley stole them not to get rich, but to destroy the system from the inside. And all that's missing is the ledger, the final piece that ties it all together. The raven…

And now they're here. On Jolene's hand. Hidden in her boat. Carried across borders.

I never thought I'd see them. Not after Bogotá. But now I know. He took them. Left them with Jolene. To keep them safe. To finish what he started.

She asked me to sail with her. She trusts me. That trust wasn't earned; I'm a liar. And worse, I'm betraying my best friend.

Wesley. My partner. My friend. My regret.

By the time I get to the marina, the stars are starting to fade. The boat's silhouette is barely visible in the early haze, bobbing like it's restless without her. Just like me.

I climb on board, crack open a water bottle, and toss myself onto the bunk. Sleep hits me like a body blow.

I wake late to a hangover that feels like punishment. The sun is high, the cabin sweltering. My mouth tastes like salt and sweat.

I groan as I push myself upright, head pounding in rhythm with my pulse. I crack another water bottle and drink like it holds forgiveness.

No Jolene.

I stagger into the tiny head, splash water on my face, and catch my reflection in the mirror. Red-rimmed eyes. Jaw clenched. Guilt etched into every line.

"You're in love with her," I say to the man in the glass.

It's not a revelation. It's a fact. Cold and permanent.

For a man who builds his life on contingencies, Jolene is a variable I never planned. I calculated routes, identities, aliases, leverage. I anticipated betrayal, bribes, even bullets. But not this. Not her.

And I resented Wesley for it. For feeling first. For acting on it. For leaving her with nothing but danger and ghosts.

But she's already in danger.

Jolene's Adonis

Me staying away won't change that. Hiding the truth from her won't keep her safe. If anything, it leaves her unarmed. And I swore I'd never leave another woman defenseless. Not after what I've seen. Not after what I've done.

The guilt I carry—for Wesley's death, for falling for Jolene, for pretending I could stay cold—it burns away like fog under the rising sun. I've spent most of my life keeping people at a distance. Clean lines. Calculated choices. Nothing left to chance. Relationships were tools, a means to an end. But Jolene… she's not a means. She's a storm. A wild, chaotic force I can't resist anymore. God help me, I don't want to.

I've tried. Tried to convince myself it's wrong, that it's too dangerous, that Wesley wouldn't have wanted this. But he told her in that letter to go on. To find love. To be happy. Would he want her to be happy with *me*? I hope so. Because what feels true— what feels *real*—is how she looked at me before she left, like she was already counting on me to follow.

Maybe this is what Wesley meant when he warned me not to let the job swallow me whole. Maybe that's why he wrote her that letter. Not just to protect her, but to hand her off to someone who could do what he couldn't. Someone who could stand in the light with her.

I'm tired of hiding. Of pretending that loving someone means letting them go. That's bullshit. Jolene doesn't need another ghost haunting her choices. She needs a partner. And I need her, not as a mission, not as an obligation, but because the moment I saw her fighting to stay alive in this broken world, I started believing I could, too.

So no, I don't feel guilty anymore. Not for loving her. Not for wanting a future that scares the hell out of me. Because love—that messy, terrifying, inconvenient thing—is the only clean truth I have left in this goddamn story. And for once, I'm going to follow it. Even if it kills me.

It's time I stop hiding.

I'm not just a shadow anymore.

I'm Franco. I'm Orlando.

And I'm hers, whether she knows it or not.

45

Jolene: Candy

Wet doggie kisses wake me the next morning.

"Okay, okay. I'm up." I pat Sadie's head and wipe slobber from my cheek with the silky hotel sheet. "You ready to go out?"

Her tail wags like mad, and she bows with her front paws stretched out in a classic let's-play pose. I roll out of bed, scoop her into my arms, and shuffle half-asleep into the living room.

"Amy!" I call as I stop outside the door of the adjoining room. "Sadie's ready for her walk. Amy?"

Sadie wiggles impatiently and launches herself out of my arms, landing with a thud on the carpet. My heart lurches as I bend down, but she's fine. She licks her paws, shakes her body, then pounces on the door like a wild animal. She scratches and yelps at the bottom, her little nails ripping into the carpet like she thinks she can claw her way through it.

I straighten and knock, brushing imaginary sweat from my brow as Sadie continues her assault on the door. Shredded threads of synthetic fiber float in the air around her. *Great. There goes the deposit* is the first thing that comes to mind, but then I remember I know the owner, and how. I sigh and reach for the handle.

"Alright, alright. Let's see if your mommy's in there."

Surely Amy would've heard all this if she were awake. But if she's anything like she was when she lived with Wesley and me, she's dead to the world. Every morning was the same: hungover, dramatic, and impossible to wake without a full-scale assault. Pillows thrown, names called. Wesley used to drag her out of bed and she screamed like we were waterboarding her. Nothing's changed.

"Amy?" I call again, more cautious this time as I ease open the door, hands raised like I'm entering a combat zone, half-expecting a pillow to the face or maybe something heavier.

But nothing could've prepared me for what I see.

I stop in the doorway; my hands still raised, and I stifle a laugh that threatens to explode.

A few weeks ago, I might've frozen in horror. But now? Now I just want to laugh until I cry.

From tiny white iPod speakers dangling by cords from the bedposts, the 80s hit *"I Want Candy"* plays at full volume. It's not exactly blasting, but loud enough in that tiny speaker kind of way that she doesn't hear me knock. Amy stands on the left side of the bed, dressed in a red camisole trimmed with white fur, licking chocolate from her finger as she serenades a very naked Pet.

"So sweet," she coos in a singsong voice, eyes locked on him like he's dessert.

Pet's wrists are cuffed—pink, fluffy ones—secured behind his head. The bed is stripped and covered in plastic, and his entire body is smeared in baked goods. Not paint. Not oil. *Pastries.* He's a living, breathing dessert tray.

Chocolate coats his chest, frosting streaks his thighs, and whipped cream is shaped into a heart that stretches from nipple to nipple and down toward his candy-coated pubic hair. A maraschino cherry—an actual cherry—is clenched between his teeth. His erection pulses beneath a line of glossy pink syrup.

Yep. That's my stepdaughter, alright.

"Sadie! No!" Amy shrieks as Sadie leaps onto the bed and starts licking the whipped cream off Pet's nipple. Amy waves her chocolate-covered hand frantically, shooing her away.

Sadie cowers, jumps down, then sits loyally at the bedside, licking her lips and waiting for praise. Meanwhile, I lose the battle. My laughter bursts free.

Amy whips around, eyes narrowed. "You think this is funny?"

"I don't mean to laugh," I say, holding up my hands in surrender. "But this... what is this? Why are you wasting so much food?"

Pet spits out the cherry. It lands in front of Sadie, who sniffs it, wrinkles her nose, and sits with her head tilted, just as confused as I am.

"We're not wasting. We're sploshing," he says matter-of-factly. "Care to join us?"

"Like hell!" Amy shouts, snatching a banana cream pie from a dessert-stacked dresser that looks like a bakery exploded on it. Pies. Cupcakes. Candy jars. Whipped cream cans. She draws her arm back like a slingshot, aiming the pie square at my face.

Thankfully I haven't made it far into the room. I spin on my heel, slipping slightly on the carpet, and grab for the door.

The pie smacks the other side with a wet *thwack*, sliding down with the unmistakable sound of foil scraping wood. I burst into full-blown laughter just as the door swings back open.

Amy stands armed with a vanilla cupcake in one hand and a can of whipped cream in the other.

I turn to flee again, but I'm too slow.

The cupcake hits me square on the back of the head. A stream of whipped cream follows, spraying everything between us like a snowstorm of sugar.

I spin around just in time to see Amy racing toward the door.

Oh, it's on!

I scoop up what's left of the cupcake and hurl it straight at her face. It hits her squarely, crumbs and frosting splattering as she stumbles back, caught off guard. While she's wiping at her cheek, I shove past her and dive toward the bed, grabbing fistfuls of desserts and shaping them into balls like I'm in a sugar-fueled snowball fight.

Amy rushes me.

I pull my arm back to launch one just as she slams into me, knocking me backward onto the bed, right across Pet's dessert-covered legs. We both burst into laughter as I swat at her playfully, smearing frosting and whipped cream across her face, her neck, her hair. She doesn't hold back either. The song plays from those tiny speakers, and the upbeat tempo somehow makes the whole ridiculous scene even more hilarious.

I reach for a chocolate cupcake and smear it onto her nose. The frosting sticks, making her look completely ridiculous.

"You look like a cuddly Christmas teddy bear with a shiny brown nose," I tell her, doubled over with laughter.

In retaliation, Amy pinches my right nipple through my robe and *twists*. The laughter dies in my throat.

"Ouch!" I scream, pushing her off and scrambling to my feet at the edge of the bed. I brush crumbs and sticky globs from my backside. "That's unfair! I didn't hurt you!"

"Who says we have to fight fair?" she says, flashing a wicked, catlike grin.

"Alright, you win," I mutter, rubbing the now-throbbing spot through the fabric.

Sadie races past us, her little legs eating up the distance to the door, until she catches the scent of banana cream pie and veers hard to the left. She dives into it face-first.

"Great! Now look what you've done!" Amy shouts, snatching Sadie away from the mess and thrusting her into my arms. Sadie's fur is now sticky with chocolate syrup and her face is slathered in cream. "Clean her up."

"She's your dog," I protest, shooting a look at Pet for backup.

He just stares at me. His eyes are filled amusement and... something else. *Hunger.*

His already-hard cock twitches and grows stiffer. The playful chaos clearly worked him up even more.

Exhibitionist. Eccentric. Total maniac. Honestly, they're a perfect match.

I throw up my hands and take the dog. "Fine. I'll take care of Sadie. He's all yours."

Amy rolls her eyes at me, then turns to him with a sultry grin. "With pleasure," she purrs.

That look—predator and playmate rolled into one—comes back into her eyes as she guides me out of the room and slams the door shut behind me, clicking the lock. So much for taking it slow. Not that I should be surprised. Amy's never listened to my advice.

I carry Sadie across the suite to the oversized bathtub, turning on the water and cradling her in one arm while testing the temperature with the other. She seems surprisingly calm in my arms, licking the remnants of cream from her face. Once there's a few inches of warm water in the tub, I lower her in and grab a bottle of oatmeal dog shampoo from the Happy Tails basket. The lather builds fast, and I rinse her with a drinking glass from the sink before wrapping her in a soft towel.

"You were so good," I whisper, rubbing her down thoroughly. Her damp fur fluffs slightly under the towel.

As soon as I set her down, she squats on the tiled floor and pees in a long, steady stream that spreads across the grout like a punishment for all the chaos.

I freeze. She looks up at me, big brown eyes wide with guilt, then shrinks into the corner like she expects to be scolded.

I kneel and hold out my hand gently. "It's okay," I say, my voice soft. "It's not your fault."

Sadie inches toward me, licks my fingers, and then trots into the bedroom. She hops onto the bed, circles once, and curls herself into the comforter like the world hasn't just exploded in whipped cream and chaos.

After mopping up Sadie's accident with a stack of paper towels and some liquid soap, I pull the handle to drain the tub and rinse it with a washcloth. Once it's clean, I refill it with steamy hot water, adding a generous splash of bubbles. While it fills, I shrug off my robe and step into the shower stall to rinse the mess from my hair.

I pour a handful of strawberry-scented shampoo into my palm and work it into the sticky, matted strands, still coated in sugary icing. It takes two full lathers and rinses before my hair finally feels clean again. With most of the damage handled, I shut off the shower and sink into the waiting tub, surrounded by a sea of bubbles.

Oh, it feels luxurious.

I throw my head back and close my eyes. It's been weeks since I've had a real bath. I miss this.

Before Wesley died, I lived for this—hot water, candles flickering around the edge of the tub, and a glass of wine in hand. After hours of sweating in a shop filled with grease and blowtorch heat, a bubble bath made me feel human again. Feminine. Alive.

Now that I'm living on the boat, all I've got is a cramped little stall. No room for bubbles. No candles. Definitely no wine. Just soap, water, and necessity. This—right now—is the first relief I've felt in weeks, maybe even months.

As the tub fills to the brim, I lean back again, eyes closed, letting that old feeling wash over me. That softness. That sensuality. It takes me back to before everything got so damn complicated. Before Wesley left.

I remember the nights he joined me in the bath, his hands sliding over every inch of me beneath the bubbles. I miss that asshole. I miss his hands. His body. The feeling of being wanted.

I try to push the memory away, but it mixes too easily with the image of what I saw in the other room, Pet, naked and tied up, chocolate glistening on his skin, that thick erection twitching. His moans. His mouth.

I wonder what he tastes like…

Selena's voice echoes in my head. *Do you bake?*

At the time, it felt like one of her many strange questions. But now it makes perfect sense. She and

Pet wanted to introduce me to *sploshing*. That's what he called it, right? It looked ridiculous. Messy. Intense.

Fun.

And right now, I could use a little fun.

My hand slides down my body, over my breast, down my ribs, into the soft, wet warmth between my thighs. My fingers find my clit while my imagination does the rest. I picture Pet with his candy-coated cock in my mouth, my tongue tracing the glossy sweetness, his hips moving with mine. I moan softly, licking my lips, eyes shut tight.

The image loops in my mind. Pet sprawled across the bed, all that decadent mess, the way his body twitched when he saw me.

But then… Amy's smile creeps in. Then Selena's with her Cheshire-cat grin from that first day.

And then Wesley's face. Not the smiling one. The disappointed one.

"Damn it!" I mutter, yanking my hand away and splashing the water in frustration. The desire drains as quickly as it came.

With a sigh, I wash the rest of my body, gently avoiding my still-sore nipple, then step out and wrap myself in a towel. I brush my hair and teeth, wash my face, and walk over to the closet to run my fingers along the beautiful clothes Bob picked out for me.

They're stunning. It's a shame I can't take them all home. But the pieces Pet bought yesterday should arrive at the marina by the time I get back. That's something.

I pull on a steel-gray designer sundress made of soft knit fabric. It hugs my body with just the right amount of stretch, the crossed bodice dipping between my breasts. I pause at the mirror and pull my hair into a loose knot at the base of my neck. Even without makeup, I don't look half-bad. My skin has that sun-kissed glow from riding my bike everywhere. My eyes—hazel and wide—look clear. Strong.

"You can do this," I whisper to the woman in the mirror.

She doesn't look convinced. She knows what's coming. She knows that once I step out of Pet's dreamworld, I'll be wading into something far more dangerous with nothing but a pair of red stilettos to ground me.

But she's not naive. She's grounded.

I shift my feet, turning side to side, then spin. The soft gray fabric lifts with the motion, exposing my legs and those bold red heels. I freeze mid-twirl in front of the mirror, skirt still swinging.

J. Jaden

The woman staring back at me doesn't look unsure anymore.

She looks like a badass.

I've got this.

46

Jolene: The Ride

Before I shoulder my purse and scoop Sadie from the bed, I reach for the hotel phone and press the button for the front desk. A polite male voice answers.

"Could you please send a dog walker to my room?" I ask.

Sadie stares at me with those big hopeful eyes, tail thumping against my arm.

"Of course, Miss. I'll send someone right away."

"Thank you," I reply, hanging up the receiver.

I run my hand down Sadie's back, stroking her soft fur as I wrestle with the thought of taking her home. Amy's clearly preoccupied, and there's no room for a dog in her strange, fetish-laced lifestyle. But what am I supposed to do with her? I'm on a mission, unsure of what George is really up to, or what Wesley meant when he wrote, *'Everything isn't as it seems.'*

He wanted me to trust his words, but how can I? Wesley lied to me about so much. Jessica, on the other hand, she's never betrayed me. And George has never given me a reason not to trust him. Not like Wesley did.

Still, I can't ignore the warning. Something's off. I'm determined to get answers over dinner with George and Jessica... and dragging a dog along doesn't exactly fit into that plan. Especially not on a bike.

Cradling Sadie against my chest, I walk back into the living room to leave a quick note for Amy and Pet while I wait for the dog walker. A tray of breakfast items sits on the kitchen bar with coffee, orange juice, bagels with a handwritten card that says "vegan" next to them, peanut butter, and fresh fruit. Everything neatly arranged. The whipped cream trail and the smashed vanilla cupcake are gone without a trace. Spotless.

My face flushes the same red as my stilettos. *Oh for fuck's sake.* Who cleaned all that up? And how did they do it so quickly and quietly? I can't even imagine what Pet's staff thinks of me. *Of us.*

Sadie sniffs the freshly cleaned floor and gives it a quick lick before scampering over to the water bowl. She drinks like she's trying to wash a regrettable taste off her tongue. She probably is. I glance down at her and try not to cringe.

Jolene's Adonis

After her drink, she hops up onto the sofa, curls into a perfect little ball, and closes her eyes like the morning hasn't been one chaotic mess after another.

Then her ears twitch, and her head pops up, her eyes locked on the door. A second later, there's a soft knock.

I walk over and pull it open just a few inches. Bob stands off to the side, and behind him, the same young man who walked Sadie the night before gives me a warm smile.

Sadie leaps into his arms and smothers his face in kisses.

"Haha!" he laughs. "You remember me, don't you?"

Her tail wags frantically, and I breathe a sigh of relief. She's in good hands.

"I'll bring her back as quickly as possible and give her a quick brushing too. Looks like she just had a bath," he says with a smile.

"Thank you. She did," I say, nodding at Bob as I push the door closed.

I toss my purse onto the sofa and settle into the kitchen. I spread peanut butter over a bagel and pour myself a cup of coffee. It's not like Chef John's, but at this point, any caffeine will do.

I've barely taken a few bites when the guy returns, Sadie cradled in his arms like she just ran a marathon. He sets her down and she flops onto the couch with a dramatic sigh. Freshly brushed, she's a big puffball. I smile and slip another $20 bill into his hand before returning to my breakfast and the barely started note.

But before I can write more than *Dear Amy and Matt*, the adjoining door opens.

Amy strolls into the room in a pale pink satin robe with a gold "D" embroidered on the chest and matching slippers. Definitely not hotel-issued. Probably another one of Pet's private collection. Her raven hair is tangled and wet, her eyes red-rimmed and puffy, proof of a sleepless night.

Sadie lifts her head and sniffs the air in Amy's direction before getting a gentle pat.

Amy crosses the room, pulls out a chair, and joins me at the table. She pours herself some coffee, glances down at the notepad, and raises an eyebrow at how little I've written. I feel suddenly exposed.

She takes a long sip of coffee before finally breaking the silence.

"So," she says, startling me slightly. "About earlier… we didn't… well, it's none of your business anyway. But we're just having fun right now. Feeling things out. Seeing if we click. You can probably guess. It's going well."

"Yeah. I'd say so." I smirk. "I heard the door open last night. Thought you left to go back to Pet's room. I didn't expect to walk in and see…"

I let the sentence trail off, realizing I just dropped a bomb without warning. *Oh well.* She's seen it all now… And she knows what I saw. No explanation necessary.

It's weird how just yesterday I was nervously backspacing the name *Pet* out of a text… and now I'm saying it to Amy like it's completely normal.

Well. *Almost* normal.

"Yeah. I know. He told me about his little nickname. And you sure got an eyeful!" she grins. "I hope you saw enough—because that's the last time you'll see anything under Sugar Lips' clothes."

"Sugar Lips?" I cringe.

"I'm still workin' on it," Amy says with a shrug. "I can't call him Pet. That's his skank-given name."

"Selena's not a skank," I snap, sharper than I mean to. "She's my friend."

Amy rises from her chair and starts scanning the floor around the table.

I follow her gaze. "Did you lose something?"

"Yeah!" She flops dramatically back into the chair. "My give a fuck."

And just like that, playful Amy leaves the building. The bitch is back. I shake my head.

"Anyway," she says, waving her hand impatiently, "the skank won't be coming back. She's served her purpose. I'm in charge now."

"In charge?" I lean forward, not sure I heard her right. "I *distinctly* remember telling you that's not what Pet had in mind."

Wait. Speaking of Pet... the breakfast setup was for three. Why isn't he here?

"Where is he?" I ask.

"He's in the shower," she says with a shrug. "Doesn't matter. He's mine now. And since you did something nice for me—setting me up with that sweet ass of his—I've decided to return the favor."

Oh no. *Here it comes.*

"What kind of favor?" I flinch a little, bracing for the ridiculous.

"I have some information that may interest you."

"What kind of information?" I want to plug my ears. I don't trust Amy with my coffee order, let alone my emotional well-being. Whatever she's about to say, it's probably cruel or manipulative, or both.

"It's about a certain someone."

I lean back in my chair and brace for impact. I know that look in her eye. This is gonna hurt.

"That guy you shamelessly threw yourself at last night."

My heart tightens. "What about him?"

"I just thought you should know he has his own agenda. It's not just about getting into your crusty thong."

"Excuse me?" My face burns. The jab at my underwear, and everything under it, is typical Amy. Belittling me seems to fuel her. I'm not even sure she knows how to speak without insulting me. But how would she know anything about Orlando? She just met him.

"Listen," she says, holding up a hand, "I'm not getting into the details. There are some things you need to figure out on your own. Clear that lust-fogged brain of yours and *be careful*. That's all I'm saying."

"Okay," I reply slowly, not because I agree, but because I know better than to argue. This is Amy. She never says anything without an angle. And she never does anything just to be nice. That's not in her DNA.

Still… why would she lie about someone she just met? It's not like she wants Orlando. She has Pet now. Well, Matt. She wouldn't need to sabotage me just for sport… would she?

"How do you even know anything about him?" I ask. "You *just* met him. And why would you tell me? What's your angle?"

"No angle," she says, shrugging again. "I know more than you think. And you're not as bad as I thought you were, so I'm just giving you a heads-up. Do what you want with it. Trust me. Don't. I don't give a fuck. I'm just paying you back. We're even."

She pauses. Her eyes narrow.

"Unless…"

I don't like the way she says that word. "Unless what?"

"Unless you take Sadie with you." She lets out a giggle, like this is all some game. "I've got my hands full here. The dog likes you, though I have no idea why."

She leans back, kicks her slippered foot onto the table like she owns the place, and gives me a smug little grin.

"Anyway, she needs time to get used to life at the marina. If I decide to live there. I don't know what's gonna happen. So just take her with you, and I'll owe you a favor."

I glance over at the couch where Sadie's curled up in a tiny fluffy ball. She's safe at the hotel, sure. The staff loves her. But let's be real, Amy's not going to walk her, feed her, or even remember she exists once that bedroom door closes again. I know what that look in Amy's eyes means. She's not coming out for a while.

"Fine," I say with a sigh. "Agreed."

Amy's lips twitch into a half-smile, clearly expecting more resistance. But what she doesn't get is that I'll always put the dog's needs before my own. Sadie didn't ask to be caught in this mess.

"Candy Man wanted me to pass along a message," she says.

"*Candy Man?*" I blink. And then I *wince*. I can't take it anymore.

Amy's trying so hard to be clever, but she just sounds ridiculous. "You're killing me, Amy. Seriously. Pet was at least kind of cute and mysterious. But now? You're turning him into a cartoon. A stripper. A punchline."

I throw my hands in the air. "He has a real name, you know. You called him Matt at the store. If you actually want something real with him, just call him Matt. It's better than anything else you've come up with."

I narrow my eyes. "And if you're smart, you'll drop the attitude about Selena. She's been around a *lot* longer than you. If Pet hears you calling her names…"

I don't even have to finish the sentence.

"Damn, you're such a nag!" she groans, rolling her eyes. "I said I'm working on it."

She pauses, then says more deliberately, "*Matt* said you can take the chopper home, or choose a car from his fleet. The bike won't work if you're bringing Sadie. If you take the car, the favor's paid. I owe you nothing. Your choice."

I blink. "I can have a car? *Choose* a car? To *keep*?"

My brain short-circuits. Pet dropping seventy grand on clothes was already outrageous. Excessive. Unnecessary. But somehow… fun. I accepted it because I knew he could afford it.

But a *car?*

I'm not even sleeping with the guy.

"Are you deaf?" Amy snaps. "I said choose a car. How much clearer do I have to make it for you to understand? It's a gift. A favor paid. It's yours. Do whatever the hell you want with it."

My eyes narrow. "A car is too much. I'll borrow one, but I'm bringing it back. I can't keep it. It's…

inappropriate." I'm saying it aloud like that'll make it feel more true.

"I said do whatever the fuck you want," she repeats, exasperated. "Honestly, he feels guilty. We pieced together that the condo he foreclosed on was Daddy's. He's trying to make it up to you with expensive gifts, very generous ones, if you ask me. Gifts you don't deserve, but here we are."

And there it is. That's why Pet—*Matt*—was in Port Aransas in the first place. To foreclose on *my* condo. I should be mad. Furious, even. But I'm not. Strangely, it might've been the best thing that ever happened to me. Of course, I'm not telling *her* that. No way. But suddenly, everything makes sense. He wants to take care of me, provide for me. And under all that fetish stuff, which might not be everyone's thing, he's actually … a decent guy.

"If it's really a gift," I mutter, "you might want to work on your delivery. It sucks."

Amy smirks.

I try to ignore the way my moral compass wobbles. Ever since Selena walked into my life with Pet on a literal leash, that compass hasn't pointed in any clear direction. It just spins, right, wrong, appropriate, inappropriate… who even knows anymore?

"I'll take the car. And Sadie," I finally say. "But you need to tell him he doesn't owe me anything else. And one condition."

Amy groans. "What now?"

"You have to quit acting like a spoiled bitch. The car is from Pet. The dog is your responsibility. I'm not saying you'll owe me, but if I'm going to take care of her, then you need to show some fucking gratitude and respect."

Amy's grin stretches wide, amused and, maybe, just a little impressed. "There's your spine. Knew it was still in there somewhere." She turns her head toward the hallway. "Bob!"

The door cracks open, and Sadie perks up like one of Pavlov's dogs waiting for a treat.

"Good morning, Miss Jolene. Miss Amy," Bob says as he steps in.

He follows Amy's instructions and leads me and Sadie down to the basement of the hotel into what I can only describe as Pet's personal garage. And holy hell!

At least a dozen cars line the walls, parked in flawless formation with just enough space to drive through the center. Bob describes the cars as we walk. "On the right are the classics: a 1950s-style powder blue Jaguar XK120 with a white ragtop, a fully restored 1939 Pontiac Deluxe Ghost Car with transparent panels and all, and a black 1934 Ford V8."

The car looks like it was pulled straight from a *Bonnie and Clyde* getaway scene.

"On the left, are your modern choices: a sleek white Maserati Spyder, just delivered yesterday, after the driver mentioned it to Mr. D'Angelo and he couldn't stand the thought of missing out, a navy blue BMW 7 Series, a candy apple red Chevrolet Corvette C5 convertible, a maroon Jaguar S-Type, a silver Chrysler Sebring convertible, and a black Toyota Prius, for the days when Mr. D'Angelo wants to blend in."

I shake my head. It's not just a garage. It's a damn showroom.

I stop in front of the Ghost Car and blink. "Wow," is all I can manage.

"That's Mr. D'Angelo's pride and joy," Bob says, stepping beside me. "The original Ghost Car. He bought it at auction for close to $400,000."

"Wow," I repeat, softer this time, still processing the fact that I'm even in this garage.

Bob leans in conspiratorially. "You're free to choose whichever car you'd like, Miss Jolene, but I wouldn't recommend the Pontiac. It's a showpiece. Drinks gas and rides like a bathtub on roller skates."

I raise both hands. "Oh, she's gorgeous, but yeah, not exactly practical."

I move down the line and pause in front of the Prius, parked next to the Sebring convertible. One screams practicality and fuel efficiency. The other promises sunshine, wind, and freedom.

I glance at Sadie, who looks far too regal for anything boxy and efficient.

I point to the Sebring. "That one."

Bob gives a small bow and retrieves a Chrysler key ring from his inside pocket. Of course he has it ready. I shouldn't be surprised.

"There's already a pet harness installed in the passenger seat," he says, gesturing toward the car. "Mr. D'Angelo remembered you mentioned having a Mustang convertible. He thought you might enjoy something with the top down."

So it's not just that I'm predictable. He listens. *Remembers things.*

I strap Sadie in, double-check the buckles, and slide into the driver's seat. It's soft, the dash smells like new money, and when I turn the key, the engine hums like it's purring just for me.

We roll out of the garage and onto the busy San Antonio streets. I crane my neck, hoping to catch a glimpse of Pet's glass balcony, but traffic moves too fast past the building.

I punch the gas.

Tires squeal as we hit the southbound highway.

"Woo hoo!" I shout, laughing as the wind whips my hair around and Sadie's ears flap beside me like tiny white flags of freedom.

I don't know exactly where this road is taking me.

But for the first time in a long time… I'm ready to go.

47

Jolene: Betrayal

The two-hour drive down the nearly deserted road between San Antonio and Corpus Christi is peaceful and glorious. For the first time in days, I feel like I've won the damn lottery.

I should feel something, sadness, maybe, over the fact that it was Pet who foreclosed on my condo. But the truth is, I suspected it. And that condo? That was the life I shared with Wesley. That chapter's over. I'm not that woman anymore. The woman I am now? She'll trade a condo for a convertible any day.

Before we hit the highway, I raise the top and crack Sadie's window just enough to let in a gentle breeze. She lifts herself as high as her harness allows, front paws braced on the seat, determined not to miss a single thing flashing past. Her ears perk up and twitch with every sound, and the wind ruffles her freshly brushed curls. But like Amy, her stubborn streak outweighs her need for rest. She insists on sitting up, alert and watchful, even as the rhythm of the road gently rocks her back and forth.

Eventually, after about thirty minutes, she gives in and settles back into the padded harness. Her head sinks down onto the strap, and within minutes, she's asleep.

"Sadie." I gently rub her back as I merge from I-37 onto South Padre Island Drive. She stirs but doesn't wake up fully. Even though she slept most of the way, it's nice having her here. Quiet company is better than none at all.

I cruise through the heart of Corpus, cross the causeway onto Padre Island, pass the neighborhood where Jessica and George live, then take the left turn toward Port Aransas. I lower the top and the wind kicks up as we get closer to the shore. I'm glad I tied my hair into a knot, though a few rebellious strands have escaped and now hang around my face.

I pull into the marina parking lot and score a space on the first row. I can't help but smile. Lisa lost her fight with management about assigning parking by slip number. Since her boat is on the first dock, she wanted the closest spot. She tried to rope Wesley into it too, since his slip was just a few spaces down from hers. But he and I were always the same—happy to park further out and get a little cardio in on the extra steps. Today, though? Today I'm grateful for the short walk. All I can think about is getting cleaned up and making it to Jessica's on time.

I adjust the rearview mirror and try to finger-comb my hair into something vaguely presentable.

Then I unclip Sadie from the harness, snap on her leash, and we hop out. I walk her to the small patch of grass just outside the docks. She does her business quickly, then heads straight down the dock toward the boat like she owns the place. For a dog who's spent most of her life in a purse, she moves with surprising confidence. I keep the leash short, letting her lead, but never getting more than a few feet ahead.

We pass Lisa and Larry's boat. I slow down a bit when we near Orlando's. Nothing. No sign of life. My shoulders sag just a little, but I keep walking.

As *My Knotty Jolene* comes into view, something feels... off. The deck cushions are flipped over, and the hatch door swings wide in the wind, creaking and slamming against the frame with each gust.

"There you are!" Lisa calls from behind me. I turn to see her jogging over. "I tried ringing you, but you didn't answer. Left you a bunch of messages. I was just about to try again when I saw you pull up in that posh convertible. Where'd that come from?"

I brush off her question and cut straight to mine. "What happened? Did Amy do this?"

I rack my brain, trying to remember what the boat looked like last night. I glanced at it when I was deciding whether to pack, and I don't remember anything being out of place.

"Early this morning, Larry heard a noise and stepped outside. He saw two blokes legging it from your boat. Their backs were to him, and they were moving fast. He reckoned they were speaking in some foreign language. Not English. Their voices were muffled, and they were gone before he could do much."

"Did anyone else see them? Were they carrying anything?" I swallow hard. *The lockbox.* Please don't let them have taken the lockbox.

"Larry said he didn't spot anything in their hands. I told him we should ring you before phoning the police, just in case they were mates of Amy's or something."

"Has anyone checked the boat? To see if anything's missing or damaged?" I glance at the flipped cushions again. It looks like someone was rummaging through the place.

Lisa shrugs. "Well… we didn't want to assume. Your boat hasn't exactly been… erm, shipshape. We weren't sure if it already looked like that."

What the hell is she talking about? I *always* keep the boat tidy, unless Amy's been here. Then it's a war zone. I press my lips together and bite back the sharp comment rising in my throat.

"Okay," I say instead. "Thanks for telling me."

But my heart is pounding. Someone was inside my boat. Someone looking for something.

And I have a sinking feeling I know exactly what.

"No problem. If there's anything else I can do?" Lisa asks, her voice sugary sweet.

I turn my back to her and step onto the deck, loosening my grip on Sadie's leash, but keeping it attached in case she gets any ideas about swan-diving into the water. She sniffs around the overturned cushions, then trots through the hatch just as the door swings open. Smart girl. I let go of the leash so she can explore inside.

"Jolene!" Lisa calls.

"Yes?" I ask, not bothering to look at her.

"There's a parcel for you at the shop. Rather large—about the size of a wardrobe. It's from some posh hotel in San Antonio."

"Okay. Thanks for letting me know." Of course Lisa knows. Lisa *always* knows. She's like the human psychic hotline of the marina. If you want to find out who's sleeping with whom or whether someone's secretly packed up their boat and bolted in the night, just ask Lisa. She knows who wintered in Aspen and who's maxed out their plastic. People think she's intuitive or "keenly aware" of the boating community—like she gives a damn. But she's just a gossip hound who gets her kicks sniffing around other people's drama.

"I can have Larry bring it to your boat, if you like," she offers.

"No, don't bother. I'll get it later. I've got enough going on here."

She probably hasn't left the marina shop all day, waiting for me to show up so she can see what's in the box.

"I wanted to chat with you about something else, if you've got a minute."

"Does it *look* like I've got a minute?" Seriously, is she that clueless?

Lisa blinks, then beams. "Like your Wesley used to say, 'You've always got a minute for me.'"

God help me. I sigh and toss a cushion back in place, then flop onto it with exaggerated drama. "What do you need?"

Grabbing the rail to steady herself, Lisa steps onto the deck like she owns it, then plonks down beside me and takes my hand. *Oh no. This can't be good.*

"Jolene, darling, first off, I just want you to know, I'm ever so sympathetic to your situation."

"Okay."

"This marina's a small world. We hear… well, everything. People talk."

"Okay," I repeat, keeping my voice flat.

"It's just… your husband hasn't been gone that long, and things seem to be moving *quite* fast with you and that… *ethnic* gentleman."

"Orlando?"

"Yes, the one with all the hair and the… you know… accent."

"Orlando doesn't have an accent."

"Oh, they all do, love."

I yank my hand away from hers and shoot her a look. She ignores it.

"Anyway, I just want you to be cautious. Larry and I worry, you know. And honestly, he doesn't seem like your type."

"Oh really? And what *is* my type, Lisa?"

She hesitates, clearly trying to find a "polite" way to be offensive. "Well… his boat is *tiny*, which probably means he's not terribly well-off. And he's not…"

"Not what? Not *Caucasian* enough for you? Not Ivy League? Not what?" My tone sharpens.

"Old," she whispers.

"What the fuck?"

Yeah. Message received. I bolt upright, and Lisa flinches like I might actually slap her. And I should. I really should.

"You bitch," I spit, standing over her. "You think I married Wesley for his money? Is that what you told Orlando?"

She opens her mouth, but I cut her off.

"You said *people* were saying that, but the truth is, *you're* the one spreading it. You always are. You just can't keep your bony nose out of everyone's business. Well, you need to keep it out of *mine*. Get off my boat. And don't come back. You hear me?"

Lisa scrambles to her feet, backing toward the railing.

"Get the fuck *off!*" I shout.

Just then, Sadie bolts out of the hatch, leash dragging behind her, and sinks her tiny teeth into Lisa's calf.

"You wretched beast!" Lisa shrieks, trying to shake her leg free.

I leap toward Sadie and pry her tiny jaws open, guilt already gnawing at me. "I'm sorry," I say quickly, holding Sadie back as she tries to wriggle free again.

Lisa crouches, rubbing at her leg. The skin's not even broken, but she wails like she's been mauled by Cujo.

"This is what I get for helping you?" she screeches. "You *set your mutt on me!* You'll be hearing from my solicitor!"

Lisa hops onto the dock and turns to storm off, slamming face-first into Larry, who just arrived. He looks delighted.

"No, she won't," he says calmly. "I've imagined this moment for years. Never thought it'd be quite so spectacular."

He turns back to his wife. "I saw everything, Lise. You earned it. As usual. Poking your nose where it doesn't belong. Now zip it and get on the boat."

"I will *not!*" she shrieks. "That dog's a menace! It should be put down! I could've caught rabies!"

"That little thing?" Larry chuckles, pointing at Sadie, now trembling in my arms. "You're fine. And we're leaving."

"*What?* Where to?"

"Up the coast. Louisiana. And this time *I'm* choosing."

"Louisiana? No! It's nothing but swamp and snakes! I'm not leaving because of *her!*"

"Then it's Louisiana or back home to London. Pick one."

Lisa gasps, sputtering with outrage as Larry hoists her up and carries her, kicking and screeching, down the dock.

"Have a safe trip!" I call sweetly after them.

Sadie lets out a tiny whimper. I cradle her against my chest, rubbing the soft fur under her chin. "That was bad behavior," I scold gently, caressing her snout.

She flattens her ears and hides her face beneath her paw.

"But you're getting a treat," I whisper.

At the word treat, her tail thumps and she slurps the air like she's starving.

Yeah… I'll make a good mom someday.

48

Jolene: A break-in

Within minutes, Larry—true to his word—unties the houseboat and motors it out of the marina into the bay. Lisa slumps dramatically across the bow, and all I can think about is Wesley. This is the day he looked forward to for years. He couldn't wait to finally say goodbye to Lisa. It's happening now… and he's not here to enjoy it.

I carry Sadie inside and shut the cabin door behind us. The interior is in the same chaotic state as the deck. My things are tossed everywhere with clothes, bags, and papers strewn on the floor. Necklaces Wesley gave me dangle from a cabinet handle, swinging gently. His old iPod sits abandoned in the middle of the table… right next to his wedding band.

Whoever tore through the boat wasn't just ransacking or looking to steal. They were searching for something specific.

The safe.

Jolene's Adonis

I dash through the clutter and into the forward cabin. Scrambling over a mess of clothes on the bed, I shove my hand into the V-shaped compartment. My breath catches, then releases, when my fingers graze the hidden latch. It's still shut. I open it just to be sure.

The lockbox is there.

Before I can lift it out, I hear Orlando's voice from the dock.

"Jolene?"

Sadie leaps onto the bench, shoving the curtain aside with her paws, barking her head off.

"Jolene, are you here? Is everything okay?"

"Coming!" I yell, carefully sliding the panel shut again. I step around the mess, close the door behind me, and meet him on the deck. Sadie's still inside.

"I just got here and found it like this," I tell him. "Did you see anything?"

"I wasn't around," he says. "I had some business in town. But I heard someone was on your boat. Are you missing anything?"

"Not that I've figured out yet. But it's a mess. I wouldn't even know where to begin."

He shakes his head. "This wasn't how it was supposed to happen. I should've told you sooner. I should've trusted you from the beginning."

He steps onto the deck. I instinctively back away, Amy's warning sounding alarm bells in my head.

"Tell me what?" I ask.

He closes the gap quickly, too quickly. My heart pounds as I stare into his eyes. Who *is* this man?

He takes my hands, trembling now. "Did you check the lockbox? Has it been touched?"

I go still. Every emotion in my body shuts down. My voice drops to a whisper. "What lockbox?"

His face twists in frustration. He runs a hand through his hair. "I'm Uncle Franco. From Mexico. Wesley told you to find me. That's me."

He points to his chest like that should mean something. Like I should suddenly trust him. But all I hear is Lisa's voice saying the intruders spoke a foreign language. Spanish, maybe?

"You did this," I breathe.

"What?"

"You and a friend. You staged the break-in to make it look like a robbery. You found the lockbox. You read the note. That's why you came after me. You don't care about me. I'm just some pathetic widow. How could I have been so stupid?"

I turn away, covering my face. "I have to go."

Jolene's Adonis

I run inside, grab the leash, and call for Sadie. She bounds into my arms. I don't look back.

Behind me, Orlando fumbles on the deck, saying something, but I don't hear him. The blood rushes in my ears like a freight train. I didn't get to look in the safe before he interrupted. He could've taken the contents and replaced the box to cover his tracks. And why would he come back? To make sure I didn't suspect him?

I strap Sadie into the harness, jam the key in the ignition, and floor it, leaving tire marks scorched across the pavement. I glance in the rearview mirror as I merge onto the highway toward Jessica's.

He's chasing me.

He jumps into a car, but I suddenly realize that I don't even know what kind of car he drives. That realization hits hard. I kissed this man. Nearly slept with him. Wanted to sleep with him. And I know *nothing* about him.

His car gains for a second, but it's no match for mine. I press harder on the gas, heart pounding as the road unfurls ahead. His vehicle disappears from my mirror.

By the time I pull into Jessica's neighborhood, an hour early, I'm certain I lost him. Just in case, I idle the car down the side driveway, tucked behind a stand of thick palms.

Hidden from the road.

I unclip Sadie and lift her carefully out of the car. She's asleep, but I need her close. I carry her around back, away from the front entrance, because if Orlando *did* follow me…

I'm not ready to find out what happens next.

"You must be thirsty and starving," I tell Sadie, giving her a quick pat before setting her down in front of the bowls in Jessica's backyard. She sniffs at the water dish, then gulps from it gratefully. Jessica's pit bull, Molly, pokes her head out of her doghouse, sniffs in our direction, then saunters back inside without a single bark or step closer.

Not surprising. Molly knows me, and Jessica's told me more than once that she's friendly with other dogs, but letting another dog into her yard to eat her food? That's generosity on another level.

Sadie nibbles at the oversized kibbles, then wanders off into the grass to do her business. "Good girl," I whisper, scooping her back into my arms. Just because Molly *seems* okay with her doesn't mean I'm taking chances.

I quietly slip into the den through the side door. The house is still—no noise, no TV, no music. The only sound comes from the kitchen at the end of the long hallway: muffled voices, low and urgent.

"Jessica?" I call out gently, easing toward the hallway. The conversation continues, only now, the volume rises. I pause. One of the voices is Jessica's, but there's something off. Her tone is sharper, her cadence heavier. She sounds… foreign. Not like herself at all.

A man with a thick accent—Russian, maybe?—responds in a language I don't understand.

Then George speaks. "Catalina! We were trying to finish the job!" Definitely George.

But what the hell are they talking about and who is Catalina?

"I told you, you shouldn't have gone through her boat," Jessica snaps. "Or her storage unit. That wasn't the deal. You had no right. I said I would handle it."

"Catalina!" George sounds exasperated.

"Jorge!" Jessica, *or Catalina?* responds. Her voice is tense, furious. The accent is more pronounced now, South American, not the polished American lilt I've always known. This can't be Jessica. But it *is*. It *sounds* like her. Still, something's wrong. *Who the hell is she, really?*

The Russian man mumbles something. It's muffled, like his mouth is full.

"I helped her pack the condo," Jessica says. "There was nothing there. And if she did hide the stones, she didn't tell me. I'm the only person she trusts. I would've known."

My stomach knots. Jessica—my best friend—isn't just Jessica. George, who isn't George, is calling her Catalina. *Is she my friend or enemy?*

I press Sadie to my chest, flatten myself against the wall, and inch forward to hear more.

"I'm telling you," George—or Jorge?—says. "We searched everywhere. That ring has a blood jewel in it, no question. Wesley had the whole collection at some point, but where the rest went, no clue. He could've hidden them. Or sold them."

The other man says coldly, "Catalina, use the trust she has in you. Get her to open up. The cartel wants those stones. Wesley should've never taken them. If she doesn't give them up, we take them. It's her or us. We've got weeks, maybe less, before they make an example out of us."

"No!" Catalina/Jessica fires back. "She's my friend. You don't touch her. There has to be another way."

"You say that now," the man growls. "But if it's her life or yours, you'll make the right choice."

"She's not some pawn," Catalina/Jessica snaps. "And neither am I."

"She should have been gone already," the Russian man growls, his voice low and rough. "If Jorge hadn't had a moment of weakness and left the fucking ladder down, she would have drowned with Wesley, just like we planned."

The sound of glass shattering makes me flinch. Sadie barks once, low and alert, a tiny growl starting deep in her throat.

A hand clamps over my mouth.

I twist, panic rising. It's Orlando. He puts a finger to his lips, eyes serious. Not panicked. Focused. Like he's done this before.

I want to scream. I want to cry. I want to run.

Do I hide with him, someone who could be working with the Colombian cartel?

Or do I burst into the kitchen and face three people—Jessica or Catalina included—who are tied up in secrets and violence and wanted to drown me?

Orlando jerks his head toward the den and signals for me to go. Quiet. Fast. Hide.

I obey.

Because right now, Orlando might be the only person not actively trying to kill me.

As Sadie and I cower in a dark corner of the den behind the sofa, I hear more shuffling and grunts, then a scream from Jessica, followed by a round of shots. My heart pounds, but it's not the sound of gunfire that scares me. I grew up on a farm. I spent hours with Wesley at the range. Guns don't scare me.

It's who might be *behind* the gun.

Several minutes pass. Jessica yells something in what sounds like Spanish.

"She's here. She's fine," Orlando assures her. "I made it just in time."

High heels clack across the stone hallway as the woman I thought was Jessica rushes into the den.

"Jolene?" she calls, breathless.

I hesitate.

"It's okay," Orlando says gently behind her. "She's working with me. The men… they're dead. They can't hurt you."

I rise slowly from behind the sofa. My body shakes. Two men are dead. Orlando or Jessica or both killed them. I don't know what *working with him* means anymore. Is Jessica cartel? CIA? Who the hell *is* she?

She runs to me and throws her arms around my shoulders. "Thank God!" she whispers fiercely. She holds me at arm's length and shakes her head. "You're early. You're never early."

She turns on Orlando. "Why did you let her come? I told you our contact was here. You were supposed to stall her so I could get a confession or something—*anything*—we could use to take them down."

Orlando shrugs. "She has a strong will. There's no stalling her."

Several men file into the house, dressed in dark suits and carrying weapons. I freeze, but Orlando tells me they're CIA. The good guys. I'm safe.

Jessica or Catalina eases me onto the sofa and gently takes Sadie from my trembling arms. "I think she's in shock," she says to Orlando.

He sits beside me and pulls a black wallet from his back pocket. Flipping it open, he shows me a badge. A golden eagle perches above bold blue letters: CIA. Underneath is an official-looking seal stamped with U.S., and the words Special Agent at the bottom.

"My name is Franco Orlando Castillo," he says. "I go by Orlando. Wesley referred to me as Franco in the letter, because only his daughter would know who that is. I work for the United States government, Central Intelligence Agency. Wesley was my partner. My mentor."

He pauses, glancing toward Catalina.

"She's not Jessica. Her real name is Catalina Vélez. She's a double agent, embedded within a Colombian intelligence unit. We were both working undercover to bring down a major jewel smuggling ring. Jorge—also known to you as George—was somehow involved. Wesley managed to intercept a shipment of blood gems from a Colombian cartel. They were meant for Jorge and another operative, but Wesley stole them and hid them. He didn't even tell me. Jorge knew you had the gems when he saw your ring."

Wait! Wesley was C.I.A.?

My head reels. "Let me think… I've had the same ring since the day Wesley proposed… except…"

"Except what?" Orlando urges.

"Wesley took it to be cleaned last year. I left it on the nightstand, and it vanished for a couple of days. He came back with it and said it had just been cleaned, but the stone looked different. Bigger. I asked him, and he swore it was the same ring. I figured maybe he upgraded it, being romantic or something."

Jessica frowns. "He must have swapped the stone, but why? That's risky."

Orlando's brow furrows. "He probably had his reasons. If he sold the original gem because he needed money, maybe he thought replacing it with a decoy would keep you from knowing. He was always cocky like that… hiding in plain sight."

I can barely process what they're saying. My heart pounds. Wesley was C.I.A. Someone tried to drown me. And now they're telling me the man I loved was caught between intelligence ops and cartels. "Wait… if Wesley didn't tell you where the stones were, how did you know about the box?"

Jessica and Orlando exchange a loaded glance.

"I found the lockbox and the jewels," he admits. "I opened it."

"Why didn't you report it?" Jessica asks him.

"We needed more than just the gems," he says carefully. "We needed a confession. Proof. There wasn't enough to charge Jorge with Wesley's murder."

My stomach twists. "When did you find the box? Wesley hid it so well. When were you on my boat?"

He hesitates. "A few times. It's not like I broke in. The door was unlocked. Look… I saw you pull it out while watching you on camera… I was only spying on you to find out if you killed Wesley."

Jessica clasps my hand, her voice cracking. "I didn't know. I swear to you, Jolene. I was devastated when I found out what happened. I asked Jorge and he told me Wesley took his own life. I believed him. I didn't think he'd ever hurt you. And I knew Orlando would come to watch over you."

Is that why Orlando was around? Just to watch me? Was that the only reason he looked at me the way he did? Did he see what happened between me and Pet? And Selena? And when I was alone…

I have to get out of here.

I rise from the sofa and reach for Sadie.

"I need to go home," I whisper, turning toward the door.

"It's not safe," Catalina says firmly. "The cartel knows you're involved. Once they find out about Jorge's death, they'll come for what he left behind. That includes you."

I turn to Orlando. "I thought you were CIA. Fine. I'll give you the box. You can do whatever you want with it. I don't need to be involved. If I give you the jewels, then I'm no longer in danger, right?"

"It's not that simple," he says quietly. "I already have the lockbox. I checked it after you left, just to make sure it hadn't been touched. It's in the car. Everything's still there. Even your money."

"Oh," I murmur. That part's none of his business.

He continues, "You're still in danger until we get the stones to the only person who can fix this and we find the ledgers to tie it all together."

"You can handle it then. Put me in protective custody or whatever it is you people do."

"No." He shakes his head. "You have to stay under my protection, and we have to take the jewels to Mexico. Wesley was wrong to put you in danger, but he was right about where they belong. The American government wants no further involvement. They won't risk more lives. One of their own stole from the Colombian cartel. A war's already started. The only way to stop it is to take them to the man Wesley trusted. That's what we're going to do. It's my duty. And I'm not letting you out of my sight again. So yes, you have to go."

"I don't *have* to do anything," I snap. I storm out of the house and march straight to the convertible. I strap Sadie into the harness and throw myself behind the wheel. When I look up, Orlando's car and a dozen black, unmarked vehicles are blocking every possible exit.

I pound the dashboard in frustration. "Dammit."

"Jolene," Orlando says, appearing beside me. He rests a hand gently on my shoulder. "You've been through hell. I know that. But try to think clearly. I'm the only one who can keep you safe."

"No, you're not. I can go back to San Antonio. I have protection there. Maybe you've heard of Matt D'Angelo. He cares about me. He can protect me. Not you. You never cared. You did your job. That's all I ever was to you, an assignment."

Tears blur my vision. My voice breaks.

He jerks the door open and lifts me from the car like I weigh nothing. He slides me down the length of his body, one hand landing beneath my ass, holding my weight steady as my feet touch the ground. Our lips are so close I can feel his breath on mine. The heat of his body... the hardness pressing through the soft knit of my dress.

"You could never be just an assignment," he says, his voice low, thick. "I want you with me. I *need* you with me. And yes, you'd probably be safer with Matt D'Angelo. He could provide for you. Give you everything you want. But not his heart."

I can barely breathe.

"Yes, I lied. I misled you. I didn't have a choice. But don't think for one second that means I don't care."

"Don't say that!" I cry. "You *had* a choice. You watched me. You used me. You thought I could be part of this—this whole mess. I *loved* Wesley. I'm not a criminal. I'm not a murderer."

"No," he says, cupping my face. "You're the most stubborn, impulsive, beautiful woman I've ever known. I can see why Wesley loved you. Hell, I wanted you from the moment I saw you on the boat, lying on your back, staring at the stars. You called me "Adonis." Then you tortured me with your need for connection, for touch. The way you moaned in your sleep. I saw it all."

"You watched me sleep?" My voice is hoarse. "Why?"

"I told you… your boat was unlocked. The doorman at your condo was easy to bribe. I haven't set up cameras in your store yet, but I found your spare key." He hesitates, then adds, "Just so you know everything, no more secrets, my goddaughter is Amy, Wesley's daughter. She didn't know about the jewels. She just wanted answers. She would've given me access if I asked. But I didn't need to."

He looks straight at me. "I monitored everything. Well, almost everything."

"No!" I slam my fists against his chest. He doesn't flinch. He just pulls me closer.

"It doesn't matter now," he whispers. "I know who you are. And now you know everything about me. There's nothing left to hide. We're the same, Jolene. We do what we have to do to survive. And I've stayed, because of *you*. I could've taken the jewels and left. I didn't. I stayed. Because I need you like I've never needed anyone."

His mouth finds mine, and I want to resist, but I don't. His kiss consumes me, fierce and aching, like he's trying to memorize the shape of my soul.

I shouldn't give in. Not now. Not after everything.

But I do.

Because even through the betrayal, the lies, the grief… somehow, I still want him.

Maybe I always did.

49

Orlando: Home

The sway of the ocean cradles us as *My Knotty Jolene* rocks gently in the open water. The world is quiet out here. It's just us, the stars, and the slow hum of the sea.

Jolene lies draped across my chest, one leg tangled with mine, her breath warm against my skin. Her fingers drift lazily over my arm, tracing the ink on my bicep.

The lone wolf.

She doesn't say anything at first, just follows the lines with a fingertip, slow and thoughtful. Her touch feels like fire and silk at once.

After a long silence, she finally asks, "Why the wolf?"

I don't answer right away. I think about the years behind me. The lies. The missions. The distance I put between myself and everyone I ever cared about. All of it.

I let out a breath.

"It was a reminder," I say. "That I was on my own. That I couldn't afford to let anyone in."

She lifts her head, resting her chin on my chest, her hazel eyes searching mine. "Did it help?"

"No," I say honestly. "But it kept me alive."

Her fingers pause over the wolf's eye. "You're not alone anymore."

I reach up and tuck her hair behind her ear. "No," I say softly. "I'm not."

She smiles. It's that small, knowing smile she only gives me. And I feel something shift inside me. Not lust. Not adrenaline. Not the thrill of a job well done.

Something real.

I press my lips to her forehead and let the silence stretch again. We don't need words right now. Her body still glows with the afterheat of what just passed between us. Her skin is damp, her thighs still tremble against mine, and I'm not ready to stop touching her.

Not ever.

She stretches a little, presses her chest into me, and moves her hips just slightly, teasing, testing.

I grow hard almost instantly. Just the scent of her, the way her breath catches when I run my hand along the curve of her back—it undoes me.

"You're insatiable," I whisper against her neck.

She laughs softly, her voice still sleepy. "Maybe I just missed you for too long."

I flip us easily, placing her beneath me, my elbows braced on either side of her as I lower my body over hers.

"Then I guess I have a lot to make up for," I murmur.

She opens her legs, wrapping them around my waist.

"You better get started," she whispers.

And I do.

My cock finds her slick, waiting heat and I slide in easily, still wet from the last time we came together. I drive into her hard, then pull out slowly, savoring the way she moans, the way her hips rise to meet me, desperate for more. The scent of her, the taste of her skin still lingering on my lips, the feel of her clenching around me, it all drives me mad. I press in and out, deeper, slower, harder, aching to lose myself in her again.

Then, without a word, she pats my arm. It's her silent signal to pause. I stop, curious. She slips from beneath me and moves to the drawer, fishing out a rolled sock. For a moment, I'm confused… until I remember that night I watched her from the deck. That sock is where she keeps her vibrator.

The sock falls to the floor, and a soft hum fills the cabin. I roll onto my back, and she climbs on top of me. And then she's lowering herself onto my cock, inch by inch, grinding her hips as she settles into place. The vibrator is pressed between us, buzzing against her clit, sending shockwaves through both our bodies.

She throws her head back and rides me, lifting and rolling her hips in that rhythm I can never get enough of. I watch her move—watch her pleasure build—watch the scene I once only imagined come to life in front of me.

That night, I saw her alone with that toy. Now she's here, riding me with it in her hand. She's not alone anymore. She's mine now. *Oh yes, she's mine.*

She screams as the orgasm hits, her body trembling, walls tightening around me in perfect rhythm. I groan, barely holding on, but I can't anymore. I release deep inside her as we shudder and spasm together, her moans tangled with mine, the sound of the sea rocking us into the moment.

And when it's over, when she collapses against me, breathless and damp with sweat, I hold her tightly and bury my face in her neck.

Jolene's Adonis

I never thought I'd find this. Not in the mess of lies and shadows I've lived in. But here she is. Beautiful. Wild. Real.

For the first time in my life, I don't feel like a lone wolf.

I feel like I'm home.

50

Jolene: A happy ending

Orlando throws the last of his bags onto the deck of *My Knotty Jolene* as he and Amy say their goodbyes.

"Are you sure you don't need anything?" Pet asks. Amy's fingers are curled around the end of a studded dog collar that dangles from his neck. It's ninety-five in the shade, and they're both dressed in black vinyl like it's nothing.

"We've got everything we need," I tell him. "I wasn't sure you'd make it in time, so I left the store key at the marina office," I say to Amy. "Please take care of it for me. We hope to be back within six months."

I hesitate, then add, "I also added your name to the account with your dad's life insurance money. There was plenty left after his debts were paid. Since he was murdered, and didn't kill himself, I was able to collect the full policy. It's half yours. It's what he would've wanted."

"I'm good. I have the trust. It will last awhile. I'll let you know. Besides, as long as he doesn't throw me out again, I'll be fine," Amy smirks, shooting Pet a look.

"We've been over this," he argues. "You're only in charge in the bedroom. Every time you're mean to someone, you wear the chain, and I'll spank *you*. Hard."

"Okay, you two." I laugh and roll my eyes. "Not in public." I lean in and kiss Amy's cheek. "Be good. And listen to him. He's a good man."

Amy pouts. "Okay."

"Where are you staying?"

"We're moving into Daddy's condo. It hasn't sold yet, and we're gonna stay here for a while."

"The neighbors are gonna love you," I tease.

"Oh, brother." Amy rolls her eyes and hugs Orlando. "Goodbye, Uncle Franco. Take care of my step-monster!"

I'll never get used to hearing her call him *Franco*. Just like I still call Matt *Pet*. Once a name sticks in my head, it stays, real or fake.

Sadie paws at my leg, and I scoop her up. She gives me one last lick before hopping into the doggie bag at Amy's feet.

"You take care of that precious dog," I say.

Amy laughs, and she and Pet wave from the dock as Orlando steers us into open water. *My Knotty Jolene* has only left the slip once since the day Wesley died—when Orlando and I took her out to stretch her sea legs—and now, as she glides across the water, the motion feels like a release. Like I'm finally breathing again.

"Did you get a chance to say goodbye to Catalina and Selena?" Orlando asks.

"We texted," I say, eyes fixed on the horizon. "I'm going to miss both of them, but it's going to take time for Catalina, or Jessica, or whatever name she's using, to earn my trust back. You both lied to me, but hers stung more. She was my best friend. I've known her for years. She never trusted me enough to warn me. She let me get close to her fake husband. Now I don't even know who she is."

I glance over my shoulder. "But… she did tell me Wesley's funeral was paid for by the cartel. We actually laughed about it. The Colombian cartel, funding a CIA agent's burial. Wesley would've loved the irony."

Orlando nods. "Yeah. He would've."

When we're far enough out, I head below deck and peel off my clothes. Then I climb back into the hatchway completely bare, posing on the stairs. "You've got a lot of time to make up for."

"I do," he says from behind the helm. "Come here."

I walk slowly, dragging it out, stopping just shy of his reach.

"Come here," he says again, firmer now.

"Make me," I whisper.

He lashes the helm into place with a rope and strides toward me, lifting me into his arms. He lowers me onto a cushion, slow and careful, like I'm something precious.

"This," he murmurs, "was the first place I touched you. You were so adorable. So drunk." He laughs softly. "I didn't know you'd already stolen my heart."

"You were my Adonis," I say, brushing his cheek. "I fantasized about you long before I ever met you."

He positions himself above me, brushing my hair from my face. "My heart belongs to you. Stamp it with whatever name you want, Orlando or Franco or Adonis, I'll answer you."

I reach up and kiss him, slow and deep. His mouth is warm and familiar now, like a place I've always belonged.

His fingers trace the curve of my breasts, the dip of my stomach, until they find the anchor tattoo just above the tender place that makes me ache for him. His touch is slow, worshipful. My eyes flutter open, and I find him watching me, those almond eyes burning into mine, his breath ragged, curls damp against his forehead.

He peels off his shirt, exposing the sculpted body I've dreamed of touching. I trail my fingers down his chest to the patch of dark hair that disappears beneath his waistband. He kicks off his flip-flops, slides off his pants, and stands before me fully bare.

When he lowers himself again, I open my legs without hesitation, inviting him in.

He accepts, sliding deep inside me, and I gasp as he fills me completely. He's thick, strong, familiar. My body rises to meet him, our rhythm falling into place like we were made for this.

He moves with control, each stroke sending pleasure spiraling through me. I arch, matching his rhythm until we're spiraling together—faster, harder—chasing that edge until we fall over it. I cry out as my body clenches around him, and he groans against my neck as he pulses inside me.

But he doesn't pull out.

He stays. His body resting inside mine, his breathing soft, lips brushing my temple.

"I just need a few minutes," he murmurs.

Grinning, I slap his ass. "It's going to be a long, hot trip. Hope you can keep up."

He kisses the bridge of my nose, then starts to move inside me again, already growing hard.

"I'll work day and night to find out," he whispers.

I wrap my legs around him, holding him close. After everything—after the chaos and pain and betrayal—I finally feel whole. Safe. Alive.

I found my peace out here.

And I found it with him.

J. Jaden

Character Sketches

Jolene Brown

Age: 33

Occupation: Blacksmith / Artisan

Location: Texas

Appearance: Long blonde hair, hazel eyes (shift between green and gold), curvy build, strong hands from years of work, approachable yet striking.

Background:

- Raised on a family farm in an ultra-conservative, church-centered community.

- Often felt out of place in her family, stifled by expectations.

- Married Wesley, a much older man, for love, not money, but labeled a gold digger by others.

- Now widowed, childless, and determined to start over on her own terms.

Personality Traits:

- **Introverted & Creative** – thrives in solitude, channels emotion through art and metalwork.

- **Empathetic & Intuitive** – reads people deeply, sometimes uncannily.

- **Resilient & Independent** – learned hard work and survival from farm life.

- **Warm & Witty** – when safe, shows humor, sensuality, and openness.

- **Shy & Self-Conscious** – struggles with trust, often withdraws when vulnerable.

Strengths:

- Skilled with tools and blacksmithing, comfortable in male-dominated spaces.

- Passionate, emotionally honest, and capable of deep connections.

- Strong work ethic; self-reliant and adaptable.

Flaws:

- Haunted by judgment and self-doubt.

- Withdraws under pressure, pushing others away.

- Sensitive to rejection, struggles to fully trust love.

Psychological Arc:

Jolene's journey is about self-acceptance and freedom. From a life shaped by rigid expectations and others' assumptions, she must learn to embrace her authentic self, silence judgment, and discover that she is enough just as she is.

Reader Appeal:

- Misunderstood, strong-yet-vulnerable heroine.

- A blend of girl-next-door charm and soulful artist depth.

- Perfect for readers who love characters that balance resilience with emotional honesty.

Orlando Castillo

Age: Late 30s to early 40s

Occupation: CIA operative / Sailor

Location: Primarily based in Texas and the Gulf of Mexico, with international ties.

Appearance: Dark hair, tanned skin from years on the water, piercing eyes that miss little, lean build, built for endurance rather than bulk. His face often carries the rough stubble of long days at work.

Background:

- Served as a CIA agent alongside Wesley, with years of experience in covert operations.

- Became entangled in the fallout of Wesley's stolen "blood jewels," cartel dealings, and intelligence cover-ups.

- After Wesley's death, Orlando's loyalty and suspicion drive him to uncover the truth.

- Crosses paths with Jolene, whose boat and life become bound to the mission Wesley left unfinished.

Personality Traits:

- **Protective & Loyal** – committed to those he cares for, sometimes to his own detriment.

- **Disciplined & Tactical** – trained to think several moves ahead, but also quick to adapt.

- **Passionate & Driven** – carries intensity in both his work and relationships.

- **Stoic Exterior** – tends to mask his emotions, but deeply feels beneath the surface.

- **Haunted & Secretive** – scarred by missions gone wrong, trusts very few people fully.

Strengths:

- Skilled in strategy, combat, and survival from his intelligence background.

- Strong moral compass, even in morally gray circumstances.

- Physically resilient, able to endure harsh conditions at sea and on land.

- Protective nature makes him a natural ally and anchor.

Flaws:

- Struggles with vulnerability; keeps his emotions tightly locked away.

- Tendency toward obsession, especially when seeking truth or justice.

- Haunted by guilt over past missions and Wesley's death.

- Can be controlling when fear of loss overtakes him.

Psychological Arc:

Orlando's journey is about trust and redemption. He must move beyond guilt and secrecy, learning to let someone in without fear of betrayal. Jolene challenges his walls, forcing him to risk not just his life but his guarded heart. Through her, he begins to believe that love and loyalty can exist outside duty and mission.

Reader Appeal:

- Brooding, protective hero with a past full of secrets.

- Balances spy-thriller intensity with romantic tension.

- Perfect for readers who love strong, disciplined men whose biggest battle is with their own guarded hearts.

Amy Brown

Age: 30 (three years younger than Jolene)

Occupation: Socialite / Seeker of comfort (lacks clear career direction)

Location: Texas

Appearance: Petite, with striking blue eyes and long dark hair. Beautiful in a polished, effortless way, though her size and presence often make her seem younger than she is. Her looks give her an air of vulnerability, even when her sharp tongue says otherwise.

Background:

- Wesley's daughter from his first relationship or marriage (unknown at this point), raised in privilege and accustomed to being the center of his world.

- When Wesley married, Amy viewed Jolene as an interloper who stole her father's attention, fueling years of jealousy and resentment.

- Spoiled by comfort and her father's protection, she learned to manipulate and charm her way through life, often avoiding responsibility.

- Wesley's death shakes her foundation and forces her to face a world where her privilege no longer shields her, and where Jolene is all she has left.

Personality Traits:

- **Entitled & Defensive** – expects life to bend to her, lashes out when it doesn't.

- **Sharp-Witted & Sarcastic** – quick with comebacks, often biting.

- **Jealous & Resentful** – especially toward Jolene, whom she sees as a rival.

- **Vulnerable Beneath the Armor** – her cruelty masks fear of abandonment.

- **Capable of Growth** – when forced to face reality, she can soften and find strength.

Strengths:

- Intelligent and quick to adapt when survival is at stake.

- Fiercely loyal once she commits emotionally.

- Has the capacity for deep transformation and redemption.

- Her wit and charm, when not used defensively, make her magnetic.

Flaws:

- Immature, spoiled, and resistant to responsibility.

- Uses manipulation to get her way.

- Prone to jealousy, bitterness, and selfishness.

- Fears intimacy and vulnerability, pushing people away before they can reject her.

Psychological Arc:

Amy begins as the antagonistic stepdaughter, her bitterness toward Jolene fueled by jealousy and grief. But with Wesley gone, she faces the truth of her fragility: her wealth and privilege cannot protect her from loss. As she grows, Amy sheds her spoiled persona and accepts Jolene not as a rival, but as her only anchor. Through this transformation, she finds humility, resilience, and the beginnings of true emotional maturity.

Reader Appeal:

- The "spoiled princess" who undergoes a redemption arc.

- Adds drama and tension at the start but pays off with emotional depth.

- Appeals to readers who love characters who transform from selfishness into loyalty and vulnerability.

Matt "Pet" D'Angelo

Age: Mid 30s

Occupation: Real estate mogul / hotel and club owner / investor

Location: Texas, with properties throughout the U.S.

Appearance: Tall, stylish, and always impeccably dressed. Blond hair, carefully groomed, with an expressive face that can shift from charming warmth to cool calculation in an instant. His presence is magnetic. Tabloids call him "the most eligible bachelor in the country."

Background:

- Comes from a wealthy Italian-American family. His grandfather started with a small Dallas motel, and each generation expanded the empire into luxury hotels, shopping centers, country clubs, and other ventures.

- Inherited immense wealth but worked to put his own stamp on the family name, known for bold investments and a taste for the extravagant.

- Though surrounded by luxury, Pet is restless, eccentric, and always chasing the next thrill.

- His world of wealth and indulgence led him into the fetish scene, where he met Selena, one of his few true equals in desire and daring.

Personality Traits:

- **Charismatic & Magnetic** – people are naturally drawn to him.

- **Eccentric & Playful** – thrives on spectacle, attention, and curiosity.

- **Restless & Hedonistic** – constantly chasing the next experience, often reckless.

- **Proud & Image-Conscious** – hates the idea of missing out; deeply aware of appearances.

- **Surprisingly Vulnerable** – beneath the bravado, he longs for someone who will treat him as an equal, not a bank account or a headline.

Strengths:

- Immense wealth and resources; can open any door.

- Confident, daring, and unafraid of risk.

- Charms people easily, often disarming with humor.

- Has vision and creativity in business and life.

Flaws:

- Spoiled by privilege; expects to get what he wants.

- Impulsive, prone to extravagance and poor judgment when bored.

- Restless to the point of sabotaging stability.

- Struggles with genuine intimacy, unsure who loves him for himself versus his fortune.

Psychological Arc:

Pet's journey is about authenticity. For years he's lived as a tabloid figure, an eccentric billionaire chasing indulgence and attention. But when tragedy pulls him into Jolene's world, Pet discovers his wealth can't protect him from loneliness and empathy. The playboy façade cracks, and he yearns for something real: a partner who sees Matt, not "Pet." Through hard lessons, he learns that true connection means giving up control, risking vulnerability, and finding worth beyond money and spectacle.

Reader Appeal:

- The eccentric billionaire with charisma, mystery, and hidden depth.

- Adds glamour, drama, and levity, while also offering emotional intrigue.

- Perfect for readers who enjoy larger-than-life characters whose masks hide very human needs.

Selena (Mistress Selena)

Age: Late-30s

Occupation: Professional Dominatrix (paid) / nightlife insider
Location: Texas, often travels to bigger cities for parties and clients

Appearance: Petite but commanding, with long, dark hair, sharp cheekbones, and eyes that glint with both warmth and authority. Her style is bold and deliberately theatrical—corsets, leather, striking heels—but she carries herself with natural confidence even out of costume. Small in stature, yet impossible to overlook.

Background:

- Born in a small village in Spain, Selena was orphaned young and raised with her five siblings. Survival shaped her, but so did her hunger for more than bare existence.

- At eighteen, she discovered the fetish scene in Madrid. A cheap corset and fishnets became her first costume, and the experience lit a fire.

- Under the mentorship of a seasoned French Dom, she learned technique, boundaries, and how power could be wielded as art.

- She chose domination not as sex work but as performance and control. She does not sleep with her clients. Her sessions are about role, ritual, and consent.

- She maintains an open, understanding relationship with her boyfriend, who accepts her professional life for what it is.

Personality Traits:

- **Confident & Commanding** – thrives in control; her voice, gaze, and presence can silence a room.

- **Playful & Saucy** – sharp humor and mischief lace her dominance.

- **Observant & Shrewd** – instantly reads clients' tells and vulnerabilities.

- **Independent & Proud** – refuses to be mistaken for anyone's mistress; her power is her own.

- **Warm Beneath the Armor** – empathetic when trust is earned; capable of genuine affection.

Strengths:

- Professional boundaries: skilled at maintaining control while protecting herself.

- Fearless, adaptable, and socially intelligent.

- Charismatic; easily draws others in with her mix of danger and charm.

- Resourceful, building a career from her passion and identity.

Flaws / Vulnerabilities:

- Can be manipulative when she feels cornered.

- Struggles with emotional intimacy outside of her professional persona.

- Jealous streak when compared to women who embody "traditional" femininity.

- Sometimes hides loneliness behind bravado and spectacle.

Psychological Arc:

Selena's growth lies in the tension between performance and vulnerability. Professionally, she's built a reputation on command, spectacle, and control, but those same qualities can keep her isolated. Through her friendship with Jolene and her ongoing relationship with her boyfriend, Selena learns that her identity isn't confined to Mistress Selena. She can be powerful and commanding while still allowing herself softness, connection, and the messy gray areas of love and belonging.

Reader Appeal:

- A saucy, magnetic Dominatrix who adds spice, wisdom, and bold energy to the cast.

- Brings glamor and edge while also carrying depth and relatability.

- Perfect for readers who enjoy unconventional, complex women who own their power but aren't defined solely by it.

About the Author

J. Jaden has worked as a professional ghostwriter and editor since 2003, writing more than 100 non-fiction books and novels during that time for a worldwide client base.

She is a wife, and mother of an adult daughter, and lives on a small farm outside of Oklahoma City. Her passions include vegan cooking, knitting, gardening, reading, and taking care of 30 winged and furry pets.

In the late 90's, she lived aboard a sailboat in Port Aransas, Texas for several months. Her love of boating and the time aboard inspired the story. The picture of the author was taken when she lived on the Gulf of Mexico.

Watch for more titles from this author on her site at JJaden.com.

The next book in the series, "Amy's Pet," will be released in late 2025.